Dark Whispers

Jo Macgregor

Other books for adults by this author

The First Time I Died
The First Time I Fell

Copyright 2018 Joanne Macgregor

This edition:
ISBN: 978-0-9947230-6-2 (print)
ISBN: 978-0-9947230-7-9 (eBook)

Cover: Jennifer Zemanek at Seedlings Design Studio
Formatting: Polgarus Studio

First published in 2014 by Protea Boekhuis, Pretoria
ISBN: 978-0-9947230-0-0 (print)
ISBN: 978-0-9947230-1-7 (eBook)

Copyright 2018 Joanne Macgregor

A QUICK NOTE

This book is set in South Africa and therefore follows UK English spelling and punctuation conventions. Words like colour, centre, metre, cosy, gynaecology, counselling, prise and realise are not spelling mistakes.

For some of the more exotic South African words, there is a glossary at the end of the book.

"Words have a magical power. They can either bring the greatest happiness or the deepest despair."

- Sigmund Freud

1
JUST PERFECT

He likes them best like this, laid out neatly in the white gowns, on the stainless-steel tables. They are still and clean, without disguise, stripped of their fashionable feathers and prepared just for him, like chicken breasts waiting on a cutting board. It is easy, like this, to see their asymmetries, their blemishes, their imperfections.

Never mind the reason why they think they are here, he knows that the real reason is to be corrected, to be made perfect. His task — no, more than that, his duty — is to fix them. It is a vocation, really, to leave them better than he finds them. They are so confused — distracted from the beauty of form by the attachment to function. They do not know what is best for themselves.

But he does.

He leans over this one now. She is so still, so relaxed, so ready. Her breathing is slow and steady, her gaze a little unfocused. He can feel his own breathing quickening, feel the heat rising from his core like a tremble of divine joy.

There is just enough time for a small whisper, a soft encouragement

1

of hope, before the darkness slides her entirely into his honing hands.

He leans over and breathes into her ear, "Just relax. I'm going to do something very special for you. And when you wake up, you're going to be just perfect."

He takes one of her hands, pats it gently. Her eyes have already closed when he murmurs, "Doctor knows best."

2
GOOD INTENTIONS

New Year's resolutions:

1. *Stop trying to save others.*
2. *Save money instead.*
3. *Embrace my extra 4 kg.*
   ("How blessed am I to live and love in this temple.")
4. *Recycle more.*
5. *Learn to cook. Anything.*
6. *Be (even more) patient with mommy dearest.*
   ("I am as a hollow reed. Troubles pass through me as the wind.")
7. *Open bank statements. Read them.*
8. *Keep one of the plants in my office alive for an entire year.*
9. *Teach Oedipus to stop drinking from the toilet bowl.*

Affirmation for the year:
   "I am a creature of conscious choice, not a victim of circumstance."

Megan Wright wondered how it was possible that, less than two weeks into January, she'd already broken each of her resolutions in some way. She sat in her car for a moment, windows open, savouring the freshness of the morning and sipping on her takeaway cup of coffee.

The hospital parking lot was littered with the detritus of the previous night's thunderstorm: small branches and castanet-shaped seed pods of the jacaranda trees which grew nearby, grey stones and gravel washed down from the flower beds on the northern embankment, leaves wrenched from trees and swirled into random piles by the strong wind, and scraps of litter blown against the palisade fences. But the air was clean, the wide African sky washed to a cloudless cobalt blue, and already the sun was hot above Johannesburg, South Africa.

Megan was just climbing out of her silver Renault, balancing the coffee in one hand, and her handbag and briefcase in the other, when her cell phone began to ring with Chicago's "When you're good to Mama" tune. The brightness of the early January morning dimmed a little.

"Hi, Mom," she said, slamming the car door closed with a swing of her hip and setting off across the lot towards the busy main entrance of Acacia Private Clinic.

"Good morning, Megan." Just the way her mother said it was irritating. "And how are you?"

"I *was* just fine, but I'm guessing that's about to change. Now, what do you want?" Megan longed to say. But instead, she said, "Fine thanks, how are you?"

"Oh, *I'm* fine."

Megan already had a good idea what the call might be

about. She headed for her usual shortcut across the small island of grass in the centre of the parking lot. There was an old pepper tree growing there, shading a small stone bench. The gnarled and twisted base of the trunk gave rise to swathes of green leaves, which always gave her spirits a lift. It was proof that life thrived — even in the disinfected and sterile hospital environment where antiseptics and antibiotics ruled supreme, and death seemed the only organic process.

When Megan didn't respond, her mother continued, "But Cayley's not."

"Big surprise," Megan muttered, taking a quick gulp of coffee and coughing as it burned down her throat.

"What's that?"

"Nothing. What's wrong now?"

Megan was on conversational auto-pilot. Their exchange was proceeding along its usual well-worn but futile path. She might as well let her mother get it all off her chest. She paused to lean briefly against the rough trunk of the pepper tree, imagining that some of its solid strength and vitality flowed into her. What she really wanted to do was press her cheek against the bark and give the tree a loving hug, but it would not do for Megan Wright, Counselling Psychologist, to be seen doing something quite so eccentric. The doctors might stop their referrals if they thought she was odder than her patients.

A small movement of brown fluff on the grass in front of her caught her attention. It was a baby bird with one wing extended at an odd angle and feathers ruffled and misaligned. It was struggling to hold its head up.

"She's not doing well at all. She seems very depressed, and

5

hasn't been to work in days," her mother was saying. "She just stays in her room — only comes out to eat and … you know."

"Oh, the poor thing!" Megan said, now on her haunches in front of the helpless creature on the grass. Placing her coffee cup on the bench, she gently cupped the bird in her hands. She could feel a rapid heartbeat beneath the downy softness squirming feebly in her fingers. "Don't panic. We'll get you some help."

"Well, I must say, I'm glad to hear a little sympathy for once!" said her mother, sounding surprised.

"Oh, right," Megan said into the phone.

She strode to the entrance of the clinic, past the Emergency unit outside where an open-doored ambulance was parked. Two paramedics leaned against the sides of the vehicle; one was smoking a cigarette, and the other had her eyes closed and her face turned up towards the sun.

The glass doors of the entrance slid open at her approach, admitting her to the lobby with its potted yuccas and palms, its gleaming brass rails and polished floors, the line of expectant wheelchairs parked alongside a bank of vending machines, and its unmistakable smell — a mixture of strong antiseptic and anxiety.

She headed for the clinic's retail pharmacy which was across the way from the intake desks with their serried rows of blue and maroon chairs.

"Megan!"

"What?"

Megan scanned the shelves in the pharmacy. Wedging the phone between her ear and shoulder, and cradling the little bird tenderly in one hand, she snatched a dropper off a rack of medical equipment and a small box of baby cereal off a shelf.

"I really think you have no love for me at all," her mother said with a sniff. "Or for your sister."

I am as a hollow reed; troubles pass through me as the wind.

The cashier, a thin woman with dark rings under her eyes which spoke of shift work, rang up the purchase, glancing from the bird in Megan's one hand, to the phone now back in her other.

"Please hold this for a sec," Megan mouthed to the cashier, handing the phone to the woman, and opening her handbag to rifle through it for some money.

The cashier, who looked weary enough to have seen most things in life and to be unsurprised by the rest, took the phone and put it to her own ear.

"Yes," she said. "Uhm-hmm … Hm-hm-hm … *Eish!*"

Megan handed over the money, shoved the dropper and cereal box into her bag, and took back the phone — resisting the temptation to leave it with the cashier, who seemed to be doing a better job of consoling Moira Wright than she had.

"Thanks," she told the assistant.

"I should say so," came the bitter response from the other end of the line.

Megan headed across the tiled foyer to the lifts. Her hands were too full today to climb the curved sweep of stairs which led up to the higher floors.

"Anyway," her mother continued, "she's losing weight again. She won't tell me what she weighs, but she promises me she's not under forty-nine kilograms."

"Oh well, if she *promises,* then I'm sure you can believe her.

It's not like Cayley would ever lie about her weight," Megan said, trying — and failing — to keep the acid note of sarcasm out of her voice.

She was slim enough to squeeze into the crowded lift when it arrived, tall enough to lean over another occupant and press the button for the third floor, and stubborn enough to avoid looking at her reflection in the mirrored control panel, sure that the irritation at her family would be clearly written on her face. Almost thirty years of skirmishes with her mother, and anxiety about her sister, was starting to show in the beginnings of fine lines at the edges of her blue-grey eyes. She shook back shoulder-length hair somewhere between darkest red and auburn-brown, and cradled the baby bird protectively against the jostles of the usual flock of white-coated doctors, and orderlies in their regulation greens. A nurse, who was standing behind an aged man in a wheelchair, left off staring at the small dent on Megan's left cheekbone and peered disapprovingly down at the bird in her hand.

"That's not very hygienic," she said.

"No," Megan said with a smile. "It isn't, is it?"

"No, it isn't — I'm glad you agree!" said her mother.

She'd been complaining at length about the treatment Megan's sister had received during her last in-patient treatment at the eating disorders unit of the psychiatric clinic where she'd been hospitalised half a dozen times over the course of the past eight years.

"I do think it's time for you to get involved again, Megan. Personally involved, I mean. Not just referring her on to one of your colleagues. After all, who knows her better than her own family? Who could treat her better than her own psychologist sister?"

I am as a hollow reed ...

With a bright smile at the sour-faced nurse, Megan stepped out of the lift and strode down the tiled corridor to her office, cuddling the bird to her chest.

"Mom, you know I can't treat members of my own family. It's unethical. We've been through all this before. Many times. Anyway, she wouldn't listen to me, and I couldn't force her — she's twenty-four, not four."

Megan stepped into the reception area of her consulting rooms. Several new potted plants — newly purchased to replace those that had died over the Christmas break — nestled between the soft seats and the side tables stacked neatly with magazines. The aroma of coffee drifted out from the small kitchenette to the rear of the reception desk where Patience Ndlovu sat, large and placid, labelling envelopes.

Megan waved a greeting, mouthed, "My mother," holding the phone up in explanation, and placed the tiny bird into Patience's big, soft hands. A small basket of wrapped mints sat on the reception counter — a moment of sweetness after the sadness of therapy for departing clients. Megan tipped the sweets out, lined the basket with a clutch of tissues and held it out for Patience to deposit the bird gently into it.

Her mother was still talking non-stop into her ear. "Mom?" Megan interrupted the flow of pleading, haranguing and self-pity. "Mom!"

"Will you help Cayley or not?" said her mother, in annoyed ultimatum. Then, with a throb of melodrama in her voice, added, "Will you save your sister?"

Hollow reed, hollow reed!

"No, I won't. Not because I don't want to, but because I can't." Megan spoke slowly, as if by careful enunciation of these words which she'd spoken repeatedly to this woman over the years, she could finally make them stick, and be understood. "I can't save her unless and until she decides she wants saving. It's her choice. While she still believes there's not much wrong with her and that we're the unreasonable ones, there's not a lot that anyone can do to help her."

"Yes, I remember the joke," her mother said bitterly. "How many psychologists does it take to change a light bulb? Only one, but the light bulb must really *want* to change."

"I'm sorry, Mom, I really am. There's nothing more I can do. Besides, I gave up saving others for New Year. No more lame ducks — apart from my patients, of course. It's one of my resolutions."

"Oh, yes?" muttered Patience, raising a sceptical eyebrow at the limp bird in the basket.

"You're prepared to help strangers, but not your own family! I don't know where we went wrong with you Megan, I really don't."

"With *me*? Where you went wrong with me? I'm not the one who's nuts, Mom."

"What a lovely term. Did you find it in one of your diagnostic manuals?"

Megan sighed, took a deep breath and told herself not to rise to the bait. "I have to go now, I have clients waiting. Love to you all."

Without waiting to hear her mother's response, she ended

the call and, for good measure, switched the damn thing off entirely. It was still early in the morning, only the second week in January, and already she felt exhausted.

"*Sawubona*, Patience," she said, greeting her receptionist in Zulu.

"*Yebo sawubona; unjani?*" Patience replied.

"Fine thanks, you?"

"*Ngikhona.*"

"Good holiday?"

"Very good."

"So, who's lined up for today?" Megan turned the large desk diary around to read it the schedule of clients.

"Mr Labuschagne first," Patience said, wiping her nose on a pink tissue and tucking it away snugly in the depths of her ample bosom.

"Then a gap, then Alta Cronjé," Megan noted. She was glad of the gap. It would give her time to review her notes on Alta and to have a think about the woman. Something was wrong there; things were not progressing as they should. "Then a Miss Nyoka — new patient?"

"Yes, referred by Dr Malan. She needs trauma debriefing for a hijacking."

"And the Taylors after her. Okay, remember to update the year date on the intake and indemnity forms, and then make a bunch of copies of each." Megan consulted the clock on the wall. Six minutes to go before her day began. "Patience, if you could find it in your most kind and generous heart, I —"

"— would love a cup of coffee. *Yebo*. But what about the bird?"

"Oh, right. Can you make some of this?" Megan fished the

box of baby cereal out of her bag and plonked it on the reception desk. "And feed it to the bird with this." She produced the dropper with a flourish. "I guess you'll have to make it quite runny."

Patience just stared at her.

"What?" Megan said.

"This bird is going to die."

"No, it's not. We can save it. Just give it some food and maybe water, and I'll nip out at lunchtime and take it to the vet. There's one on First Avenue."

"Even a very good vet cannot save this bird: it is not strong. It is going to die, but first it will suffer. I think it's better if I just break its neck."

"No!" Megan said, shocked. "It just hurt its wing, that's all. Probably got blown out of its nest by the storm last night."

She took a worried peek at the bird. It seemed to be moving less than it had earlier. Was it just less panicked than before and resting, or was it weaker?

"Maybe its mother kicked it out, when she saw how weak it is."

"Patience — just feed the bloody bird, okay? Keep it alive until lunchtime and I'll take care of it from there."

"If you say so," said Patience, unconvinced, but already taking the bird and food to the kitchenette. "But we better not leave it here, or the patients will think you're no good at saving and fixing," she added over her shoulder.

Patience always got the last word in, Megan reflected. And, almost always, she was right.

3
ALTA

Megan's office was a mix of soothing neutrals — a calm background for the pain and horror which was released daily in the space. Scatter cushions added a pop of pale mauve — a colour one of her more sandals-and-candles patients had told her was associated with healing in the world of crystals and auras — but the overall feel was light, airy and uncluttered. At the far side of the office, backed by high shelves of books and journals, stood her desk, its surface half-covered with files. Resting on top of a pile of papers was a paperweight: a fragile dandelion seed head trapped in timeless perfection inside a heavy glass cube.

Brilliant summer sun streamed in through the single window which overlooked the outside parking lot with the pepper tree, and the remaining office wall was hung with a large abstract oil painting. A long couch, a two-seater and a single wingback chair were grouped between the desk and the door, together with two small side tables — one topped with a dried flower arrangement and the other with a large box of tissues.

"Mr Labuschagne is here," Patience said, coming in and putting a large mug of strong coffee on the desk. She used the moment of relative privacy to bend over and rearrange her bosoms in their double-D-cup bra.

"Problem?" asked Megan, a little fascinated with these adjustments. Her own specimens had room to spare in a B cup.

"New bra. Too tight."

"Uh, okay. Does he want any tea or coffee?"

"No, nothing. As usual."

"You can send him in."

Henk Labuschagne, photocopier repairman and weekend pigeon racer, had so far spent four sessions with Megan, supposedly to deal with his marriage. Every time, Megan had suggested that it would be easier to address the issues in the relationship if both he and his wife were present, but her client had fervently resisted any attempt to allow his wife to join his sessions. It was time to turn up the heat a little.

He sat before her now, short, with thinning grey hair and a round pot belly, rattling off the inconsequential details of his week. He hardly paused to take a breath, but rubbed his hands nervously over his meticulously laundered and ironed jeans. He was probably afraid she'd ask some hard questions if he gave her half a chance, and was consciously or unconsciously keeping her at bay with an endless stream of prattle.

"Henk," she interrupted. "Why do I get the feeling that you're telling me everything except what you really came here to talk about?"

He tucked his chin back in surprise. His mouth opened and closed silently a few times.

"It's okay to tell me, you know. What you tell me is confidential. I won't tell anyone else. And" — she gave him an encouraging smile — "I've probably heard it before."

"Well, doc —"

"Megan," she automatically corrected.

"Megan," he said, and rubbed his legs again. "I did it, doc. I'm ... I'm an infidel."

"Sorry?"

"I've been an infidel."

Whatever Megan had been expecting, it wasn't this. She had no idea what he meant. Had he joined another religion, or engaged in some occult practice?

"I'm not sure I understand."

He stared back at her, a desperate pleading in his gaze.

"I committed infidelity."

"Ohhh." The penny dropped. "You're saying you were unfaithful to your wife?"

"Yes, doc. With a Chinese ... er ... massager. There by Cyrildene."

"You had sex with a worker in a massage parlour in Chinatown?" Megan clarified.

There was a sheen of perspiration on Henk's forehead now.

"I didn't mean to — have sex, you know? My friend Piet told me they give great massages. Eastern style, he said. And my back was killing me from bending over the machines all the time, so I thought why not, hey? And I got the address from him and I went there, but the girl didn't speak too much English, so maybe she didn't understand what I meant. And I couldn't help it, doc, honest, when she started touching me and

15

stuff. And she smelled so good, like flowers. And she was very pretty. So, when she started massaging me I got a —" He glanced at Megan, alarmed.

"You got an erection?" she guessed.

"Yes, that! And then I was lost, a goner. I couldn't stop, doc, I just couldn't. It felt too good. But then afterwards I felt so bad. Because Carol is a good woman, a good wife. And she doesn't give me a hard time, and it's not right what I've done. And now," his voice began to tail off, "I don't know what to do about it."

"First things first," Megan said, keeping her tone brisk and business-like. "Did you use a condom?" Please say yes, Henk. Please say yes, or else things are about to get a whole lot worse.

"Yes, she didn't even ask, Doc, just rolled it on my … you know … thing. She was very professional. Very good. Verrry good." He paused for a moment and seemed in danger of getting sucked back into the erotic memories. But, yanking himself back into the guilty reality of the present, he said, "But now I feel terrible! What must I do? Must I tell her what I did? Or mustn't I?"

Suppressing a sigh, Megan said, "Let's start by examining the choices you have, and what the potential positive and negative consequences of each of those might be. When you have a clearer idea of those, then it might be easier for you to make a decision."

Then again, maybe not. It would be nice, she thought, to be a mechanic. To be able to pinpoint exactly what was wrong in an engine, and to be able simply to clean the dirty pipe, or reconnect the detached alternator, or replace the faulty fan belt, and then pronounce it "fixed". Human beings were a lot more complicated and a lot more messy. And, even after therapy, they were never entirely as good as new.

"Tell me how you would feel about telling your wife, and what you think would happen if you did," Megan began.

She was soon into the swing of the day and the rhythm of the session. The outside world faded away as she focused all her attention on this fearful man sweating his way through the cock-up — a literal one, she realised — that threatened to destroy the relationship he valued. Her mother, her sister, and even the helpless bird with its tiny fighting heart were forgotten in her total absorption.

Forty minutes later, Megan saw Henk Labuschagne out of her consulting room. Patience would sort out the payment and book his next session for the following week. Megan flopped down in the comfortable chair behind her desk and sifted through the pile of client files which Patience had efficiently laid out for the day's consultations. She wanted to review her session notes on Alta Cronjé and plan for her next steps in therapy.

Megan began rereading her notes from their first session together, almost six months previously.

> *Alta Cronjé, 31yrs, computer programmer*
> *Married (Johan, 35yrs, electrician)*
> *1 child, daughter, (Marlien, 4yrs)*
> *Grandfather (maternal) was an alcoholic. No other family*
>   *history of alcoholism, depression or other psych*
>   *conditions.*

Presenting problem: adjustment problems post-surgery
(gynaecological, Dr A. Trotteur at Acacia).
Secondary insomnia (early morning wakings), nightmares
Generalised anxiety
Labile affect: anger → weepiness, irritability & temper
outbursts
Concentration & short-term memory problems (negative
impact on work performance → undermining
motivation)
Weight gain (+7 kg)
Unwillingness to be physically touched
Problems in sexual relationship with husb, incl loss of desire
and pain during intercourse.
→ problems in marriage. Husb doesn't fully understand,
though has been supportive and accepting of her phys
changes.
Low-grade depression
Assessed for suicidality: reports passing thoughts of death, but
no clear intention. Husb & children plus faith
(Christian) = strong inhibiting factors. (Joked that
would take a bottle of pills with a bottle of French
champagne if ever changed mind.)
Prelim. diagnosis: Adjustment Disorder / PTSD, possible
Mild Depression

Megan read through all the process notes from the regular weekly sessions with her client which had followed that intake interview. Some things had improved for Alta over the course of therapy. She was now functioning better at work, she was able to hug her family members again, and had managed to implement many of the anger management techniques she'd learned in therapy.

But, frustratingly, other symptoms had not faded. On a separate sheet of paper, Megan listed the problems which had persisted, resistant to her best therapeutic efforts to eliminate them.

Weight gain (no loss since start of therapy)
Nightmares (themes of threat, torture, powerlessness)
Mood swings
Sense of physical numbness
Sexual problems (loss of libido, battles to relax, pain during sex)

Alta Cronjé had been operated on in Acacia Private Clinic for a lesion on her genital labia. Prior to the surgery, she hadn't known both labia were extensively affected and was therefore shocked by the amount of tissue which had been removed. But although the experience had surely been a crisis, and the recovery — especially of her sex life — had been painful, it didn't fully account for the clinical picture Megan was seeing.

Alta had developed Post Traumatic Stress Disorder, despite the treatment which should have prevented this. Either, thought Megan, her treatment approach to Alta had been ineffectual — always a possibility — or something else was at work. Something deeper, perhaps cloaked in amnesia, or repression, or one of a dozen other defence mechanisms, was driving the ongoing presence of these symptoms. Simply stated, Alta should be much better by now. Perhaps it was time for a different approach.

Megan studied her client carefully when she arrived for the session. Alta was shorter than Megan, and plumper. There were dark shadows, like black arcs, beneath her brown eyes. Her hands fidgeted constantly with a tissue, tearing off small bits and rolling them into tiny balls which she placed in a small pyramid on the arm of the couch where she sat. When the tissue was completely shredded, she sighed with irritation, swept the balls into her hand, walked across the room, and tossed them into Megan's dustbin, before grabbing another tissue from the box on the coffee table, and starting again.

"I think that we should take some time to recap things before we go on," Megan said. "Is that okay with you?"

"*Ja*, sure," Alta said, unenthusiastically. She kept her eyes on her busy hands, saying nothing while, aloud, Megan reviewed why Alta had come to therapy, what they'd done in their sessions so far, what had and had not improved.

"By now you should be feeling much better than you are. So I'm worried that there's something else underneath all this, something which is preventing you from healing."

"What sort of something?" asked Alta, showing her first sign of interest in the session.

"I don't know. And I don't think you know either — at least, not consciously. Which means we can talk and talk until the cows come home, but we may never figure out what it is unless we try a different approach."

"What do you mean?"

"I think it might be useful to try some hypnotherapy."

"Hypnosis? Never!"

Inwardly, Megan sighed. She was sure she was about to hear

some of the many misconceptions about hypnosis that abounded, and which made her work much harder than it needed to be. But she kept her expression neutral and merely said, "Tell me your concerns."

"Hypnosis is mind-control," Alta said firmly. "That's why they tell you at the church never to do it. It empties your mind completely. It drives out the Holy Spirit. And I don't want to end up eating onions and quacking like a duck — no, thank you very much!"

"Alta, you've been seeing me for six months now. Do you honestly think that what I want for you is to eat raw onions and quack?"

"Well, okay, no. But what about the mind control?"

"I can't control your mind — not when you're fully conscious and not when you're in trance. No one can. If hypnosis was as powerful as people seem to think, then why would we psychologists bother talking and listening to you at all? I could just have knocked you out in the first session, said, 'Right, you feel all better now, wake up and back to normal!' and you would have been fixed."

"Hmmm," Alta said, apparently still unconvinced, but not as certain as she had been.

"And as for the Holy Spirit," continued Megan, knowing how important it was to work within her clients' worldviews, "if I don't have the power to make *you* change, I surely wouldn't have the power over God. Besides, why would I want to drive away the Holy Spirit? I want you to hang on to anything that helps you feel and get better."

"I'm still a bit scared."

"Of what?"

"Of not being in control, of not knowing what's going on, what you're doing to me. It will be like another general anaesthetic."

Megan, who had long since mastered the art of writing while still maintaining eye contact with her clients, made a note on her pad of paper while she said, "Alta, when you're in trance, you're very relaxed, but you're not asleep or unconscious. And you won't be amnesic for what happens. Anyway, I won't be "doing" anything to you — all hypnosis is self-hypnosis, and if at any time you want to stop, all you have to do is tell me, or open your eyes."

"Really?"

"Really."

"Well, I guess you can try, but I don't think you'll be able to get me to go under."

Megan allowed herself a small smile; the battle was half-won. In her experience, those clients who believed themselves impervious to hypnotherapy made the best candidates and went into trance most easily. She thought this might be because they had good defences and were determined to protect themselves against being taken advantage of and knowing that a part of their mind was keeping a wary eye on proceedings paradoxically allowed them to relax more fully.

She said, "Let's give it a shot next session and see how it goes, okay? I actually think you'll be very talented at hypnosis, because you're clever and creative. The only folks I battle with are those with lower intelligence, because they battle with abstract thought and symbolic images."

This was true. But it was also a therapeutic double bind that she often used when preparing clients for hypnotherapy. They either had to go into trance, or admit that they were not intelligent. Invariably, they chose the former option.

"Okay, I'll try it," Alta agreed. "I'm ready to try anything. I'm so sick and tired of feeling like this, you know? I just want to get better." Her eyes were moist with tears.

"That's all I want for you, too." After a pause, Megan asked, "What's your take-away from today's session?"

Alta thought for a bit and then said, "Maybe there's something else. Something else wrong with me."

"Yes, and I guess that's a bit scary. But it can also give you hope, because if there *is* something, and we can find out what it is, then we can try to fix it."

She ended the session there, telling Alta to book another appointment with Patience as soon as possible — before some unhelpful soul talked her out of trying hypnotherapy — and wished her goodbye.

Reviewing her notes, Megan inked a large asterisk in the margin next to one of the lines, then circled the asterisk for good measure.

Fears loss of control — connects to loss of consciousness and experience of gen anaesthetic: "What you're <u>doing to me</u>" ???

Underneath she wrote: *Next session: hypnotherapy (already prepped), regress to operation and gen anaesthetic. Check if any repressed memories.*

Then she took a deep breath, and focused on trying to clear her mind before the arrival of her next patient.

4
LAST TIME

When Megan opened the door to her townhouse that evening, Oedipus ran up to greet her — barking, yelping and dancing in circles. He was a fat and lazy Golden Retriever ("more doughnut than dog" according to Cayley) who didn't stir himself easily, but who always had these moments of madness when Megan or Mike came home from work.

Her townhouse was compact, but gave the impression of space, perhaps because it was largely under-decorated. She'd moved in a year ago and though he spent more nights than not at her place, Mike still kept his own apartment in Sandton. Somehow, she'd never gotten around to adding those little touches which would give it a more homey feel. Gardening and home decorating magazines littered her bedroom, the two bathrooms and the small kitchen, brightly coloured post-it notes marking pages with inspiring photos of designer spaces. But Megan never quite managed to find the time or energy to connect the dots between inspiration and execution. Tables, chairs and couches were where they should be, but the walls were mostly bare, and the place had an unlived-in feel which irritated her.

Oedipus leapt against her legs, demanding attention.

"Sit!" she said firmly, then leaned over to give the dog a loving pat. Everyone should have a dog, if only to have someone so glad to see you at the end of the day.

Mike's greeting was less exuberant.

"Howzit," he called from the couch in the living room where he sat facing the television.

A back on form Tiger Woods was putting on a green somewhere in the world, and the laptop propped up against Mike's knees was open on his Facebook page.

"Hi," Megan said, leaving Oedipus to rumple Mike's fair hair and plant a kiss on his lips.

He craned his neck around her to catch a putt on the screen, groaned in disappointment, and then smiled up at her.

"Good to see you. Finally."

"I know, I know — I'm late. Did you start supper?"

"No, I was working," he said gesturing to his laptop, now displaying a page from a conveyancing contract.

"So was I," she replied, vaguely nettled.

Oedipus jumped up on the couch beside Mike and stared up with adoring, chocolate brown eyes. He was a real charm monster, alright.

Megan dumped her bags, helped herself to a glass of wine from the bottle of Merlot sitting on the low table, and pushed the dog aside to squeeze in next to Mike. Her first sip was a big one, and it was followed by a deep sigh.

"Bad day?" Mike asked.

"Not great. I had some hard sessions and a new client. And then there was the bird."

Mike glanced up from his keyboard to check on Tiger's progress. "Bird? What bird?"

"There was this tiny, baby bird that I found under the pepper tree in the parking lot at work. It must have fallen out of its nest during the storm last night," she said, now tickling the pale fur of Oedipus's soft belly. Every time she paused, the dog writhed and kicked a paw to get her attention.

"Don't tell me you —"

"I couldn't just leave it there."

"Yes, you could. That's exactly what you could've done. *Should've* done. It would've made a nice meal for some cat — all part of the natural order." He typed something on the keyboard and snuck another look at the golf.

"I thought maybe we could save it."

"We?"

"Okay then, me. Anyway, I took it to the vet at lunchtime, but it was already so weak and she said there was no real hope, and so she —"

"— sent it to the great seed bar in the sky? Oh, my poor Meggy. Mad about all creatures damaged and deranged." Mike set aside the laptop, got up and kissed her forehead. "Come on, let's go make something to eat." He took her hand, pulled her up and pushed her towards the kitchen.

She opened the fridge and stared inside. On the top shelf stood a bottle of milk and another of wine. Scattered below were the dried remains of a ready-roasted chicken from the nearby deli, some wilted celery she'd bought with the vague idea of making a Waldorf salad, a tub of liver pâté with a furry grey-white film creeping across the surface, and a few eggs still in their brown cardboard box. Bottles of sauce, gourmet mustard, curry paste, tapenade and pesto — most of them still unopened and a few already past their expiry dates — stood on the door shelves, staring at her like the reproachful evidence of good intentions.

Beside her, Oedipus also stared hopefully into the fridge. He gave a sharp bark, perhaps of disgust.

Megan sighed. "*Oefs* ala Meg?" She tossed the mouldy pâté and the limp celery into the bin.

"Scrambled eggs, *again*?"

"Or you could order pizza."

"You know, Meggy-babes, you won't be able to rely on your looks forever. You really need to learn how to cook," Mike said, pinching her bum.

Irked, she slapped his hand away. "So do you!"

Megan knew she was a hopeless cook. Cooking had always been Cayley's thing. Cayley, who cooked perfect food for others. Cayley, who knew the nutritional content and calorie count of every morsel she allowed herself to swallow, but the pleasure of none of it. Cayley, who'd never known the sensuous joy of a delicious bite unseasoned by guilt. Cayley, who kept everyone else out of the kitchen, and herself away from the table.

Scrambled eggs and spaghetti bolognaise, learned in some long-distant class at high school, were about the extent of Megan's repertoire. She knew she should improve her skills —

eggs for supper at her age, for God's sake, like some hard-up, hungover student living in digs. It was even on her wretched list of New Year resolutions, but it irritated her to hear Mike state the obvious, and in a way which implied it was her job to do the cooking, her job to take care of him.

"Chauvinist pig," she muttered, whisking the eggs.

"Maybe. But you love me anyway, because I'm so cute and handsome!"

And he was — tall, blonde hair, baby blue eyes, and a tight butt. In spite of her irritation, Megan grinned, denting her left cheek where the odd dimple marked the result of a childhood accident. She stirred the eggs while he put toasted bread on two plates.

"Eat up, cute and handsome, it's all you're getting," she said, sliding the rumbled yellow mess onto the toast, and plonking one plate on the oak kitchen table in front of him.

They spoke a little about his day. Mike was a conveyancing attorney whom she'd met when he'd handled the transfer of her townhouse. It wasn't a field that Megan found particularly interesting, but she knew Mike was passionate about his work.

"The good news is," he said, washing down the last bite of toast with a swig of wine, "that we're probably going to get the deal for all the units in that housing development in Cape Town."

"That's fantastic," Megan said, smiling and clinking her glass against his. A thought occurred. "Could you do it from here? Or would you need to be based down there?"

"I'd have to be based in Cape Town. I could stay there for the duration of the project, or else fly down for the weekdays and return every weekend. Or maybe every other weekend."

"Charming."

"What?"

"It won't be too fantastic for us, Mike. We'll hardly see each other."

"You *are* in a bad mood today. Here," he said, pouring her another glass of red. "Have a little more — atta girl — and then we'll go to bed. And I'll kiss it all better, all over."

"You know, sex doesn't fix everything."

"No," he conceded, winking lazily. "Just most things."

As soon as she'd finished the excuse for supper, he took her hand and pulled her to the bedroom, closing the door firmly in Oedipus' hopeful face. He kissed her softly on her cheek, deeply on her mouth. He smelled of toast, and tasted of wine and familiarity. Unbuttoning her blouse, he reached in to cup her breasts with warm hands, while nuzzling the soft hollow at the base of her throat. They tumbled slowly onto the bed where he slid off their clothes with practised speed, but slowed down to slip on the condom with great care.

"Don't want a repeat of last time," he murmured.

They went through the usual touches, kisses and caresses, and, as usual, it was good. But Megan was left feeling strangely unsatisfied. Tired as she was, she lay awake for a long time thinking about her relationship with Mike, her work, and her New Year resolutions before eventually drifting into a restless sleep.

She dreamed of Alta Cronjé lying in a hypnotic trance on a couch littered with dead birds.

5
TRANCE

"So just *relax*. Lie back, make yourself completely comfortable, take a deep, deep breath, and try to find a spot on the ceiling that you can stare at without blinking," Megan began.

Alta Cronjé relaxed back in the couch, her feet resting on a footstool, her arms lying on the soft mauve blanket draping her lap and legs.

"Now as you stare at that spot, trying hard not to *blink*, perhaps you could imagine that your eyes are like tension magnets, pulling all the stress and tension from all parts of your mind and body up into your eyes, leaving your body so comfortable and so relaxed."

Alta's eyes blinked slowly.

"And soon you may find," Megan continued in a monotonous, sing-song voice, laying emphasis on the words that acted as subliminal suggestions, "that your gaze begins to glaze over or that your eyes begin to feel tired and heavy. And when your eyelids feel so tired — so tired and so heavy that they would really rather close — then just allow them to *close*. And if your eyelids would prefer not to close, then just allow them not to *close*, whichever is more comfortable."

Alta's eyes took one final slow blink and stayed closed.

"And as you relax even deeper and deeper, focusing on your breathing and my voice and just allowing the rest of the world to drift off and away, perhaps you could imagine, now, that a warm, heavy, soothing sensation is entering your body, through your toes. And as it enters your feet you can just allow them to relax and become warm and heavy and relaxed, all tension melting away …"

Megan's voice soothed in calming tones, in slow sentences which had no beginning and no ending, as she guided Alta in the progressive relaxation up through her body. Alta's feet went limp and turned outward, her arms slumped heavily to her side, her shoulders dropped and the tension eased from her face.

"… and just let that warm, relaxing sensation flow over your face. Find the muscles between your eyes and around your eyes, and let them smooth out, soothe out. Find the muscles in your jaw, where you store so much tension, and just allow them to relax … And, finally, find the muscles in your eyelids and allow your eyelids to become so heavy — so heavy, so comfortable and so relaxed — that it's just too much effort to open them, and when your eyes are so heavy and so relaxed that you can no longer open them, just let one of your forefingers lift and lower so that I know."

Megan leaned forward and stared closely at Alta's hands. The right forefinger on her right hand twitched and lifted a few millimetres before moving back down.

31

"Thank you. You're doing wonderfully well. Now, while you allow your body to *relax* deeper and deeper with each breath, and your mind to become soft and deep like folds of velvet, perhaps you could focus on my voice and listen carefully while I give you the protections to keep you safe in hypnosis."

Megan repeated the standard set of commands which would protect Alta while she was in trance, then went through the other usual steps in first inductions — a deepener to get Alta into an even more concentrated trance, setting up a beautiful "safe place" in the subconscious mind where she could rest while in trance; confirmation of *yes* and *no* fingers for signalling; and, as they had earlier discussed, the installation of a command suggestion for Alta to relax deeply and immediately in response to Megan saying the word "sleep".

Megan concluded, "Remember, the word 'sleep' when used in ordinary conversation or by anyone else will have no effect on you, only when we're working in hypnosis and you know it to be appropriate. So for now, just do that, just *sleep*."

Alta's head lolled to one side on the cushion. Her breathing was slow and even, and Megan was satisfied that the trance was deep enough to begin the planned regression.

"Well done, Alta, you're doing very, very well. Now I would like you, if you're willing, to imagine that you are staring at a calendar. And this calendar has one page for every day, and it's open on today's date, Monday the twelfth of January. But this is a very special calendar, because it works backwards and it takes you backwards. So, if you tear off the top page, you will see yesterday's date: Sunday the eleventh of January. Do that now, see yourself tearing off the top page and going back to yesterday." Megan paused a moment before checking, "Can you see the calendar? Can you see how it goes backwards, how it takes you backwards? Let your fingers tell me."

Alta's yes-finger twitched.

"Excellent. Now I'd like you to start tearing off the pages, one by one. And as you tear them off, you'll find yourself carried back in time, back in time with the pages. Nice and slowly now, as you relax even more deeply, go back to Saturday the tenth, and then Friday the ninth, and Thursday the eighth."

Megan kept her voice in its rhythmic, melodic cadence, lulling Alta into the serene calm which would allow her to return to her traumatic experience.

"And perhaps, as you continue looking at that calendar, the pages begin to tear themselves off, one by one, and you just allow yourself to be carried back, day by day, so comfortably, so easily ... And after a while, perhaps even right now, those pages begin to tear off and flutter away more and more quickly, page after page. And it's so relaxing to see them flying off so fast, it's almost a blur ... And they go and go and go, back and back and back, through December and November and even earlier ... And you go back in time with them ... And after a while it starts slowing down, slowing right down until it stops, and brings you to that date in July last year when you had the operation. And when you're there, on that day, let your yes-finger lift and lower so that I know."

A pause. Then the finger signalled.

"And perhaps you could read off that date to me, Alta."

Megan waited for several moments. It was usual for people in trance to have a delayed response, particularly when the trance was this deep. When it seemed that no response was coming, she suggested, "You'll find talking easy now, Alta. Tell me what date the calendar has brought you to."

After a few more seconds, Alta mumbled, "Twenty-second of July."

Megan checked her notes. That had indeed been the day of the operation.

"Very good. And I wonder if you would just allow yourself to look around, and be aware of where you are. See the lights and the colours, allow yourself to hear the sounds, and see who's nearby. And then just tell me what you're experiencing."

The answer came quickly this time. "Pain, so sore." Alta's body twitched in the seat.

"Just sleep, now Alta, so deeply asleep and comfortable," Megan said. When her patient's body relaxed again, she asked, "Where are you?"

After a pause, Alta said, "Recovery room."

"You're in the recovery room, after the operation?"

"Mm."

"And you're in pain?"

She kept her voice neutral even though it seemed strange to her that Alta should have felt pain so soon after the procedure. Surely she would've been given medication to keep her pain free once the general anaesthetic wore off? Perhaps this might be the reason why Alta had subsequently been so traumatised, and so sensitive to touch in the weeks and months that followed.

"So sore," Alta whispered.

A single tear from the corner of one eye slid over her face

and down her neck, leaving a thin trail through the make-up on her face. Megan knew from experience that one tear on the outside usually meant that the client was weeping intensely on the inside, so she hurried to intervene.

"For now, you can just allow that pain to become much, much smaller, Alta, almost as if you were turning down the volume control on your pain. There is no need to feel it now, just turn it right down, and *sleep* deeply.

Alta sighed.

"Now tell me what happens next."

"The doctor comes to me."

"The one who operated on you?"

"Mm."

"And what does he do or say?"

Alta gave a little gasp, then said, "Smiles ... pats me on the head."

"He pats you on the head?" Again, Megan kept her tone dispassionate, but silently she thought, *patronising git.*

"Mm. All done, all perfect now."

"Say again?" Megan leaned forward to catch the softly mumbled words.

"All done, all perfect now," Alta repeated.

"Do you say that or does he say that?"

"Him."

Megan sat back, nonplussed; the words seemed peculiar to her. She would have expected the doctor to say something like, "You'll be feeling better soon," or "I'll come back and check on you later," or "The op went well, you can relax now." But "all perfect now"? It gave her an odd feeling. Still, it was her job to help her clients, not judge the doctor's bedside manner, so she reframed the words into something more constructive.

"So it's all finished, and you can go back to your bed in your ward, and just relax and know that you will recover very well. Right now, all is well."

Something niggled at Megan, preventing her from ending the regression. All practitioners knew the sensation of therapist's intuition. When you were trained, the lecturers warned you against following your instincts, and urged you to stay instead on the straight and narrow path illuminated by theory and research, but Megan didn't know a single therapist who didn't, on occasion, follow the lead of their inner voice. She followed hers now.

"Okay, Alta, you've rested for a while, and you feel very relaxed and comfortable. With each breath that you take, just allow yourself to *sleep* even deeper and deeper, more and more relaxed. And perhaps you could just allow yourself to go back to earlier in the day, before the operation. Would it be okay to do that?"

When she got the affirmative signal, Megan continued, "And, again, look around and tell me what you see."

"Lights."

"You see lights?"

"Light ... light ... light."

"Okay, and what do you hear?"

"Click-click ... click-click."

"Where are you?"

"On trolley ... in corridor. Wheeling me."

"You're lying on the trolley, in the passage of the hospital, and you can see the lights passing overhead and hear the clicking as you're wheeled along. And how are you feeling?"

"Muzzy … fuzzy."

"You're feeling muzzy and fuzzy. Do you know why?"

"Gave me a pill."

"I see. They gave you a pre-op tranquiliser to keep you nice and calm — is that right?"

"Mm."

"And do you feel calm?"

"Mm, feels nice," Alta said, her tone lifting a little.

A smile dimpled Megan's cheek. "Yes, it feels very nice to be calm and relaxed. And then what happens?"

"Get to the operating room."

"You get taken into operating theatre. And what's that like?"

Alta shivered. "So cold."

"Yes, the operating theatres are kept very cool. Who's there, Alta? Have a look around and tell me."

"Nurse."

"There's an OR nurse. And who else?"

"Anaesthet— Anaes—"

"The anaesthetist is there. Anyone else?"

"Dr Trotteur."

"Is he your doctor? Your gynaecologist?"

"Hm."

"Does he say anything?"

There was a long pause before Alta responded. "Not to worry."

"He tells you not to worry. And then?"

"Tells nurse to go."

"The doctor tells the nurse to go?" Megan repeated, checking she'd heard right.

"Not needed … is simple procedure. Doesn't need help… She must go to C, help Dr Williams with Caesar."

"I want to be sure I understand, Alta. The doctor sent the OR nurse away. He told her he didn't need her help with the surgical procedure, and she should rather go and assist Dr Williams with the caesarean section in operating room C. Have I got that right?"

"Uh-huh."

Megan was no surgeon, but she found this very unusual. Surely it was standard procedure always to have an OR nurse present at an operation — particularly one of the gynaecological kind? A bad feeling was starting to take root just under her chest.

"And what's happening now?"

"She's gone." Alta's left hand twitched where it lay, and a foot moved under the blanket.

"The nurse is gone. So, it's just Dr Trotteur and the anaesthetist?"

"Uh."

Megan wasn't sure if she was imagining it — or projecting her own rising unease onto the woman in front of her — but she thought she heard a tremor in Alta's voice.

"Where is the anaesthetist now?"

"My head."

"He's sitting at your head," Megan repeated. "And what's he doing?"

Alta mumbled something softly. It sounded like "ko."

"What was that? Say again?"

"…'uko."

"You'll find it easy to speak more loudly and clearly Alta, because it's important for me to hear. Now tell me again, what is the anaesthetist doing?"

"S'duko."

"He's playing sudoku?" Megan heard the indignation in her voice and took a deep breath to steady herself.

"Yes."

"And what is Dr Trotteur doing?"

"He's putting the tools straight."

This time Megan was sure she hadn't imagined it. There was a definite quiver in Alta's voice, and the pitch had risen, too.

"He's arranging the instruments for the operation."

"There's a knife!" Alta shuddered.

"A knife? Is it a surgical scalpel?"

"Yes," Alta said and seemed to relax just a little.

"Then what does he do?"

"Smiles. Touches me." Alta's chest was beginning to rise and fall faster.

"Where?" Megan asked shortly, "Where does he touch you?"

"… forehead."

Not *that* then.

"He smiles and touches you on the forehead. Does he say anything?" Megan asked.

Alta said nothing, but her body stiffened. Her feet flexed and her fingers curled into tight fists. Megan could tell she was on the verge of a strong negative reaction, but she was loathe to interrupt the regression. Best to get it over with as quickly as possible.

"What happens next Alta, tell me quickly."

"Anaesthetist puts a needle in my arm, and there's a tube … He injects into the tube …"

"He's getting ready to give you the anaesthetic. Does he say anything?"

"Count backwards, from one hundred. See if you can get to zero," Alta said in a voice deeper than her own.

"And then?"

"He looks at Dr Trotteur," Alta said, her voice catching on the last two words. Her feet twitched under the blanket.

"He looks to Dr Trotteur to give him the go-ahead?"

"Uh."

"And then? Tell me now — what happens then, Alta?"

Alta rolled her head from side to side against the back of the chair, and jerked her elbows in against her sides. Her knuckles were white ridges of bone on her tight fists.

"Don't want to," she whimpered, tears now sliding freely down both cheeks.

Megan's heart thudded in her chest. She was desperate to ease Alta's suffering, but knew that the truth was perhaps just moments away from being revealed. "Tell me quickly and then we'll go away from here and be safe. What happens then? Tell me now," she urged in a commanding tone.

"Doctor leans over me, leans on me, on my boobs. He says … he says —" Alta broke off and pushed herself back into the couch, as if cringing away in fright. Her legs drew up against her body.

"What does he say?"

"Too much!" Alta gasped.

"He says too much?"

Alta gave a single sob from deep in her throat. "No, too much of *me*."

"He says there's too much of you?" Megan checked, alarmed.

"Whispers."

"He whispers? What exactly does he whisper?"

"Don't want to listen, I want to go. Want to go. *Please*," Alta begged.

"We'll go soon, I promise. Just a few seconds more, and then we can leave. As soon as you tell me exactly what he says."

Looking at Alta squirming on the couch, Megan wondered if she was pushing her too far. She was just about to call it quits when Alta spoke in a clear, deep voice.

"There's way too much of you, my little bitch. But not for long. I'm going to cut it all away and make it neat and perfect. Doctor knows best."

6
GUT FEEL

"**N**ow, Alta, just *sleep!*" Megan commanded. "It's all over. Just sleep and go back to your safe place and rest there, safe and sound."

Immediately, Alta stopped sobbing. Her head lolled to the side, she took a deep breath and sank deeply into the couch.

Megan rubbed a hand across her mouth, thinking frantically. Was this a real memory, or some drug-induced hallucination that Alta only thought had happened? It seemed very real to her, but Megan could not be absolutely sure.

Alta's extreme distress was undoubtedly genuine. Megan wanted to help her feel better, but would that be possible without interfering with the memory? If the experience had really happened, Alta might want to pursue a legal case and then she'd need all the details to be clear and accurate. Megan knew that with all the prejudice against hypnosis, and all the disinformation propagated by the so-called "false memory" organisations, she had perhaps already compromised her patient's memory in the eyes of the law. Inwardly she cursed herself for not taping the session as proof that she hadn't planted suggestions, or introduced inaccuracies.

Bringing her mind back from useless regrets, she applied herself to the question of what she could do now to help her client. Ordinarily she worked to diminish the distress associated with the experience, or she'd reawaken her patient and use a trauma technique to desensitise the memory, but these were methods which would invariably reduce the clarity of the memory. What she did now depended on what Alta would want to do going forward. It was time to finish up this session.

"Okay, Alta, as you rest, I want you to know that the experience you had in the operating theatre is over. All over. It happened many, many months ago. It is *not* still happening now. See the calendar again, see it gaining pages day by day as it moves you forward in time, day by day, to the present here and now. See yourself sitting safely in this room, today. The operation is over, you are safe and sound, feeling calm, and you are no longer in physical pain. Right now, you're safe and all is well. And when you come awake, you'll be able to remember the exact details of the experience you've recalled today."

Megan moved on to the reawakening and reorientation of Alta to the present, and gave her a few moments to fully wake up. Alta opened her eyes and sat up straight.

For a minute, the two women simply stared at each other, then Alta said, "What the *fuck*?"

"Yes," Megan replied, keeping her voice calm. "It's very shocking."

"What the fucking hell did that man ... that ... that monster, do to me? And why?"

43

"Okay, Alta, take a deep breath and let's just talk for a moment about what you've remembered. And about what it may or may not mean."

"What do you mean?"

"Hypnosis is not what you see in the movies, Alta. It's not a scene-by-scene accurate replay of precisely what happened in reality. It's a subjective record of what we remember happening, all mixed up with our feelings and thoughts about what we think happened. It's a subjective perception, not an objective record — do you understand?"

"What are you trying to say? That I imagined the whole thing?" Alta was getting angry again, leaning forward on the couch.

"Not at all. I'm simply cautioning you that, that …" What *was* she trying to say? Was she merely attempting to manage her own anxiety by casting doubts on the accuracy of Alta's memory? That would be unconscionable. "I'm just saying we need to go slowly here, and cautiously. A memory recovered in hypnosis doesn't count as evidence of anything — you need to know that."

Alta's face was bleak. "Do *you* think it happened?"

"Gut feel? Yes, I do."

Alta slumped back and was quiet for a few moments. "So what now?" she asked, starting to crumble a tissue again.

"That depends on what you want to do. If you want to take this further, lay a charge — of assault, I guess — against Dr Trotteur at the police, or make a complaint against him at the Health Professions Council, then it's important that we don't tamper with your memories. I would support you through that process, though it won't be easy on you emotionally to dredge it all up for others to hear. And I'm thinking it would be a difficult case to prove. But if you do manage to nail him, then you would be doing something tremendous to right a wrong and to stop him, because … there might be others."

"He's done this to other women?" Alta was clearly distressed by the thought.

"If he's done it to you, then quite possibly, yes. But it's your choice, Alta. If you simply want to forget all about it, if you want me to help you dull the memories and heal the pain, you're within your rights to choose that course of action. And I'll support and help you in that, too."

Alta sighed and it seemed to Megan that the breath came from the very depths of her pain.

"Why don't you take some time to think it through? You don't have to decide immediately. Think about what it will mean to you either way. Think about what, in five years' time, you'll wish you had done now. Maybe chat to Johan about it and see what he thinks. And we can talk it through next time."

"All right." Alta picked up her handbag and got ready to leave.

"Are you okay to go?" asked Megan.

Alta nodded.

"Call me if you're not coping."

"Maybe I'll take the week off and we can spend some time at the farm, and get my head straight on all this. Just the three of us — Marlien and Johan and me."

"That sounds like a good idea. It'll be better if you're not alone too much right now."

Once they'd said their goodbyes, Megan flopped into her chair and blew out a breath she felt she'd been holding for the last half hour. Her hands were trembling and her heart still beat unpleasantly fast in her chest.

She knew, just knew, that Alta's memory was real. That somewhere in this hospital there was a very disturbed and dangerous doctor, and a slew of vulnerable women. Whatever Alta Cronjé decided, Megan knew that she herself would need to take this further.

What she needed first was more information.

That night, little though she felt like it, she set about finding out more. After an afternoon of demanding sessions with three more clients, one of whom spent the whole hour complaining that therapy wasn't working for her, yet insisted on making another appointment, Megan was exhausted and wanted only to research the softness of her bed and her pillow. But her session with Alta Cronjé still weighed heavily on her mind, so she booted up her laptop and settled cross-legged on the couch, a piece of salty Siciliana pizza in her free hand.

"Surfing the web?" Mike asked, snagging the last piece from the box and peering over her shoulder while he ate it.

"Sort of."

"The Health Professions Council of South Africa," Mike read off the screen. "Ooh, exciting stuff."

"I've just got to look something up."

"Aren't you all registered and paid up?"

"It's not for me."

"Oh, a *client*." He said the word with heavy emphasis as he plopped onto the couch beside her. "One of the crazies."

"Don't call them that."

"So why this site — is the client a doctor? Or a dentist?" he asked, trailing fingers lightly over her knee.

Megan twitched her leg away; she hated being tickled. "Nope."

"Hmm, a mystery …" Mike tickled her other knee and moved his exploring hand up her thigh until she swatted it away. "So that must mean —"

"Haven't you got something else to do?" Megan asked.

"Well, yes, babes. But I'd need *you* for that." He grinned and wiggled his eyebrows suggestively.

"Mike, I'm so tired that it would technically constitute necrophilia."

"Reminds me of a limerick I once heard," Mike said, a teasing glint in his eyes. "Only poetry I could ever remember. Goes like this: There once was a caveman named Dave, who kept a dead whore in his cave. He said, 'I admit, I'm a bit of shit, but think of the money I save!'"

"That's disgusting."

"Oh, lighten up! It's a joke — remember them? Things that make you laugh and smile. Or have you forgotten how?"

Megan ignored him. She had no energy for arguing tonight.

After a pause, Mike began again, "So if the client isn't the doctor, that must mean … that the client has a problem *with* a doctor. And you're trying to check up on the doctor."

"Dammit!" Megan said.

"I'm right!" Mike crowed.

"No, the website just crashed."

"Oh, come on, Meggy, I think you've got something to say to me." He sang it to the tune of the Rod Stewart classic, *Maggie May*.

"You know I can't."

"Just a few juicy details. What's the deal with the doctor? Or is it a dentist? I've always figured only dodgy people want to spend their lives with their hands shoved inside other people's filthy mouths."

"Just let me finish this, okay?" Megan said, irritated.

She retyped the address of the Council in the search engine, but the system hung for a while and then returned the message "Gateway Timeout". She tested her search engine on other sites, which all loaded without a problem, and then tried the Council's again, double-checking the address as she keyed it in.

"What difference can it make if you tell me? They wouldn't know," Mike said.

"I'd know," Megan said. "It's unethical. I won't be telling you anything, so you may as well stop nagging me."

"Is it a doctor at the hospital — at Acacia?" Mike said suddenly.

Megan was so surprised that she glanced up quickly, startled. Mike took this as confirmation.

"It is, isn't it?" he said gleefully. "What's he done? Or is it a she?"

"Mike!"

"Oh-oh, shenanigans in the consulting room, I'll bet! Have they been playing doctor-doctor?" He reached out with open hands as if to examine her breasts. "Should *we*?"

Megan swore. The website had failed to load again, and the links to it from other websites weren't working either. Why were government websites always so hopeless?

"You could be the naughty nurse, who's just done something *wery badd* …"

"You have a one-track mind, Michael Welsh," she said, pushing his hands away.

"So do you. It revolves around work," he snapped. He stalked out the room, slamming the door behind him.

Megan swore again.

7
RIPPLES

He smears the butter from side to side, evenly and right up to the edges, not neglecting the corners. His morning ritual of bread and tea is soothing. This mass-produced, ready-sliced bread tastes like nothing, of course, but each slice is perfectly rectangular and white. Nothing else in the day that follows will be as neat as this. The anchovy spread must also be evenly distributed — no lumps or swirls can remain to disturb the surface. He picks up a chef's knife — its sharper, curved edge is better for this job than the serrated edge of a bread knife — and cuts off the crusts with four swift swipes. He wipes the mess of butter and spread off the blade and cuts again, twice across, twice down. Nine equal bites. He eats them.

Palesa, who has already washed the dishes, wiped the counters and put his laundry into the washing machine, enters the kitchen. Her black and white domestic worker's uniform is spotlessly clean and neatly ironed; she knows this is important to him. Her face is beaming with pride as she beckons her son into the room.

The boy is twelve, on the cusp of his mutation to manhood, and *he is a delight to look at. His features are symmetrical, his skin a smooth, unblemished brown, and his teeth are straight, even and white. Oh, that they could all be this way.*

"Tshepo got his report yesterday. It is all A's. Even for maths — an A!" Palesa says.

"Perfect!" He bestows a smile on the child. "Simply perfect. Congratulations."

The boy grins and squirms, both pleased and embarrassed.

"What do you say to the doctor?" Palesa prompts her son.

"Thankyouveryverymuchforpayingmyschoolfees," Tshepo says. It comes out in a rushed, uneven utterance. The child looks better than he speaks.

"Would you like to see his report?"

Not really, but it seems it must be done. Things cannot always be as perfect as the boy's results, as unspoiled as his skin.

"Go fetch it, Tshepo," Palesa urges.

The boy runs outside, to the room at the back of the house, and his mother lays the tray for tea. Cup, saucer, milk jug, teapot and sweetener tablets in the bowl — all white, all placed in their correct places on the linen tray-cloth.

He always has his tea directly after his breakfast. Routines are important. He hates it when something, or someone, disrupts his routines and his plans. Glitches, mishaps and disruptions leave lingering ripples in the smooth flow of his days. He drops sweeteners into his tea — one, two — stirs precisely five times, sips.

It is time to choose another.

He must do better this time, select more carefully. He has made some unwise choices in the past which came back to disturb his ordered existence. That distressing — abusive, really — phone call yesterday, for example. They usually have a better respect for authority, the Calvinists, but she might be one of the stroppy ones, and she had, he now knew, an uncouth husband. He wishes he could cut the disturbing phone call away from his day as easily and thoroughly as he cut the crusts off his bread. He must not let these flies in the ointment get under his skin.

He picks up the linen napkin, dabs at his mouth, feels, as he always does, that almost imperceptible ridge on the bottom of his chin. No. He will not think about that.

He stares out at the garden, sipping his tea. In future, he must investigate better, know more before he makes his decision. The student had been a mistake, too. He had assumed from her earrings and bohemian way of dressing that she was an arts student — a know-nothing, do-less. But he discovered — afterwards — that she was a law student.

Not good enough, he chides himself. He must be more meticulous.

His hand strays back to his chin, strokes the line. It feels longer — could it be growing? No! That is an intrusive thought, an impossible, erroneous one. He will clear it from his mind. Nevertheless, he finds himself walking to the bathroom, standing at the basin, pulling the magnifying mirror out on its extendable arm to check.

There, see? It is not bigger. It is almost invisible.

But still, it is *there.*

"Are you ready?"

A girl, a swing, a fall, a cut. His mind pulses with the images.

He spins around on his heel, bellows, "What did you say?"

Palesa stands in the open doorway, clutching a white sheet of paper. She retreats a step, her face alarmed.

"Are you ready? To see Tshepo's report?" her voice is barely above a whisper.

He slams the door in her face. Stupid woman!

"Are you ready? Are you sure?" The voice again.

It is not real. It is not now. *But, it is strong enough to carry him back a quarter of a century.*

He is little again.

"Are you ready?" the girl asks.

"Oh, yes," he says, climbing onto the swing, eager to get going.

Red paint peels from the seat's rough surface, and splinters prick him as he wriggles, but these things do not bother him. He is about to be pushed by Sara, the oldest child in the home. Sara is big and has thick arms, and when she gives you a Chinese bracelet on your wrist, it feels like your skin is being ripped off. Everybody tries to stay on the right side of Sara — and here she is, offering to push him on the swing.

"Are you sure you're ready, Attie?"

She speaks in a strange way, drawing out his name slowly. Her teeth gleam and her eyelids droop over her deep-set eyes when she grins.

"Yes, yes!" He takes a firm hold of the chains.

All the other children draw closer to watch. One of the older boys nudges Sara and whispers something in her ear that makes her giggle. The smallest child in the house, a runny-nosed girl whom everyone calls Beany, peeps around one of the poles at him, and smiles shyly.

"Then let's" — Sara pulls back the swing until the seat tilts — "begin!"

She thrusts it forwards, pushing so hard with both hands

against his back that he almost loses his grip on the chains.

"Up you go," Sara shouts. "Up." Shove. "And up!" Shove.

Higher and higher he rises with each thrust. It's like flying! The little ones below gasp as his skinny legs and bare feet sail up into the air, and his head tips back with each lift. Over there is the red-brick house where they all live with their house mother Tannie Elsa. He soars higher even than the corrugated tin roof winking silver in the late afternoon sun, as high and light as a bird. If he lets go of the chains, he will swoop through the air, free and strong.

And still, Sara pushes him higher.

"Look," she cries to the others, "pigs can fly!"

"Pig-gy, Pig-gy," they begin to chant the hated nickname.

"This little piggy went to market, *this little piggy stayed at* home,*" she pushes in time to the chant, her thrusts like blows on his thin back.*

"This little piggy had roast beef, and this little piggy had none." She is yelling the words up at him now. "And this little piggy cried wee-wee-wee all the way home!"

The swing seems to pause at the top of each lift — to stop and hang suspended in the air before it plummets down with an unsteady back-swing. With each pause, his bum lifts off the seat, and with each drop, something cold swoops in his stomach. Sweat trickles down his face, but he dares not let go of the chains to wipe it from his eyes.

"Stop it! Stop it, I don't like it."

She ignores him.

The seat of the swing wobbles and jerks from side to side. Any moment now, it might loop right over the bars which hold it up. The poles creak and strain against bolts already loose in the base of old, cracked cement. What if the whole thing pulls loose and topples over? What if his sweaty hands slip and he falls down onto that hard, red earth?

"Stop! Please, please!" he whispers.

Air roars in his ears. Tears blur his eyes. He wants to scream, but every time he opens his mouth, the wind races in and snatches his breath. Far below, Sara and the others chant and laugh. He cannot hear, cannot breathe. His whole being is one whispered scream. Stopstopstopstopstop!

A gong sounds, and the chant falls silent. The children run away up the slight rise of grass to the back door of the house.

The swing veers and rocks. He clings on, whimpering, cursing. As it sways slower and lower, he sticks his feet out, drags them hard against the hollow of ground and stones beneath the swing, until it judders to a halt. He topples down onto his knees in the dirt, gasping and trembling.

When he can breathe again, he sits up and fists the tears from his eyes. His feet hurt. They are scraped raw front and back, and the nail of one big toe is torn away from the bloody nail bed. Tiny bits of grey and white gravel pit the grazes on his knees. A warm, wet stain spreads across the front of his shorts.

There's a small noise to his right. He swings around, sees Beany still standing behind the pole. She takes a step towards him.

"Sorry, Attie," she says.

A fierce hotness begins to throb in him. That she *should feel sorry for* him *— this puny, snot-faced girl, with her too-short dress and stupid voice. She saw what they did to him.*

And she saw what he did to himself.

He wants to yell and run away from here. He wants to smash and break and bruise. Blood beats in his ears as all the world becomes this moment, this rotten place.

"Come here, Beany," he says, taking a ragged breath and forcing his lips to twist into a smile. "It's time for your turn on the swing."

The little girl smiles and clambers onto the same seat, seeming not to mind the wetness he left behind. Dirty girl. Dirty, rotten, stinking girl.

Now he is the one behind the swing. Now he is the one pushing — hard and high. It doesn't take long for Beany to get panicky. The swing is hardly high at all when she starts to shriek like a mad thing, a high-pitched scream of terror which rings in his ears and drills through his head.

"You shut up," he screams. "You dirty —"

"Attie! Stop that!"

He turns for just a second to see Tannie Elsa charging down the rise toward them, and in that instant, the red swing with the screaming girl swings back down at him and clips him on the chin. His teeth snap together with a sharp click. He flips backwards through the air and lands hard on the ground, banging his head on the red earth. Then he feels and sees nothing more.

When he opens his eyes, he is lying on the back seat of a car. There is blood in his mouth. It tastes tinny and sharp like the two-cent pieces he puts in his mouth to hide from the other boys. It trickles down the back of his throat and makes him feel sick. Tannie Elsa sits next to him, pressing a cloth against his chin and mouth, and something against the back of his head. Someone, a man he does not know, is driving the car.

"Are you awake now? You banged your head and cut your lip, so we're taking you to the doctor to get stitches," says Tannie Elsa.

"What?" He feels confused. Her face above him is too big. He tries to bat away the pressure at his chin. "Hurts."

"We're taking you to Dr Biddle — so he can check you out and sew you up again."

"Don't like him … hurts me."

"Now don't talk nonsense. We always take you kids to Dr Biddle and he sorts you out fine, doesn't he?"

"Gonna puke …"

"Don't —"

He retches. A thick clot of dark blood, chased by a stream of vomit, spills onto the seat, onto Tannie Elsa's dress. His throat burns, his head is going to split.

She makes a noise of disgust. "Now look what you've done, Attie."

He stares at the black leather of the seat. Blood and vomit run in rivulets down the stitched grooves. The darkness takes him away again.

He lies on his side on a hard, high bed in the doctor's office, on top of a green rubber sheet which sticks to his bare legs. A strong smell catches in his throat. He stares at the jumble of silver instruments lying on a metal tray on top of a small table beside the bed.

The doctor wears a white coat and he smells funny, too. "What have you been doing to yourself, my boy? Getting into all sorts of mischief again, hey? You've got yourself a nice cut here on your chin." The doctor reaches out a thick finger and pokes.

"Eina!" Attie pulls his chin back.

"And he's got a cut on the back of his head here, too, doctor," says Tannie Elsa from behind him. *"And he's been vomiting and passing out."*

"Hmmm ... probably got concussion. Let's see the back of his head."

The doctor whistles and clicks his tongue against his teeth. "We're going to have bit of a problem here, because this cotton wool is stuck onto the cut."

"I was trying to stop the bleeding, doctor."

"Well, it worked, but now the blood's dried and the cotton wool is all stuck on. See, when I try to pull it off?"

Sharp pain tugs at the back of his head. It feels as though they're trying to pull off his scalp.

"Eina!"

The doctor laughs at him. "That's not sore, not for a big boy like you. Come on, sit up now."

Attie wants to explain that for sure it is sore, but he already knows that the doctor won't listen — those stubby fingers are too busy pouring a splash of disinfectant into the shiny metal basin of water resting on the bed. The water turns milky white and a sharp smell fills the air.

The doctor dips a wad of gauze into the white mixture and rubs at Attie's chin and lip. The cloth hurts, the antiseptic burns and when Tannie Elsa starts plucking the cotton wool off the back of his head, it feels like tufts of hair are being torn out of his scalp. His throat pinches closed and hot tears spill over.

"Why are you crying? It's not so bad. Don't be such a baby, now," says the doctor.

Those hurting hands come closer. There is a threaded needle between the thumb and forefinger. He jerks away, back into the softness of Tannie Elsa.

"Can't we give him an injection, doctor, so it won't hurt so bad?" she asks.

Attie nods his support of this idea, even though moving his head hurts.

"No, no. It really doesn't hurt that much, just a little pinch. I've sewn up kids half his age who haven't shed a tear. He's just making a fuss to get attention. He's as bad as a girl! Besides, by the time the anaesthetic starts working, we can already be finished here. Trust me, Elsa, doctor knows best."

Attie waits for Tannie Elsa to stop the rough fingers with the sharp needle, waits for her to insist that the doctor take away the pain. But all she does is clutch his head tighter back against her chest and say, "Doctor knows best, my boy. Now, sit very still or you'll get sewn up skew."

A sharp pain burns his chin like ice, like fire. He feels each hot stab as the needle twists in and out of his skin, each sharp throb as the thread tugs and pulls tight. His whole face aches. He tries to keep his lip and chin still, tries not to start crying again, but he can't stop himself from groaning.

The doctor tuts, ties a final stitch and says, "There you are — good as new! Better actually, since I cut off that ugly mole at the same time. Okay, now turn around and we'll do the cut at the back of your head."

"No," Attie says, though it hurts to speak and he cannot move his lips properly. "It's too sore."

"Stop being such a baby!" The doctor sounds cross, now.

He twists Attie's head around roughly and yanks off the remains of the dried cotton wool, ignoring the sobs.

Tannie Elsa pulls Attie's face gently against her chest and whispers, "Shhh now, shhhh … The doctor says it doesn't hurt, it'll soon be over. Just shhh and be still."

"Why do you believe him and not me? It's my head. I know what it feels like. It hurts bad. It feels like my head is on fire. Make him stop!" he wants to say, but they'll never listen, not to him, so he says nothing, merely burrows his face deeper into the softness of Tannie Elsa's bosom.

She smells like sweet flowers, and he can see a fine dusting of white talcum powder on her skin. She holds him tight to her, and kisses the top of his head. He no longer needs to cry. He pushes what is happening at the back of his head to the back of his mind. It is happening to someone else, somewhere else. The doctor is hurting another little boy far away. He, Attie, is here, nestled against the soft pillows of Tannie Elsa's breasts.

Strange tingles of hot and cold begin to buzz through his body, coming from somewhere deep down. He wants something more, needs something more. He wants to climb right inside the woman, to burrow deep into her soft sweetness. His hands creep from where they clutch her back, move around to her front. She gives an odd sort of giggle and pushes them away.

"Now just the tetanus shot … and … there you are — all done. Won't even leave much of a scar. Didn't I tell you it wouldn't be so bad, eh?"

A burning pain sears through his left arm, but it is nothing compared to the burn behind his eyes — a heat which has nothing to do with tears.

Maybe the doctor notices, because the disgusting man blinks and takes a step back.

"She believed you. She listened to you.*"*

"People listen to their doctors, Attie. That's because doctor always knows best."

Instructions are given to Tannie Elsa about bringing him back to have the stitches out. But he is no longer listening to the doctor.

He is thinking.

8
VERDICTS

"Any messages?" Megan asked Patience after she saw Lindi Nyoka out at the end of her session. The trauma debriefing was going well and the client would need only one more appointment.

"Yebo," Patience said, holding up three pink slips. "Cayley called. Plus, the Taylors late-cancelled because she's got a tummy bug."

"Good." Megan caught Patience's look of surprise, and explained, "Not that she's sick — I'm just glad to have a free hour. I've got some important admin to do."

"And the transplant board wants to know if you can take another potential recipient evaluation."

"What for?"

"Liver."

Megan considered a moment. She had an idea that investigating Alta Cronjé's case wouldn't leave much time to assess and write reports on potential transplant candidates.

"No, I think let's decline this one. But ask them to keep me on the referral list. I still want the work, I'm just too busy at the moment."

"And then a call from my favourite honey."

"Wade?"

Wade Alden, Megan's long-time best friend, had winkled his unique way into Patience's affections over the years.

"I like that boy." Patience handed over the message slips, then fished around inside her massive handbag, brought out a pack of chewing gum and popped one into her mouth. She offered one to Megan, sniffed in response to her refusal, and returned the crumpled cardboard pack to its hidey-hole. "He's kind and polite and good for you. And so handsome! You should marry him."

"Patience, you do know he's gay?" It was hard to miss.

"Thcha," Patience clicked her annoyance. "Sex! There's more to love than that. You want a man who can listen to you, who can comfort you when you're sad, who can be strong when you are weak." She took a big sip of tea the colour of mahogany and sighed in pleasure.

"I'm not weak," Megan pointed out.

"That's your problem — a woman can be too strong," Patience said, with the confidence of one presenting an argument-clincher. "That's why you're still alone."

"But I'm not alone," Megan protested. "I've got Mike."

Patience made a dismissive movement with her hand as if brushing off a fly. "How are you going to get a decent man, a *strong* man, if you're so strong you don't need one?"

Megan rolled her eyes.

"Besides, Wade can *cook.*"

"Look, just give me the number for the HPCSA, won't you?"

"What about —"

"I'll call Wade later, I promise."

Patience looked up the number in her dog-eared index book, wrote it on a slip of paper and handed it over, saying, "You think about what I said."

Megan merely sighed. Sometimes, one needed lots of patience for Patience. Back in her office, she dialled the Pretoria number. It rang for several minutes before being answered by an unenthusiastic voice. Megan asked to be put through to the department which handled complaints and disciplinary matters.

"What Board?" asked the voice.

"Medical."

"Please hold, s'busy."

Megan wedged the phone between her shoulder and neck, and sorted through papers on her desk. *Greensleeves* played on repeat in her ear, interrupted every few minutes by the voice: "Still busy, please hold."

It was twelve more minutes before someone finally answered the line.

"Good day, my name is Megan Wright. I'd like to enquire whether any charges for unprofessional conduct have been laid against a certain medical doctor."

"No, you've come through to the wrong extension. This is the Dental Therapy and Oral Hygiene Board. Hang on, I'll put you back to switchboard,"

"Wait!" Megan said, but it was too late.

The bored operator came back on the line. "You holding for?"

"Complaints against doctors — medical doctors, not dentists," Megan said as clearly as she could, and with forced politeness.

"Same Board, please hold."

After another few rounds of the same, tinny music, a tired female voice answered.

"Medical and Dental, Mrs Mdluli speaking, how can I help?"

Megan repeated her spiel.

"Why do you want to know?" asked Mrs Mdluli.

"I'm thinking of changing to this doctor," Megan improvised. "And I want to be sure that he's good, that he's had no problems before."

"What's the doctor's name?"

"It's Dr A. Trotteur." Megan spelled out the surname.

"Hang on, I'm just looking him up on the system."

Megan heard keyboard clicks in the background.

"Here we are … an obstetrician-gynaecologist?"

"That's the one."

She pushed the telephone hard against her ear, eager to hear what Mrs Mdluli had found, but there was only silence on the other end of the line.

"Hello?" Megan said, fearing she'd been cut off.

"Yes, I'm still here."

"Well? Have there been any complaints against him?"

"The Board does not disclose whether there have been complaints against practitioners, as these may be inaccurate or unfounded," said Mrs Mdluli, sounding like she was repeating a regulation for the umpteenth time. "I can tell you that there have been no verdicts against Dr Trotteur."

"None?" asked Megan. She'd been so sure there would be something.

"No. No *verdicts*." Had there been a slight emphasis on the last word?

"So … no verdicts," she persisted. "But have there been any complaints laid? Any disciplinary hearings held?"

"I'm sorry," said Mrs Mdluli, and she sounded it. "I can't give you more information about that. Is there anything else you want?"

"No, but —"

"Goodbye." The line went dead.

Megan replaced her handset and stared at the telephone, wondering. Wade was always good for encouragement and advice. Now seemed like a good time to return his call.

"How goes the world of advertising?" she asked.

"It's magnificent, fabulous, wonderful! But wait, that's not all!" he said, imitating an infomercial voice-over. When Megan gave only a feeble laugh, he asked, "How are you, sweetheart?"

"Crap, since you ask."

She tucked the receiver under her chin and began playing with the paperweight on her desk, passing it from hand to hand, feeling its heft. She loved the contrast of the fragile dandelion seed head and the sharp-edged cube of solid glass. Usually, what stood out for her was the beauty of the delicate puffball, and the promise of regeneration and new life, but today it was the heaviness of the glass that registered.

"That bad?"

"Yes, I'm worried about a client some of the time, fighting with Mike lots of the time, and exhausted all of the time."

"Oh, my poor girl!" Wade said and the real concern in his voice brought a lump of self-pity to her throat. That was another thing he was good for, thought Megan, sympathy. Patience should add it to her list of his attributes. "Anything I can help you with?"

"Nah. I'm just really worried, I've got a feeling a doctor did something really bad to a patient, but when I tried to check, the official at the Council just said there were no verdicts against him. She said it like that: 'no *verdicts*'. I don't know, I just get a sense there's something there, but I don't know what to do next."

She could talk to Wade about work. He never pressed for names, wasn't curious about the gory details, and he was a bottomless well when it came to keeping secrets.

"Why not go there?" he suggested. "In person, I mean. You could turn on the charm and use your Spidey psycho-powers to winkle the information out of her."

"That's actually not a bad idea," Megan said, putting down the paperweight and sitting up straighter.

"I'm full of them. And here comes another one — trust your intuition."

Sitting in the small and cluttered room at the HPCSA offices in Pretoria a few days later, though, Megan reflected that intuition seemed a very insubstantial basis for her visit. Mrs Mdluli was an older woman with short, greying hair framing a round face set in grim lines. She seemed just as resolute about not divulging any further details in person as she'd been on the telephone.

"All the guilty verdicts of our hearings are public record. They're published on the website. But I'm not permitted to disclose any further information about this member," she said, tapping the buff-coloured folder on the desk in front of her. It looked thick. Surely it couldn't be so full unless a number of complaints had been laid against Trotteur, even if none of them had resulted in a guilty verdict?

"So there *is* further information which you could —"

"Which I could *not*," Mrs Mdluli said firmly.

Megan was beginning to feel desperate. It was infuriating that the information she sought was a mere arm's length away, and yet was out of reach. She wondered what would happen if she just snatched the file and made a run for it. A hearing of her own, no doubt. One which *would* result in a negative verdict.

"I wonder," she began, unsure if she were following the promptings of intuition or insanity. "I wonder if I could perhaps make it worth your while to share some of that information."

Mrs Mdluli stared at her.

"I mean, really worth your while."

"Ms Wright, are you trying to bribe me?" Mrs Mdluli's face was unreadable. Was she insulted, or tempted?

"Er …"

"You people!" Mrs Mdluli virtually spat out the words. "You think just because I'm black, I'm corrupt."

"No!" protested Megan. "I just —"

"All blacks are lazy, dishonest, potential criminals — is that it?" Mrs Mdluli leaned forward across the desk, fury in her dark eyes.

"No, really, it has nothing to do with race," gabbled Megan. "I'm sorry, really sorry, Mrs Mdluli. I'm just desperate. Please, just listen."

Mrs Mdluli said nothing. Pursing her lips tightly, she sat back fractionally in her chair.

"I have a traumatised patient, and I think, from what she remembers, that she was seriously abused by Dr Trotteur. Emotionally tortured and physically maimed. And I think he did it deliberately. I'm scared that he may have done it to other women, that he might do it again. And I need to know whether other women have laid complaints. I'm sorry I insulted you by implying … I'm sorry. I just don't know how else to get the information I need. If I'm right, he must be stopped — surely you can understand that?"

The official stared at Megan for a long moment, then she narrowed her eyes and said, "I'm afraid I can't help you. I am not permitted to disclose confidential information. You must please excuse me — I need to go to the bathroom. I will be back in five minutes, so please ensure you are gone by then. And I remind you, you are not permitted to read this file." She pushed the buff folder a few centimetres across the desk towards Megan. "Not under any circumstances. Do you understand what I mean?"

Mrs Mdluli got up from behind the desk and left the office, clicking the door closed behind her.

After a moment's immobilised surprise, Megan seized the

file and opened it, paging quickly through the contents — notes of preliminary disciplinary hearings, official forms which looked like charges and, towards the bottom of the file, letters to the Council complaining about Dr Trotteur. She was scanning these last pages, shooting glances at the office door every few seconds, when her gaze was caught by a bullet-pointed phrase, "… that Dr Trotteur did, unnecessarily and with no medical basis, surgically over-tighten the opening of my vagina and cut out my clitoris".

They were real words, written in the grammatically correct order, but still they made no sense. Megan reread the sentence slowly, swallowing down the bile rising in her throat. Cold sweat beaded her top lip.

Loud voices outside the office made her look up quickly, clutching the file to her chest, but it was just two people walking down the passage. She could see their shadow moving past the frosted glass of the door. She needed to hurry. Grabbing her phone, she opened the camera function and swiftly took photographs of the letters of complaint. There was no chance to capture more of the details in the file — she was running out of time. At any moment, Mrs Mdluli might return.

Megan closed the file, replaced it on the desk and, grabbing her bag and stuffing her phone into it, exited the office. In the corridor, she passed Mrs Mdluli walking back in the opposite direction. The eyes of the two women met for a moment. Megan silently mouthed the words, "Thank you," and Mrs Mdluli gave a small nod.

Megan hurried down the corridor, pushed open the door of

the fire escape stairwell and raced down the stairs, out of the lobby and towards where her car was parked in the hot sun of Vermeulen Street. She was still two car lengths away from it when her stomach convulsed. Bending over a rubbish bin, she threw up, retching until there was nothing left but dry heaves.

9
SURELY NOT

"I'll have the carrot cake with cream cheese icing, please, and a café latte," Megan said, handing the menu back to the waitress.

"Uhm," said her sister, "just give me a minute." She seemed to be reading and carefully considering every item on the menu. "I'll have the ginger *rooibos* tea to drink — no milk or sugar — and …" She returned to scrutinising the menu.

The waitress chewed on the already splintered end of her ballpoint pen. Megan glanced around. They were trying out a new coffee shop in Parkhurst's main drag for their regular coffee morning catch-up. Too many uncomfortable wrought iron chairs and tables were crammed into a cobbled courtyard with a few scrawny olive trees giving scant shade. The rough brick walls were hung with words shaped in twisted wire: *peace, forgiveness, dream, love.* It was all a little chi-chi and underwhelming, except for the prices, which were impressively steep.

The waitress cleared her throat and looked at Megan. Megan looked at her sister.

"Cayley?"

"No, nothing for me, I think," Cayley said, passing the menu back to the waitress who gave a barely suppressed sigh and retreated to the shadowed interior of the restaurant.

"So, how's life?" Megan asked.

"Same shit, different day. But I might be getting a new job."

"Oh, yes?" Megan tried to sound enthusiastic rather than cynical. Her sister had run through at least half a dozen jobs in the previous two years. Nothing lasted long in Cayley's life — except her obsession with food and her body.

"Yes, it's quite exciting actually. There's this catering company called Juicy Morsel. It's owned by one of mom's friends, and they've said they'll take me on as a ... well, not a chef, exactly, but a catering assistant, I guess you could call it. Helping with the food prep, and plating up at functions and stuff. They do corporate shindigs and weddings, Bar Mitzvahs, all sorts."

"Mom got you a job. At a catering company?"

"Why do you say it like that?" Cayley said, sounding defensive.

"Like what?"

"Like you think it's a bad idea."

"Isn't it?"

"You're so negative, Megs. It's a good job. I'll enjoy it, earn some money, pay off my store cards. What's the problem?"

"The problem, Cay, is that you have an eating disorder —"

"I do not!"

"— and a job which involves thinking about and working with food all day, will only feed your obsession with eating and weight!"

"I don't have an obsession."

The waitress arrived, put their hot drinks down in the middle of the table, and an enormous wedge of cake, topped with cream cheese icing and a mini marzipan carrot, in front of Megan.

Cayley stared at the cake with an expression of longing. "That looks really good."

Here we go again, thought Megan. "Are you sure you don't want a slice? I can easily call the waitress back."

"No. I couldn't. But I wouldn't mind testing a crumb — just to see if it's moist. Carrot cakes can be very dry, you know. It's hard to get them moist without making them claggy."

She crumbled off a small piece of cake, sniffed it, and then deposited it carefully on her tongue, as though it was the rarest of exotic foods.

"Mmmh. It's not at all dry. Maybe they used crushed pineapple. Some recipes do, you know. And some include sour cream. This one's really good." She ate another small piece.

Megan grabbed a fork from Cayley's setting and stabbed it into the top of the cake. "Let's share. Help yourself."

"No, I mustn't — I've already eaten today," said Cayley, but moments later her hand, like some shy creature not fully part of herself, crept across the table top and broke off another small morsel. She looked up at Megan with a mischievous grin. "This way it doesn't count. If you break it up and eat only the crumbs, then by the time it gets to your mouth, all the calories have oozed out. It's been scientifically documented. It's officially called 'calorie leakage'. I saw it on *Discovery*."

Megan smiled, but it was a sad smile. She was all too aware

how their chat had narrowed, as it always did, down to Cayley's relationship with food. Her gaze travelled down her sister's slight frame to where her thin arms rested on the table. They were covered with lanugo — the anorexic's tell-tale light fuzz of downy hair.

"Is there any point in telling you that you do not need to worry about calories?"

"None at all," said Cayley, sneaking another bite. "Why aren't you eating? Don't tell me the mega-mentally-healthy Megan has started worrying about *her* weight?"

"I think you do enough of that for the both of us. Here, you have it." Megan pushed the plate of cake across the table. "I'm feeling a bit queasy, actually."

The whole issue with Alta Cronjé and Dr Trotteur was really bothering her — enough, apparently, to turn her stomach, especially when she thought about that letter in the file at the HPCSA, that poor woman.

"*Babelas?*" said Cayley, tucking into the chunk of cake.

"I am *not* hung over."

"Maybe it's food poisoning," Cayley teased, sucking icing off her fingers. "With your cooking skills, I wouldn't be surprised."

"Lately, I've been so busy and so tired that we've been living on take-aways, so I guess it's possible that I picked up a bug. But I haven't had a runny tummy or anything, and I don't feel sick all the time, just at odd moments." She sipped at her coffee; it tasted bitter and smelt strange.

"Maybe you're pregnant," Cayley said, and — at Megan's horrified look — added, "Kidding!"

As they both laughed, Cayley caught the waitress's attention and ordered a slice of Black Forest cake. "What the hell, in for a penny, in for a few pounds!"

They spoke for a while about their parents ("Mom's taken up scrapbooking now, so the whole house is covered with ribbons and stickers and home-made calendars, and Dad's AWOL as usual — Atlanta, I think."); Megan's work ("When are you going to settle down and get a real job, Megs? Kidding!"); and Megan's relationship with Mike ("Sounding a little rocky, there, sis.")

"Anything to report in your love life?" Megan asked.

"Nah, all the good ones are dead, married or gay. As for the rest — arseholes aplenty. Tell me this, sis, if they can send a man to the moon, why can't they send them all there?"

Cayley's cake arrived and she began to eat it quickly, gobbling down forkful after forkful, without pausing for breath or even appearing to taste it. Absorbed as she'd been in eating it, she seemed surprised when she noticed it was finished, and a dull flush suffused her face. A heaviness settled across Megan's chest as she watched her sister. She knew what was coming next.

"Excuse me, I just need to go to the loo."

"Cayley, please don't do this," Megan said urgently, laying a hand on her sister's arm.

"Do what?" said Cayley, all innocence. "I just need to pee, okay?"

"*Please*."

"Oh, stop smothering me, Megs. One overbearing, over-controlling mother is more than enough."

She stood up, spun around and flounced off in the direction of the toilets, her short skirt swinging above her impossibly thin legs. Megan watched as her beautiful sister's course across the courtyard drew admiring glances from the men and envious looks from the women.

If they only knew, she thought. But I am not going to follow her. I am not going to storm into that bathroom and yank her head out of the toilet bowl. Not again. I am going to sit tight. I gave up rescue missions for the New Year. I cannot help someone who insists she is not lost or stuck. I am going to sit here and drink my coffee and think about something else. Unbidden, Cayley's throwaway phrase bubbled up from the subconscious depths Megan had shoved it to: "Maybe you're pregnant."

It bubbled up again late that night, and it was the words — surely not true, surely not even possible — and not Mike's uneven snores, that kept Megan awake in the darkness.

10
IMPERFECTION

He can feel the pressure rising, building inside him, expanding, stiffening the muscles of his back and tensing his scalp. It is getting harder to contain.

All around him, all he sees is imperfection. Flaws and blemishes. Uneven, unbalanced defects.

That man over there, with the front tooth missing from his puckered mouth. That woman, her thick make-up and long, heavy fringe failing abysmally to conceal the port wine birthmark blotting her forehead and temple. The fat child gripping the can of cola, rolls of flesh bulging over the belt of her jeans.

The children, in particular, bother him. He believes as a matter of principle that they should be given the chance to outgrow their imperfections — their purple-budding acne, their uneven teeth, their swellings of puppy fat. But with such bad beginnings, what hope do they realistically have of emerging from the cocoon of childhood without deformity? Already they are incubating ugliness.

It is a defective world. It causes him pain — an actual physical ache that seems to press against his chest from the inside, to squeeze and squeeze inside his head.

He pushes his fingers hard against his eyeballs until the phosphenes explode across his visual field. He tries to expand his chest, to breathe against the compressing weight that robs him of breath and makes him dizzy. He rubs his chin.

He needs relief. He needs the release — the grounding — that only a scalpel moving through flesh, cutting into and away, can bring.

And he needs it soon.

11
ZUMA'S LAW

Patience stuck her head around the door to Megan's office.

"Mr Labuschagne is here," she announced.

Megan glanced down at her watch; she still had a couple of minutes.

"Okay, I'll see him in a moment, just come in for a sec."

Patience stepped inside and, at Megan's gesture, closed the door behind her.

"Do me a favour, won't you," Megan asked. "Will you get the names and numbers of all the gynaecologists at Acacia? Make a list for me. And while you're at it — ask around to find out who's good."

"Gynaes!" Patience said, visibly swelling with curiosity. "Is there something you want to tell me?"

"No," Megan said firmly. "I just need a check-up, okay?"

"And you don't want to go to your usual doctor? To Dr Khumalo? You said you liked her."

"I thought it would be easier to see a doctor here at Acacia."

"Hmmm." Patience was clearly unconvinced.

"Just do it for me, okay? Please?"

Patience gave a shrug which Megan took for assent.

"You can send in Mr Labuschagne. I'll get the doctors' names from you after his session."

An hour later, she stared at the list of five names. The last one immediately caught her eye, but she made herself ask Patience what she'd gleaned about each of them.

"This one — Dr Weinberg — I have written him at the top, see? Because the nurses tell me he is the best one. Very gentle, very good. They say he has the most natural births." Patience gave Megan a significant look. "Do you want me to make an appointment for you?"

"First tell me about the others."

"Dr Gebhardt is no good for you."

"Why?"

"They say it is a funny thing, but every one of his patients has a pelvis too small for normal delivery and she must have a Caesar."

"I don't need to know about their birthing skills, Patience, I need a gynae."

"That *wabenzi* Dr Maseko also. The doctors who make too much money? You must stay away from them."

"And Dr Williams?"

"They say she's good, but she's not taking any new patients now, she's about to go on leave to have her own baby."

"What about this one?" Megan pointed at the last name on the list.

"Dr Trotter?"

"Trotteur, I think." Megan pronounced the name with what she thought was the correct pronunciation. It looked French.

"They wouldn't say much about him. But they didn't say nice things, like they did about Dr Weinberg."

"Did they say anything bad?"

Patience gave Megan a sharp glance. "They didn't say anything specific, but Sister Mercy called him *indoda engalungile.*"

"There's a sister called Mercy?" Megan laughed, momentarily distracted.

"*Yebo.* But you're a psychologist with a receptionist called Patience."

"Fair point. Anyway, what they called him — a dodi-whatsit — what does that mean?"

"It means you should go see Dr Weinberg," Patience said, adjusting her bra-straps with an air of finality.

For a moment, Megan was tempted to schedule an appointment with Dr Trotteur. She wanted to see him, to assess him for herself, but only an idiot would walk directly into a situation she knew was potentially dangerous. It was better to discover what she could quietly, subtly and indirectly.

"Make me an appointment with Weinberg, will you?" Megan said. "As soon as he can squeeze me in."

"They'll want to know what it's for," Patience said, still looking curious.

Megan smiled. "Nice try, Patience."

The receptionist shrugged and ambled back to the front office, sticking her head back around the door to announce that Alta Cronjé had arrived for her appointment.

"Send her straight in," Megan said.

Alta's appearance had improved. Her hair was freshly washed, the shadows under her eyes seemed less pronounced, and her face was less pinched than it had been.

"You're looking better than when I saw you last," Megan said, after they'd exchanged greetings. "Did your break at the farm do you some good?"

"*Ja*, it was great to get away, you know? It's so quiet there, so peaceful. It was just Johan, Marlien and me. And we just took it easy. I slept better."

"That's great."

"I told Johan."

"About what happened that day? What you remembered in hypnosis?"

Alta nodded.

"And?"

"He went mad. Nuts. Chucked a lamp on the floor and shouted. And then …" She puffed out a breath. "It was horrible."

"Did he hurt you?"

It was always touch and go how men would react to the rape or abuse of their partners. As often as not, their rage found focus in blaming the woman herself.

"No, man! Hell, you always think the worst, hey? Must come with the job. No, he's never laid a hand on me. Well, not like *that*, anyway. But he started crying, like sobbing. Hard. And I felt so bad for him, that I wound up comforting him! It's a terrible thing to see a big, strong man cry."

"He was really shocked and upset," Megan said, falling back on the old therapeutic technique of reflecting back to the client what she'd just said.

"You can say that again. And when he stopped crying, then he got *really* angry. He went so red in the face I was scared he'd have a heart attack. He wanted to jump in the car then and there, drive back to Jo'burg and kill that doctor. Said he wanted to cut off his balls first and see how *he* liked it!"

"He felt powerless about what had happened to you, helpless that he couldn't prevent or fix it. He wanted revenge."

"Exactly. I swear, if we'd been in Jo'burg, the doc would be dead by now. It was only because we were on the farm, and I told Johan that he couldn't leave me and Marlien alone — it's not safe with all the farm murders — and so he calmed down a bit and stayed put. But we could only talk properly the next day."

"How did he respond then?"

"Well, he still wanted to kill the guy, and painfully. Me too, actually. But I made him think and see that that will only get *him* locked up for murder. 'Cause that's how it works in this place — the real killers and rapists walk free. But the good citizens who put one foot wrong? They get caught and locked up. Murphy's law. Ha!" She gave a cynical laugh. "Or maybe Zuma's law."

"Is he calmer now?"

Alta grinned. "Worried he's gonna come here one night and do something to the doctor? No, he's calm now. But we both want to take this further. Charge the doctor, or whatever."

"Are you sure?"

"Ninety per cent sure. We're just worried that it's just gonna be his word against mine, you know? And it's too late to get a second opinion about whether the surgery was necessary because the … the part that was supposed to be diseased is gone, isn't it? There's no, like, evidence."

"Well," Megan said slowly, thinking carefully about her next words. "I've been doing some digging."

"And?" Alta leaned forward and looked intently at Megan.

"I found out that there have been several other complaints laid against Trotteur, two of which resulted in charges being brought by the Health Professions Council of South Africa — the Board that governs and disciplines doctors."

"Charges? What for?"

"Pretty much the same as happened to you. He mutilated them — there's no other word for it. I didn't get the full details, but on one of them, he tightened the vagina way too much and … and cut off her clitoris."

"Fuck!"

Megan gave Alta a moment to take in what she'd just heard.

"So how come he's still practising? How come he's not locked up in a jail cell with other monsters?" Alta said, her voice hard with anger.

"There hasn't been a verdict against him," Megan explained. "When a complaint is laid, they investigate a bit and then hold a disciplinary hearing if they think it's warranted. If there's enough clear evidence against the doctor, then he gets a verdict against him and a fine or maybe a suspension, or if it's really serious he's deregistered and can't practise anymore."

Alta looked appalled. "A fine! Deregistered — for what *he* did?"

"I don't know what they would do in a case like this. Maybe they'd be obliged to report it to the police if there was a guilty verdict. And then there might be a criminal case, or the victim could bring a civil claim. In any event, it never came to that with Trotteur; I don't know why. Maybe there was insufficient evidence. I'm not even sure it came to a proper hearing stage."

"Can we find out?"

"I can try. If we're going to get him, we'll need more evidence. We need to know why the other women's complaints didn't result in guilty verdicts, so we don't make the same mistakes."

"I want to get him, Megan. I want to nail this bastard, this butcher."

"Okay, I'll see what I can find out, leave it with me. In the meantime, let's shift our focus back to you. Tell me what else is happening in your life. Because you are so much more than this one trauma, Alta. You are a whole person — a mother, a wife, a programmer, a funny, clever, creative woman. Don't let's reduce you to this one thing that happened to you; don't let him have power over your mind like he had power over your body."

"You're right." Alta rubbed a hand over her face as if scrubbing away all thoughts of Trotteur. "D'you know that Marlien had her birthday while we were on the farm? She turned five — my little baby is five years old!"

Alta fished her cell phone out of her handbag, tapped the screen and held it up to show Megan the photograph of her daughter. The little girl's hair was the same shade of brown as her mother's, but her smile was more carefree than any Megan had ever seen on Alta's face.

"She's gorgeous! And she's not such a baby anymore."

"No, she's a proper little girl. She's growing up so fast; she'll start big school next year. You know, I've been wondering ..."

"Yes?"

"She doesn't need me so much now. And Johan is better with her since she's a bit older — I think he was scared of breaking her when she was so little. But now they can kick a ball and play games together and stuff. So, I have more free time. And I thought, maybe, that I might volunteer. Like a counsellor, you know? Do a course and help other people who are having problems, who just need someone to talk to. But maybe it's a stupid idea," she said, looking almost shyly up at Megan, as if for approval.

"I think it's amazing that you'd like to help others. And I think you'd be good at it."

"You do?"

"I do. But I also think that before you start helping others, we need to make sure that you're as healthy and strong as you can be. Because it's hard to hear other people's pain when you're still dealing with your own issues."

Which, Megan thought wryly, just about disqualifies every psychologist I've ever known. Including myself.

12
PROBING

There were three other women in Dr Weinberg's waiting room on the second floor of Acacia Clinic. They all had large bellies bulging out front, and expressions of glazed placidity on their faces, and they sat quietly, smiling benignly at each other, occasionally stirring to rub their baby bumps with gentle, proprietary hands. One was knitting — something Megan had not seen anyone do in years.

By contrast, Megan battled to sit still; she alternated pacing the small confines of the room with perching on one of the pink chairs lined up against the pink-painted walls. It was like being inside a rosy womb. A patient — not pregnant, from what Megan could see — emerged from the consulting room, and one of the waiting women was called in.

Megan's objective for the consultation with Dr Weinberg was to get more information about Dr Trotteur. She tried to come up with a subtle and plausible way of fishing for details, but none occurred to her. How did one unobtrusively weave into casual conversation questions about a medical colleague deliberately botching surgeries? *So, tell me, Doc, have any of your colleagues maimed or tortured patients lately?* She would just have to wing it when the time came.

There was another exchange of patients to and from the consulting room, and a young couple came in and reported to the reception desk. There was only one patient ahead of Megan now. Thinking that perhaps reading would help settle her nerves, she shuffled through the pile of magazines on a side table covered with lacy cloth in the ubiquitous pink, trying to find one which would interest her: *Living and Loving, Your Baby, Your Pregnancy.* A phrase on the cover of one of them caught her eye: "Are you, or aren't you? Symptoms of pregnancy".

She turned to the article and scanned the list of symptoms printed in a pale pink text box. Did the whole world go pink when you were pregnant?

Nausea — check.

Tender breasts — not that she'd noticed.

Dizziness — nope.

Missed period — check. Maybe.

Fatigue or exhaustion — check with a vengeance.

Increased need for urination — immediately she felt the need to go.

Food aversions — check, she'd totally gone off coffee and wine.

A definite pattern was beginning to emerge. She felt her anxiety spike and her stomach clench, but maybe that was just symptom number ten: *heartburn and indigestion.* The whole thing sounded like some horrible disease — why did the women sitting alongside her look so smugly contented?

"Mrs Wright? Doctor will see you, now," the receptionist said.

Megan looked with some surprise at the third, heavily pregnant woman who she'd assumed was ahead of her. Perhaps the mother-to-be had no appointment. Perhaps she just wandered into the rooms from time to time to bask in the rosy glow of bountiful fecundity.

Dr Weinberg stood up behind his desk to greet Megan and shake her hand when she entered his consulting room. He was a slight man of about her own height, with silver hair and sharp eyes behind rectangular steel-rimmed spectacles.

He read through the patient history forms which she'd completed and asked, "So how can I help you today?"

"Oh, just a check-up. No real problems."

"How long has it been since your last pap smear?"

"I can't remember," Megan lied. She knew exactly when it had been because every year she scheduled her annual pap smear in the week before her birthday, but that had only been a few months ago and she needed a valid reason for this visit, and enough time to ask some questions. "A couple of years, I think."

"It's important to have a pap smear regularly — that means annually, Mrs Wright," he chided gently.

"It's Miss, but please, call me Megan."

"Right, Megan," he began. She noticed that he did not invite a similar informality with *his* name. The old doctor-patient power imbalance still held sway. "Anything else bothering you?"

"Not really. Except …"

"Except?"

"Well, I've been very tired recently — though work's been hectic and it could just be that. And I've been nauseous, even though I haven't been ill."

"Have you missed a period?"

"I think I'm late, by two to three weeks, but I'm not sure. My cycle isn't very regular."

"When was the first day of your last period?"

"About six weeks ago, I think. I don't keep records." She felt like a small girl confessing her guilt on some crime, and it irritated her.

"Hmm," said Dr Weinberg, pushing his spectacles up his nose. "Let's do the check-up first and then we can do a pregnancy test."

A nurse in blue uniform escorted her into the adjacent examination room through an interleading door, and handed Megan a floral-patterned gown. It was pink.

"Everything off, please, and put the gown on so that it opens to the front. You can put your bag and clothes on this chair. I'll be back in a few minutes," the nurse said brightly and left, closing the door behind her.

Megan stripped, hung her clothes over the chair and slipped into the gown. The cotton was cool against her flesh. Hopping onto the examination table, she positioned herself on the disposable linen-saver, and pulled the white blanket over her. An ultrasound machine hummed beside the bed, and a tray of gleaming metal speculums with a half-squeezed tube of KY jelly rested on a stand alongside, together with a container of thin wooden spatulas and a box of disposable gloves. A stainless-steel lamp with a long, bendy neck was clamped onto the side of the bed, ready to illuminate her insides.

"I'm ready," Megan called.

Dr Weinberg came into the room, followed by his nurse. After he'd taken her blood pressure and pronounced it satisfactory, he asked her to open the gown so that he could perform a breast examination. With her arms held first up above her head and then down by her sides, he firmly palpated each breast, working in circles from the outside inwards towards the nipple. It was uncomfortable to the point of being painful. Did Dr Khumalo usually press so hard?

"Do you check your breasts regularly?" Dr Weinberg asked.

They must teach them in medical school to ask this question, Megan thought, because they all do it, every time.

"Oh, yes, definitely. Every month just after my period."

She'd long ago learned to lie to avoid the stern talking-to otherwise invariably followed, a lecture which prolonged the trial of lying exposed and cold on an uncomfortable surface, with a stranger's hands pressing hard on your naked breasts, while pretending it was a perfectly normal and pleasant activity. In reality, every time she felt her breasts, *all* she felt was a network of lumps which both worried her and inclined her to fall back on repression — one of the more useful defence mechanisms.

"I see you have a nurse present when you do the examination?" she said.

"Oh yes," he replied. "Always."

"Do all gynaecologists work that way?"

"The male ones do, or they should do. It's considered ethical and careful practice. It puts the patient's mind at ease, but it's also for the protection of the doctor."

"How so?"

"As obstetricians and gynaecologists, we have to be very careful," said Dr Weinberg, positioning her right hand behind her head and palpating the area under her arm. "We examine very intimate areas, which can lay us open to charges of improper conduct, so the nurse is the witness that we did nothing inappropriate."

"Do you always have a nurse present in your operations as well?"

"Oh, yes. Well, mostly she's needed to assist, of course. But more can go wrong in an operation than an examination, so we also need someone to be present, witnessing what we did."

"Surely the anaesthetist …?"

"He's at the other end of the operation — the head — while we're at the tail, so to speak." He smiled and closed her gown. "All fine there, let's do the pelvic exam now. Please bend your knees."

Megan bent her legs, let them fall open and stared at the ceiling. Dissociation was the defence mechanism called for in this part of the examination — a splitting off of the conscious self so that it was free to drift off to a peaceful place far away from the vulnerable body displayed like a frog on a dissecting table.

"Just relax now," said Dr Weinberg.

Megan always wished she had the guts to reply, "I'd like to see *you* relax while someone inserts a cold metal implement into your most private part, cranks you open, and then inspects by

93

spotlight while someone else looks on!" But she merely took a deep breath and tried consciously to relax her muscles while the chilly speculum was pushed inside her and opened.

"That all looks fine," said the doctor.

Megan felt the small internal pinch that signalled the pap smear being taken. Dr Weinberg passed the spatula to the nurse, who smeared it onto a glass slide, sprayed the surface with something from an aerosol can, and then put another glass slide over the top of the sample. Megan felt the speculum being closed, the discomfort of its withdrawal.

Now she could feel his fingers entering her, moving up and around — presumably to feel her cervix — while his other hand pushing down on her lower pelvis. Images of Alta Cronjé's ordeal flashed through Megan's mind.

"Relax again, please."

The gynaecological examination was surely the ultimate in patient vulnerability, and it was worse being examined by a male doctor. Without medical training, how could a patient be sure that every touch was justified, every inspection not voyeuristic, every squeeze not actually a grope?

"All done," Dr Weinberg said at last, closing her knees.

Megan could not repress a sigh of relief.

He peeled off his latex gloves, tossed them into a waste bin and handed her a small plastic bottle with a green lid. "We need a urine sample. There's a bathroom in the next room; just leave the bottle there for the nurse to test. We can talk in my office when you're all dressed."

She did as instructed, and when she returned to his office a few minutes later, he was making notes in her file.

"Everything looks fine. You can call for the results of your pap smear in three days," he said. Just then, the nurse entered the office. Dr Weinberg looked questioningly at her.

"It's positive. Congratulations!" she beamed at Megan, before leaving, closing the door behind her.

"What?" Megan said. "What did she say?"

The sudden cold swoop in her stomach was definitely not indigestion.

"Your urine test was positive. You're pregnant," he said, his voice neutral.

"Are you sure? I mean really sure?" she heard herself say in a high voice. "I can't believe it!"

"We'll confirm it with a blood test — here are the forms for the path lab on the ground floor — but these days the urine tests are very accurate." He studied her carefully. "Are you all right, my dear? It sounds like this was unplanned."

"I'm just battling to take it in." Megan rubbed her hands over her face. "I'm a little shocked, I think."

He took a couple of leaflets off the shelf behind him and passed them to her. "Here are some brochures on the options open to you now."

Options?

"Have a think about it, give it a few days for the news to settle in, discuss it with your partner, and then come in for another appointment and we can decide what to do next."

"Okay," Megan said slowly. "I'll do that."

Her mind was racing, thinking ahead to the implications for work, what her mother would say, how Mike would react. Oh God, Mike.

"Was there anything else, Megan?" Dr Weinberg made a final note in her file and closed it.

She tried to stop the swirling in her head, tried to force herself to focus on the other reason why she was here. Denial — that was the defence she needed to employ now, to block out what she'd heard and to focus only on the real purpose of her visit.

"Yes, actually. Uhm, while I'm here, I just wanted to ask you … your opinion on one of the other gynaecologists here. Dr Trotteur."

Dr Weinberg arched an eyebrow. "Planning on changing doctors again, so soon?"

"No, no, nothing like that. It's just that sometimes one has to refer a client to a specialist and one would like to be sure that he's … beyond reproach."

"Beyond reproach? What does that mean?"

"You know, competent, compassionate, ethical."

Megan was finding it hard to find the right words. The only word that seemed to be in her brain and on her tongue, was *pregnant.*

"I mean, if there was anything against him, any complaints or question marks, then I'd like to know before referring a client to him."

"Have you heard something against him?" Dr Weinberg asked.

"I can't really remember. Maybe just some hospital gossip."

He stood up and frowned down at her. "Dr Trotteur" — he pronounced it *Trotter*, as Patience had — "hasn't been at Acacia for very long, less than a year, I believe. But … I know of no formal complaints against him." He spoke slowly and it sounded to Megan that he was choosing his words very carefully. "In any event," he said more quickly as he escorted her out of his office, "I hope you'll return to me for your care. Goodbye, Miss Wright."

Megan made her payment and then walked down the corridor in a daze, clutching the path lab form and pamphlets in her hand, wondering about what Weinberg had not said, and about what he had. *Pregnant!*

A few doors down, her glance was drawn to a brass nameplate beside another medical suite: *Dr A. Trotteur, Gynaecologist/Obstetrician*. She stared at it for a long time, then took a step back away from it and continued down the corridor.

I'm pregnant, she thought. I really am.

13
ANY MOMENT NOW

"I'm pregnant."

The words hung in the silence, heavy as fear, light as hope.

"You're what?" Mike asked, his face blank with shock, his blue eyes round.

Megan cursed herself inwardly. She'd meant to soften him up with a glass of wine and a hug, lead him gently into a conversation about their future, and draw out a sense of his intentions. Instead, she'd opened the door to him and just blurted out the two words that had been playing pendulum with her feelings all day, swinging her from terror to elation and back again.

Now Mike closed the door, hung his keys deliberately on their hook, and placed his briefcase on the table. Oedipus leaped up against his legs, but Mike ignored him. He stood directly in front of Megan, looked her straight in the eye and said, "What did you say?"

"I'm pregnant."

He stared back at her. The silence between them drew breath and expanded, seeming to push back against her chest.

"Sorry," she added, though she hardly knew what she was apologising for. For being fertile? For being a woman?

Mike stepped around where she stood paralysed by a growing dread.

"I need a drink before I can deal with this," he said, heading to the kitchen. "Maybe two."

She trailed after him, Oedipus trotting behind her, and watched as he poured wine first into a glass and then down his throat. He poured a second glass and turned to face her, grim-faced.

"How could this happen?"

Denial again, thought Megan. "That time when the condom tore … I think."

"But one time — c'mon!"

"That's all it takes, Mike," she said aloud, but inside she was having a different conversation with herself. Any moment, any moment now he'll pull me into his arms and hold me. He'll kiss me on the forehead, and tell me not to worry, because everything will be all right, that he's excited to become a father. And then he'll smile that great big smile that splits his face and radiates joy, and he'll swing me around in the air and whoop, "A baby! We're going to have a baby, Meggy!" Any moment now.

Instead, Mike stayed where he was, leaning up against the kitchen cupboards opposite her. He tilted the wine bottle towards her in silent invitation to join him, but she shook her head, her eyes locked on his face.

"What?" he challenged. "You're not drinking alcohol now?"

She said nothing, determined not to be diverted.

"So," Mike said, topping up his glass and returning the bottle to the fridge. "What are you going to do about it?"

"What am *I* going to do about it? Don't you mean *we*?"

"Well it's your body — isn't that what you women are always saying?"

"*You women*?" she echoed faintly. The slightest ripple of anger was beginning to stir her becalmed numbness.

"It's your body," he repeated, "so it's your decision."

"But it's *our* baby!"

"It's hardly a baby, Megan, don't get all dramatic. It's just a cluster of cells."

She stared at him. She felt as though she was seeing him truly for the first time. Some of this must have shown on her face, because he said, "What did you expect — happy congratulations? Sorry, no can do. I'm supposed to be running that project in Cape Town, remember? What do you expect me to do — just turn it down? And what about you … *your* career? How are you going to balance this?"

"Oh, please don't pretend your horror is on my behalf."

"It's a fuck-up, Megan, and no two ways about it."

"So, you think I should …?"

"If it were up to me, I'd say end it, right now. But it's not up to me, this is your —" he stopped abruptly.

"— my baby?" Megan finished for him.

"It'll be you who has to, you know …"

Now he was using rationalisation — all the defences were having their boxes ticked today.

She didn't wait to hear what it was that *she* would have to do. She already had a pretty good idea. She would have to do it *all*, probably, whichever way she chose. She walked out of the kitchen, whistled for Oedipus, grabbed her phone and the lead hanging next to Mike's keys, and headed out.

They walked through the streets of the townhouse complex, Oedipus anointing his usual spots in between dragging Megan along.

The walking helped her think. *A cluster of cells.* Maybe so, but a cluster of cells which seemed to have pushed the rest of her life out of focus and into the blurry background. The fact of a life — newly, but deeply, rooted inside her — was all that was clear now. A strangely important heaviness anchored her to her life. Difficult, maybe; inconvenient, certainly. But also solid and real.

Her phone rang. Perhaps it was Mike, calling to make nice, to beg her to come home. But the screen displayed a different name.

"Hi, Wade."

"Howzit, sweetheart. What's up?"

"I'm pregnant!"

The briefest of pauses, then the words she'd craved to hear all day. "Oh, Megan, how wonderful! I'm so happy for you!"

The kindness, the genuine joy in his voice undid her and she started to sob, walking blindly behind Oedipus, tripping over the uneven paving.

"What are you blubbing for?"

"Mike doesn't want it."

There was silence for a long moment. Wade had never said

a bad word against Mike, though Megan suspected that he was strongly tempted at that moment.

"No problemo, because your little one will have me as its one and only fairy godfather." The words were light, but his tone was fierce and protective.

"We— I haven't decided what I'll do yet, Wade."

"Megs, this is me you're talking to. Of course you'll have it."

How did he know her so well? And Mike know her so little?

"And it will all be fine. More than fine. It'll be fabulous! And I will be there for you — every step of the way. Do you hear me?"

"I love you, Wade."

"Love you, too, Megs. Call you later?"

"Please."

Oedipus stopped and sat on Megan's feet. She realised they'd walked the entire circuit of the complex and were back outside her front gate. It clicked open as she reached for the buzzer. Mike stood in the frame of the front door, neither inside nor out. Story of his life.

His eyes questioned her.

She sighed. "There's the logic, Mike, and then there's the pull."

He tugged her against his chest and held her there. But he said nothing.

14
CHOICES

H*e stares at the board nailed above the hissing coffee machines.*

Americano, Latte, Espresso, Cappuccino

Short, Tall, Grande

Chai, Macchiato, Red Steamer, Frappuccino

Choices, choices. An action as simple as buying a cup of coffee has become endlessly complicated.

"Yes?" the woman behind the counter asks.

"I would like a cup of coffee, please," he says.

"Filter or espresso?"

"Filter," he says, and before she can ask how he wants it, he adds, "With milk."

But still she finds a question: "Full cream, semi, skinny or soy?"

"Full cream."

"Flavour?"

"Coffee," he says contemptuously, and watches with derision as she turns to consult the board where the absurd flavours are listed — hazelnut, mocha coconut, salted caramel, gingerbread — to

confirm the unfamiliar varietal, before she gets it.

She gives him a look, a tight smile. He sees at once that her teeth are uneven. She has an overbite and her right incisor has edged forward and a little over the left, like pertly crossed legs. It bothers him. He wants to reach out and thrust the erring tooth back into its proper place.

He realises that she is offering him yet another choice. "What was that?"

"Short, Tall, Grande?" she repeats.

"Medium," he says, refusing to capitulate to the absurd jargon.

She gives him another look, this time without the lopsided smile. Be thankful for small mercies, he thinks.

"That'll be with wings — take-away," she says. It sounds more like an instruction than a query, but he is more than happy to comply. He is eager to get away from this place — the noise of shouted orders and fizzing machines, the hot push of people in the queue behind him, the mess of milk puddles and coffee grounds on stainless steel.

While he waits, he looks at the confectionary displayed in the glass-fronted counters: cheesecake, chocolate cake, pecan pie. All available by the slice. It strikes him as significant, these phrases — a slice of cake, a slice of the pie, a slice of life. It is the slicing, the cutting into and off of, which is important, not that which is removed or left behind.

A cup of his preferred choice — tall, white, Americano with wings — is shoved towards him and he carries it to the counter where he must further tinker with it. First, he pulls a handful of serviettes from the dispenser and sweeps the offending spill of sugar and scatter of empty packets into the litter hole in the centre of the counter. If only all that offends the eye could be disposed of so easily.

He is just about to add sweetener to his cup, has just ripped open the little blue sachet, when someone jostles his elbow. The white powder falls in a moving line across the foamy surface of his coffee, the curled rim of the cup, and the just-wiped countertop. He turns to face the offender, recognises him immediately.

"Oh, hello," Dr Weinberg says.

"Hello, Gavin."

"Getting your caffeine fix?"

"Trying to."

He stares at Weinberg, who pours two sachets of sugar into his cup, and stirs it with a plastic stick that looks like a long, white needle. Whatever happened to teaspoons? His critical scrutiny seems to unsettle Weinberg. He often has that effect on people; it pleases him.

"So, have you been up to something you shouldn't have?" Weinberg asks.

Is it his imagination, or is his colleague looking at him very keenly?

"What on earth do you mean?"

"Someone was asking about you the other day." Weinberg takes a slurp of coffee, leaving an unsightly line of foam on his upper lip. The steam fogs the lenses of his spectacles. "Practises here at Acacia and may refer to you, and seems to give more credence to hospital gossip than she should. She wanted to know what you're like with patients — sorry, 'clients'." Weinberg puts a sarcastic emphasis on the last word. "Whether there have been any complaints."

He turns away, ostensibly to tear another sachet of sweetener, but really he needs a moment to soothe the spasm that he can feel momentarily twisting his features.

105

"Who?"

"Who what?"

"Who was asking?"

"A patient. No names, no pack-drill."

His heart begins to beat faster but his features — now back under his control and long-schooled to reveal what he is not feeling — crease and wrinkle to convey bewilderment.

"I can't for the love of me think what that could be about," he says.

"Probably nothing. But keep your nose clean."

Is there a warning in the words?

"I'll do that," he says, pulling back his lips to reveal his own, even teeth.

Weinberg nods back, unsmiling, and walks off.

I'll do that — that, and more, he thinks.

15
STORM

Rainbow rolls, fashion sandwiches, tuna sashimi, edamame, eel maki — the small plates with their plastic domes rotated around the turntable. The sushi bar had been Mike's choice.

Megan's thoughts were far away. It was uncomfortably hot and muggy in the restaurant where the air-conditioning was failing to tame the sweltering February afternoon. Outside, where the smokers' tables spilled out onto the piazza, heat shimmered off the paving and mosaic floor art, and a few withered plants baked in their terracotta pots. But hulking above, storm clouds — dark and bulky as thugs — were beginning to muscle out the sun.

She wished it would rain. The enervating heat had sapped her energy and slowed her thoughts to a sluggish torpor. According to *What to Expect When You're Expecting*, your body's temperature ran higher when you were pregnant. Too bloody right, Megan thought, pulling her hair off her sweaty neck and securing it into a rough bun with a hair tie. The book also said that the little tadpole inside her was as big as a small strawberry and now had arms, legs and a beating heart. Bigger than a cucumber maki, not yet as big as one of the California rolls sailing past her gaze.

Mike slid into a high stool beside her. "Hello, gorgeous! Miss me?"

Several replies vied for escape at Megan's lips:

No.

Where were you?

Don't you know it's rude to keep a lady waiting alone in a restaurant?

But in the interests of preserving peace, as well as reducing the levels of her stress chemicals — she'd read about that, too, in the book — she merely said, "Hi there."

"Oh, excellent, they have butterfish today," Mike said, extricating a black plate topped with slivers of white fish from the passing parade. "Jeez, it's hot. Have you ordered some wine already?"

Megan tapped the glass of mineral water in front of her. "No booze for me," she said.

"I'll just have to drink for the both of us," Mike said, scanning the wine list he'd just been handed by the waiter. "A glass of the Porcupine Ridge Chardonnay, please."

He snapped open his bamboo chopsticks and stirred a nugget of jade wasabi into his bowl of soya sauce, then snared a slice of the pale fish, dipped it in the sauce and dropped it into his mouth. Megan watched him eat. He was undeniably good-looking. His blue shirt brought out the colour of his eyes, and his hair — in need of a trim — flopped rakishly over one eye. He looked like a cool surfer in search of a beach.

She looked away. Outside the light had turned the peculiar acid yellow of an impending Johannesburg thunderstorm. Perhaps it would hail. She hoped Oedipus would take cover under the portico at the back door; he wasn't the most intelligent of dogs.

"Excellent," Mike enthused again, after he'd eaten the last piece and sipped deeply from the glass of wine now at his elbow.

He turned his attention to the turntable, in search of the next morsel, and Megan returned her gaze to the neat slices and perfect cross-sections on display. It was very soothing, very relaxing to watch them approach from a distance, pass slowly by for her perusal, and then disappear off down the line again. It was almost hypnotic — sushi conveyer belts could probably be used as a trance induction method, she mused.

"What's the matter? You not eating?"

"Hmm? Oh, no, I can't."

"Heat killed your appetite?"

"No. It's sushi — I can't eat it."

"But you love sushi," he insisted, pouring soya sauce into a salmon hand roll and taking a large bite.

"Mike, I'm pregnant. You can't eat raw fish when you're pregnant. It can have parasites and bacteria."

Mike mumbled something, but a deafening crack of lightning muted his words. The long electric rumble of thunder which followed ushered in the cool breeze Megan had been craving all day.

"You can have one with a prawn, can't you? They're

cooked." Mike pointed at a coral prawn, bisected along its underside almost all the way through to its spine, and draped open over an oval of pressed rice. The transverse coral lines looked like the ribs of some flayed creature. "Or a yaki-whatsit." He gestured to a skewer of grilled chunks of chicken drifting past on one of the turntable plates.

"Yes, but look," Megan said, nodding to where the three sushi chefs in the central preparation island were filleting and slicing fish with long, sharp knives, and sculpting balls of rice with their fingers and palms. "They use the same knives and boards for preparation, and they don't seem to wash their hands between touching the raw fish and the cooked food."

Mike caught the waiter's eye and indicated with an impatient gesture that he wanted his wine replenished.

"Now you're just being ridiculous," he said.

Was she? She didn't think so. It seemed stupid to take the risk of getting ill when you wouldn't be able to take medicine to get better. There was so much you had to avoid for the sake of the developing baby: not just sushi and alcohol, but also camembert and blue cheese, coffee, X-rays, hair highlights, and headache tablets — she could have used one of those right now. The oppressive heat seemed to be pushing in on her skull, squeezing her brain. She cricked her neck to loosen the tension locked in her muscles there, and ordered a Greek salad from the hovering waiter.

"I saw Dr Weinberg again today."

No response.

"I figured I may as well stay with him, it's more convenient than driving all the way out north to see Dr Khumalo."

Mike smirked. "I thought Doc Khumalo was a soccer player. And who's Dr Weinberg?"

"Mike, are you deliberately trying to piss me off, or are you so far stuck in denial that you won't even allow yourself to remember that he's my gynae? You know, the one who'll be delivering *our* baby come September?"

Mike said nothing. He lifted a plate of shredded crab salad off the turntable, inspected it, and plonked it back on the belt. He checked his phone.

Outside, the rain finally broke. Hard heavy drops pockmarked the piazza with dark splashes, sending shoppers scrambling for cover. The outside diners grabbed their plates and glasses, and ducked inside, laughing and shaking water from their hair. Steam rose off the paving and the heady scent of rain on parched earth drifted in to where Megan sat.

"I have to work in Cape Town next week, on the new project," Mike said, his chopsticks toying with the pale pink shavings of pickled ginger.

"The foetus is about so big." Megan held her thumb and forefinger apart to show him. "I'm apparently about seven-and-a-half weeks along." She had to raise her voice to be heard above the rain now drumming on the roof.

"I'll be working flat out, and I'll have to be there for the following week, too."

"The first scan will be at nine weeks. Will you be here for it? They'll give us photos from the scan, even a DVD if we want," Megan said in the direction of the dissected segments of fish and sliced flesh passing her line of vision.

Mike spoke to them, too. "So, I thought I'd just stay there

over the weekend. Save the cost of another flight and get some work done."

Megan swivelled in her stool to face him. "So, this is how it's going to be? Like this. Really?"

Mike looked at her and shrugged. "Your choice."

He downed the remains of his wine and signalled for the bill.

16
ANXIOUS

Megan scanned the list of the day's scheduled appointments.

"Who's this?" she said, pointing at the name written in the first slot of the day.

"Mr Thomas," Patience said. "New client."

"But haven't I already got a new client today? Here." Megan tapped the last slot where the name Dr Smith was listed. It was one of her rules that she saw only one new client per day. First sessions were more demanding and tiring than follow-ups. They also often ran over time and she liked to schedule them at the end of the day so that they didn't make her run late for other clients.

Patience shrugged. "He said it was urgent. And your first appointment had cancelled, so I put him in."

"All right. Buzz me when he's here and has filled out the forms."

"*Yebo*. And I must leave early today. My cousin in Newcastle …" She produced a crumpled black and white photo of a suited man posing earnestly beside a straight-backed chair. The man looked young, the photo — a formal, studio shot — looked a century old.

"Fine. It's fine — just let me know when you go."

In her office, Megan sat at her desk and sipped the coffee. It still tasted peculiar to her, oddly metallic, so she set it aside and spent a few minutes trying to prepare her mind for the day ahead and for the clients she would be working with. Soon her thoughts strayed to Mike, the fight they'd had the previous night, how they'd lain afterwards, back to stiff back in the suddenly vast bed. From there, it was a short mental hop to baby beds — Moses baskets and antique cots with brass fittings and snowy bedding. She was thinking about tiny white baby clothes when Patience announced her client. It seemed a long journey back to the reality of the consulting room.

Mr Thomas looked to be in his early forties. Megan's first impression was of a very attractive man. He was tall, slim, clean-shaven, with thick dark-blonde hair swept back from a high forehead. The irises of his eyes, which were the dark brown of aged port, didn't quite touch the rim of his lower lids, giving his eyes an enigmatic appeal. He wore dark grey trousers with a pale blue shirt open at the collar, the sleeves rolled up casually to just below his elbows. His hand, when he reached out to shake Megan's, was cool and dry, his grip firm.

"Mr Thomas, er ..." Megan shuffled through the completed intake and indemnity forms which he'd handed to her, trying to find his first name.

"Please, call me Tony."

"Hello Tony. You can call me Megan."

"Where should I sit?" he asked.

"Wherever you're most comfortable."

It was her standard reply. She liked to study her new clients in these first uncertain moments and to form hypotheses about them depending on where and how they sat. Tony Thomas sat, as most clients instinctively did, in the chair facing the door, with his back to the wall — symbolically facing the opening of the cave, ready to fight or flee the threat of anticipated therapeutic challenges.

"You have a lovely office," he said, looking around the room. "The colours are very calming."

"Thank you. Before we begin, can I just get a few details?" Megan launched into her usual list of questions: about his age (forty-five), family structure (single, never married, no children, parents deceased), and occupation.

"I'm an artist."

"Really?" Megan said, interested. "What kind?"

"Photography, mostly," he replied. "But I also do some sculpting from time to time."

"Should I have heard of you? Are you famous?"

"No," he gave a modest laugh and ran his hand through his hair, smoothing it. "No, I'm not well known at all. I do mostly landscapes, but celebrity portraiture is where the fame is — Annie Leibovitz, David Bailey, Lord Lichfield."

Megan finished drawing the simple genogram that was the first entry in any client's file, thinking how nice it would be to chat to a man whose idea of high art was not the perfect putt or drop-kick. Mentally chastising herself for these wayward thoughts, she raised her eyes to give him her full attention.

"So, what brings you here?"

"A friend recommended you, but …"

"But?"

"Honestly? I was reluctant to come."

Megan held the silence, sure he would continue.

"I'm a very private man. The thought of spilling my guts to someone, the thought that others would know or find out …" He stared at her intently with those dark eyes, as if trying to assess her trustworthiness.

"Maybe it would help to know that psychologists are ethically and professionally bound to maintain the strictest ethics, particularly when it comes to confidentiality. We're not allowed to share any details of your treatment — even the fact that you are in treatment — with anybody, without first getting your express and written consent. We're not allowed to do or say anything which might breach your anonymity or confidentiality."

"No exceptions?"

"That's a good question. There are just three exceptions to the confidentiality rule. By law, we're obliged to report if and when we have knowledge that a client is actively intent on killing themselves, or on harming or killing someone else, or where there is ongoing abuse of a child." She paused to let him process the information before continuing, "Does that reassure you?"

"Yes, that seems safe. I'm sorry to be so neurotic."

"Not at all. It's important for you to be comfortable, to be able to trust me and this process."

"It's hard for a man to admit he has problems and needs help."

"It is. Why did your friend suggest you come?"

"To talk through some issues," he said hesitantly, shrugging and looking a little embarrassed.

To Megan, it hardly sounded like it merited an urgent appointment, but she knew that when people got up the guts to call a psychologist, they often did so in a now-or-never state of mind. By the time they sat in front of her, however, their problems often seemed less critical and they felt silly discussing them.

"What sort of issues?" she pressed.

He tilted his head, thinking. "I have a bit of a temper, it gets me into trouble sometimes. Oh, not beating up people, or road rage, or anything like that," he said quickly, smiling in response to her raised eyebrows. "It just interferes with how I relate to people."

She waited.

"And, I apparently have 'unrealistic expectations'." His fingers sketched quotation marks around the phrase. "Or so I'm told."

"Who told you that?"

"More than one ex," he said, with a self-deprecating smile which made his eyes twinkle with a sherry-coloured light.

"So, it sounds like you've had some relationship problems, partly due to difficulties in managing your anger and your expectations," Megan reflected.

He nodded. She continued probing for a while, asking for details and examples, and making a note of the issues which would be targets for therapy. She would teach him strategies for anger management, then explore his typical patterns of

117

interaction in romantic relationships.

It seemed a simple enough case, but she'd practised for long enough to know that no "case" — no person — was simple at all. With this client, she'd need to track back through his past to find the real source of his anger, the origin and true function of his exacting standards. But there'd be time enough for that in later sessions, once he trusted her more.

Don't go too deep, too soon — you'll scare off the punters. Megan could still hear the voice of her first supervisor. It had been sound advice.

She outlined some preliminary goals and the framework of a treatment plan with Tony Thomas. He seemed relieved to have a plan of action.

"I'm so glad I came today. I was in two minds, you know, but then I decided to meet with you and I feel so much better." He grinned. It really was a charming smile.

"I'm glad. But fair warning, there's a lot of work ahead."

"I'm sure there will be. But I feel I understand and can put things in a much better context now. So, thank you, really."

A little embarrassed, she let him out to the reception where he eagerly booked a succession of appointments.

Tony Thomas's calm air and pleasing manners could not have been more different to that of her last client of the day, whom Patience ushered in at precisely five-thirty with an adjustment to her petticoat and a reminder to Megan that she was leaving early and wouldn't be there to book follow-up appointments at the end of the session.

Dr Arthur Smith hesitated on the threshold of her office for a moment before taking two deliberate paces inside. He was thin and of medium height, dressed in a navy suit worn with a plain white shirt and a conservative grey tie. His grey hair, cut short, fell evenly on either side of a defined middle path. His eyes, which scanned the room in a series of quick glances, were an icy blue and his mouth was set in a grim line.

"Dr Smith." Megan reached out a hand to shake his.

He took it after a moment's hesitation, looking reluctant.

"May I call you Arthur?"

"I suppose." The pale eyes came to rest on her.

"Won't you sit down? Wherever you'll feel most comfortable."

Arthur Smith immediately sat down in the tall wingback chair with its back to the door. The power-seat, Megan noted, usually taken by either the supremely confident wishing to dominate the process, or the desperately insecure seeking a sense of protection in the chair's high back and armrests. She wondered which Smith would turn out to be. Of course, he could always be both — it wasn't unusual for both personality positions to coexist uneasily in the psyche of one troubled individual.

Megan sat in the two-seater nearest him, tossing a cushion which was in her way onto the adjacent couch. She headed the top page of her notepad with his name and the date and started as usual.

"Before we begin, may I just get a few details?"

"If you must."

He pulled his gaze back from the couch at which he'd been staring, and turned his head to look at her. He seemed almost to study her, from the top of her auburn hair — pulled back from her face with tortoise-shell clips — to her strappy black sandals.

He frowned at these. Megan felt faintly uncomfortable. If he was so unenthusiastic and planned on being uncooperative, why had he come?

Diligently she noted her feelings on the paper. *Counter-transference: irritation, feeling judged.*

"It helps me understand you better if I know your family context," she said. "How old are you, Arthur?"

"Fifty."

He stood up abruptly, moved jerkily over to the couch and arranged the jumble of scatter cushions into a straight line with a mauve cushion on each end, and the tan one precisely in the middle.

"It was bothering me — the mess," he said, sitting back down in the wingback.

"I see," Megan said. "Is there anything else in the room that bothers you?"

"The picture." He jerked his chin twice in the direction of the painting hanging directly behind her desk.

"Would you like to …?"

"Yes." In an instant, he was out of his seat to straighten the painting, stepping back to check and making several minute adjustments before he said, with a kind of grim satisfaction, "There you are — perfect."

No, there *you* are, she thought, studying him as he settled himself back into the chair. She wondered just exactly what she was seeing: extreme anxiety — possibly even obsessive-compulsive disorder — or a further attempt to dominate the session by controlling the space, to dominate *her* by implying that she was untidy?

"Do things like that often bother you?"

"I'm here, aren't I?" he snapped tersely.

"Right," she said slowly. "We'll come back to that in a minute. First, I do need to get the basic details. I see from this," she said, holding up the intake form which he'd completed in neat black capitals, "that you're a doctor?"

He merely nodded.

"Any speciality?"

"I cannot see how that's relevant. I suppose you want to know if I'm married, have children, that sort of detail, too?" He rubbed the knuckles of one hand against his chin.

This time, it was she who nodded.

"I was married to the same woman for twenty-four years. We have two children — a daughter of twenty-three and a son of twenty years."

"You say you *were* married?"

"Maureen passed away five and a half years ago. Cancer."

"I'm sorry to hear that. How old was she at the time?"

"Is it really necessary for you to know all this?"

"Yes, Arthur, it is."

He crossed his legs first one way and then the other. "She was fifty-two years old."

Megan noted the details.

"I suppose you're doing the sums, writing up all sorts of Freudian theories now, like why I married a woman older than myself? And what that says about me, that I married a mother figure?" he almost sneered the words.

"Did you?"

"No!"

"Right, then." Megan checked the genogram. "And did Maureen work?"

He hesitated, then said, "She took care of me. And the house, of course. I like it to be neat and tidy. I have a domestic worker now."

"Let's talk about that." Megan pointed to the row of cushions on the couch, and asked, "Why is it important that things are neat, tidy, ordered, and" — she pointed at the painting — "straight? What happens inside of you when things are messy, uneven, or untidy?"

She listened very carefully to his answers, but Arthur Smith seemed intent on yielding the bare minimum of information. By the end of the session, she was still not sure what she was dealing with. He might just be a deeply anxious man suffering in the self-imposed trap of obsessive-compulsive anxiety disorder, overcome by a compulsion to impose order on a world which threatened him with its entropy and unpredictability. But there was a chance he was something altogether more problematic and troubling. She could not rule out that she was seeing a man with obsessive compulsive *personality* disorder, a man who wanted to control others, to force them to fit his template of how the world should be, a man who might resort to intimidation, even abuse, to maintain the illusion of control which protected his fragile sense of self.

Megan was suddenly aware of the complete silence outside, and that she was alone in her offices with this man with the hostile eyes.

"I think we'll leave it there for today," she said.

He looked surprised.

"Next time I think we should explore if you have any rituals — any behaviours or habits which you feel compelled to do to help discharge some of your anxiety. So, you can think about that in preparation for our next session."

"You think I'm anxious?"

He had a peculiar expression on his face, somewhere between humour and derision. He rubbed his chin again.

"Yes, I do," she said. She stood up, feeling a compulsion of her own: to open the door and flee into the corridor as soon as possible.

They moved into the reception room, Arthur stepping aside to let her precede him. She sensed a quick movement behind her and felt the hairs on the back of her neck rising. Taking a long, quick stride away from him, she stepped behind the counter, and spun around to face him.

"You can pay for today next time," Megan said.

She noted that the glass sliding door to the corridor was closed, the latch of the Yale lock clicked into position by Patience to prevent anyone from wandering into the rooms while she was consulting. Megan felt an urge to run to the door and fling it open, but Arthur stood at the end of the counter, blocking her path to the door.

"I'd prefer to pay now," he said.

He reached into a breast pocket of his jacket and withdrew a leather wallet. Extracting a silver-coloured credit card, he held it out to her, but just as her fingers touched it, he jerked it back out of reach. The sudden movement made her jump.

"Cash," he said, counting out notes instead and tossing them onto the counter in front of her. "Cash is king."

Why hadn't he wanted her to take the credit card? Every instinct told her to get out. Now.

"Goodbye, Arthur," she said, stepping resolutely towards him in the hope of shepherding him towards the door. He took a single, small step back, and then stopped.

"Aren't you going to make another appointment for me?" he asked, his lids narrowing over his cold blue eyes.

"Yes, of course. I forgot. I don't usually make the appointments," she babbled. Opening the large desk diary at the following week, she chose an empty morning slot at random and said, "How about next Wednesday at nine-thirty?"

He shifted his weight from one foot to the other, and then back again, and knuckled his chin. Then he reached over, grabbed the diary from her hands, slammed it closed and thumped it back down on the counter.

"I don't think so, Megan," he said, straightening the diary so that its edges were perfectly aligned with those of the counter. "I'm not sure I want another appointment. I was determined to meet you, to see for myself … But I'm not sure you can help with what's wrong with me."

Normally, Megan would encourage a reluctant client to give therapy a few sessions before deciding whether it was likely to be beneficial. Normally she would have tried to talk a client out of coming only once, to dissuade them from sliding back into avoidance and denial. But this didn't feel normal. She wanted nothing more than to get away from him.

"Right. Fine." She grabbed her handbag and keys, pushed past him to the door, and fumbled the catch open with trembling fingers. "You can call my receptionist if you change your mind."

He walked up behind her just as she slid the door open and stepped outside into the corridor. It was deserted, the lights dimmed to their after-hours setting. This wing was home to the offices of specialists who consulted during office hours, far away from the hustle and bustle of the hospital wards. Arthur Smith stepped out to stand beside her, pulling the door closed behind him and giving her a sideways glance.

Megan stepped around him to lock the door. "The lifts and the exit are that way." She indicated down the corridor.

"I'll walk with you," he said, his pale eyes glittering in the subdued light of the corridor. "You shouldn't be here alone at this time of day."

She set off in the direction of the lifts, walking briskly and feigning a confidence she didn't feel. His legs kept easy pace with her stride and she noticed that he never stepped on the join line of adjacent tiles. Each step fell precisely in the centre of a tile. Was that intentional?

As soon as she reached the bank of lifts, she jabbed the down button. After a moment, Arthur reached forward and pushed the up-button.

She stared at him. "Are you going upstairs?"

"No." He tucked his chin in. "It just bothered me … the one light."

The lift doors opened and Megan stepped in immediately, taking up a position right next to the panel of buttons. With her left hand, she punched the button for the ground floor. She held her right hand behind her back, threading the sharp keys between her fingers in a makeshift knuckleduster, trying to do it without allowing them to clink.

Arthur stood too close to her, examining her face. His eyes lingered on the dent in her cheek. The doors slid shut slowly and the lift seemed to pause in the absolute silence before beginning to sink slowly down. Arthur looked from the display of lights above the doors to Megan, and then to the panel of buttons. She felt the skin on her scalp tighten.

He took a sudden step right up to her, his ice-blue eyes blazing in his taut face, and spoke, his voice loud and urgent in the metal cube. "I must —"

The lift stopped, the doors opened, and a young couple holding the hands of identically dressed twin toddlers stepped in, bringing with them a burst of noise and motion.

Arthur shrank back into the corner of the lift. Megan smiled at the family in weak relief. She stuck close to them when they exited on the ground floor, merely nodding a greeting to Arthur when he said goodnight. She kept her eyes on him as he strode across the foyer, paused at the automatic sliding doors, looked back over his shoulder at her for a moment, and then stepped outside.

17
REVENGE

Megan bent over the bunch of roses and inhaled. No fragrance — they were perfectly shaped hothouse blooms the colour of antique lace with the faintest trace of dusky pink in their swirled centres.

"They're lovely, Alta, thank you."

"Just, you know, to say thank you. I'm doing so much better, and I wanted you to know how grateful I am," Alta said.

She did look a lot better. The tightness had left her face, she was taking more care with her appearance, and she was smiling happily. It was for the reward of seeing previously depressed patients smile like this that Megan did the work she did.

"I'm so glad." Megan freed the roses from their cellophane straightjacket, and put them into the vase which Patience brought into her office. "But you don't need to thank me or give me gifts."

Therapists were not supposed to encourage their clients to show their appreciation. To Megan, it had always seemed to be both better manners and more sensible simply to receive such small gestures with good grace, rather than to challenge a client's kindness with a psychodynamic interpretation that her gift was an unconsciously manipulative attempt by the psyche to ingratiate itself with the Kleinian "good breast" in the form of the therapist.

It also meant she could keep the flowers.

"So, what have you been up to this week?"

Megan gave her a smile. "I thought that was my line."

"No, I meant with, you know …"

"I know. I've been asking around, but I haven't found out anything specific. Nobody seems to want to say anything. I've booked Monday off and I'm going to visit the two women who laid complaints with the Board, although I've only managed to contact one of them. I've set up an appointment to see her. The other woman's phone number gives me a 'no longer exists' message, but I have her address, so I thought I'd just take a chance and swing by there. I'll chat to them both, find out what happened to them, why their hearings didn't proceed and, of course, whether they'd be prepared to try again."

"That sounds good," Alta said. "I've thought a lot about it, and Johan and I have discussed it. And I've decided I'm definitely going to go ahead with a complaint."

"I see." Megan tried to let her face show neither her satisfaction nor her concern.

"I've started working on a letter — can I bring it for you to look at when I'm finished? I'm not sure about the language and stuff, maybe you can help?"

"I'd be happy to take a look. So, do you want to talk about that today? Or is there something else you'd rather do?"

"What I'd like to do," said Alta with a wide grin, "what I'd *reeaaally* like to do is to kick a cop!"

"Huh?"

"Kick a cop! Poke a popo, push over a pig!"

"What the …?" A giggle was building inside Megan. Some clients were so much easier to like.

"So I'm driving here, right? And you know I've got some serious stuff to worry about without some fat pig of a cop adding more worries to my life, right? And at this bloody stop street here — down the road from the clinic" — she pointed south — "I sort of pause and cruise through, because it's a boom opposite and no road on the right, so the only other cars come from the left and I'm turning left, so it's hardly dangerous. I don't even know why it's a stop street instead of a yield sign. Wait! No, I do know. It's so some fat lazy pig of a popo can meet his traffic ticket quotas without having to get off his arse and catch the real criminals out there. So, he jumps out and waves me over, right? I swear, Megan, there was a moment there when I was totally tempted just to put foot and run him right over, squash him flat as a pancake." Alta smacked her hands together in a glancing blow.

"But you didn't? Please tell me you didn't."

"Of course not! What do I look like — a killer or something? No, but then he hangs all over my window, sticking his stupid hands inside my car, checking my licence and stuff. And then — get this — he wants a bribe! Hell, but I wanted to kick him so badly. Just here" — she tapped the centre of her shin — "and hard!"

"He asked for a bribe?"

"Not directly. No, he says he's so hungry and it's so hot here in the sun and maybe I could help him buy lunch, how 'bout it? I mean, have you ever?"

Megan was beginning to enjoy the story immensely. It was a delight to see Alta so animated and feisty. Who knew there was such a thing as crooked cop therapy?

"What did you do?"

"I said to him, 'Better yet,' I said, 'maybe I could buy you a box of condoms for when they send you to jail for bribery and corruption! How 'bout *that*, officer?' I swear he swelled up even bigger and wrote me up probably the biggest fine he could — R900, for that! But it was worth it. What an arsehole!"

"It made you feel better to challenge the injustice?"

"Well, I felt a little bit better then, but I was still pissed off, right? So, I couldn't just leave it like that."

"What did you do?" asked Megan, delight vanishing in the face of rising anxiety.

"I went to the shops down the road and bought some big sheets of cardboard, and a fat permanent marker and some duct tape. Then I made a few posters. Like 'Crooked Cop Ahead', 'Cop at the Stop Street!', 'Poke a Popo!' and — hell, I couldn't resist it — 'Kick a Cop Today!' Then I drove back around the block and stuck them up on the lampposts coming up to the stop street to warn other decent motorists like me!" She laughed loudly. "So then I stop at the stop street, wait a good few seconds before moving off and turning left and I drive past the fat bastard again, waving and smiling like the queen." Alta heaved a deep, satisfied sigh. "Hell, it felt good!"

18
WHAT REMAINS

"Thank you for agreeing to see me, Mrs Cole," Megan said.

"Technically, I suppose it's Miss Cole, now. Or Ms. Maybe just call me Stacey."

They were sitting in the living room of Stacey Cole's Norwood house. It should've been a beautiful room, with the sun streaming through its bay window and turning the Oregon pine floors a golden-pink, but the space between the wooden floor and the pressed steel ceiling was clogged with clutter. Uneven columns of books and magazines teetered alongside baskets of laundry and old take-away food containers. Piles of paper, unopened mail and old newspapers were strewn across every surface. Megan could see that the passage beyond the room was similarly congested with mounds of clothes, stacked shoe boxes and black plastic storage bins. The whole house seemed filled up and weighed down by the clutter.

Dust puffed up in a cloud when Stacey flopped heavily onto her couch, sending sparkling motes dancing in the sunlit air, and dulled the surface of the bread-baking machine box on the floor beside the couch. Rows of empty, dusty wine bottles were lined up in front of the decoratively tiled Victorian fireplace which dominated the room.

Stacey Cole seemed weighed down by herself. She was short, yet probably a good forty kilograms overweight, Megan estimated. The fingers which pointed at the tea tray on the table ended in badly chipped nail polish.

"I made tea," Stacey said, in a voice as lifeless as her unwashed hair. "Help yourself." She leaned forward with some effort and took three Oreos from a serving plate.

"Thanks," Megan said.

She poured herself a mug, more out of politeness than desire; the tea was probably already cold. She took a sip — it was. She set the cup down on a side-table crowded with used coffee mugs and four framed photos. The largest of these, in an ornate silver frame, showed an attractive woman, dark hair glinting in the sun, looking with loving eyes into the face of a smiling young man. The woman was wearing a long white dress, embroidered with lace and crystals; the man wore a tuxedo.

"That was me. It's the *before* picture." Stacey gave a harsh laugh and ate half an Oreo, watching as Megan carefully replaced the photograph. "It's hard to believe, isn't it?"

Megan leaned over the tea things and handed Stacey her business card. "I'm here because I know that you laid a complaint against Dr Trotteur, and I'd be very grateful if you could tell me more about your experience."

"How'd you find out?"

Megan hesitated, then opted for the truth. "Inappropriately," she said. "Possibly even illegally. I looked at a file that I wasn't supposed to."

"Why? What's it to you?" Stacey brushed crumbs off her chest. They landed in her lap.

"As you see, I'm a psychologist. One of my clients, a young woman, was, I think" — she searched for an appropriate word — "maltreated by Dr Trotteur."

"*Maltreated*. That's a nice word for what he does. What's he done to her?"

Megan was reluctant to give details. This wasn't her story to tell, but on the other hand, it was a big ask to expect this damaged woman to give details of her own ordeal without sharing some confidences in return.

"I think he mutilated her. Unnecessarily removed almost all of her labia."

"That all?"

"All!" repeated Megan.

"She got off lightly," said Stacey in a voice bleak with bitterness. She must have seen something of Megan's shock on her face, because she sighed and continued, "Sorry. I don't have much compassion left for others. I'm too busy feeling sorry for myself."

"What happened to you? What did he do?" Megan asked softly.

"What did he do? Let's see … First, he told me exactly what he was *going* to do, whispered it right into my ear just before the anaesthetic kicked in. He said — I haven't forgotten the words, you see, *can't* forget them, and believe me, I've tried. He

133

said, 'I'm going to neaten you up, dear Stacey. Cut away all the unnecessary bits down there and leave just what's essential. Because that's all you are, just a hole. But I'll make that right and tight, too. And if I find that your uterus is dirty and stinky, I'll clean up there as well. Doctor knows best'."

Megan stared back, open-mouthed with horror.

"Next, he cut off my labia and my clitoris, and removed part of my perineum." She nodded when Megan flinched involuntarily. "Then he did a thermal ablation of my uterus — do you know what that is?"

Megan shook her head, shocked into silence.

"They crank open your cervix and pour very hot saline water into your womb. It burns the lining, destroys the endometrium permanently. No more messy periods after that. No more chance of messy babies, either."

"Oh, God, Stacey."

"Then he stitched up my vaginal opening *really* 'right and tight'. No more messy sex either." She paused, looked down at the brown crumbs in her lap. When she looked up again, tears were coursing down her cheeks. "I should have listened to my intuition. The first time he examined me — in his rooms, before the operation — he extracted the speculum roughly and said, 'You're not very tight. You have a lot of sex, I can tell.' It gave me the creeps, but I thought I was just being silly, a prude. I even signed a consent form, giving him permission to tighten my vagina. And of course, you sign forms that if they find something malignant while operating, they can cut it away right there and then.

"I guess you could say he cut away — what's his word for

it? *Excised*, that's right. He excised my husband, too. What's the use of a woman who can't have sex, a wife who can't have children? Who can't do anything much but pile on the mess, inside and out."

Megan could feel tears rising in her own eyes. "Stacey, I'm so sorry. So very, very sorry." The words seemed worse than inadequate.

"Well, that makes two of us. Because *he* certainly wasn't sorry."

"You confronted Trotteur?"

"Of course — once I figured out what he'd done to me, the extent of the damage, the permanent pain. He reminded me that I'd given consent for the procedures, insisted it had all been necessary, that the excised tissue had been malignant. But when I wanted proof, he couldn't give me any. Said the lab had lost the results and he hadn't kept a copy. Said I'd imagined him whispering that shit to me. All lies, of course. So, I laid a complaint against him at the HPCSA. Figured once I had a ruling in my favour there, once he was stopped from practising, and then I could lay a criminal charge of assault or negligence or whatever. Maybe even a civil claim."

"What happened?"

Stacey sighed heavily. "It took ages to get the hearing, almost a year, and then it basically boiled down to my word against his. And when I told them what he'd said, and it took everything I had to say those words out loud, you could tell they thought *I* was completely delusional. Or maybe I'd been imagining it because of the anaesthetic and medication. They couldn't believe that of a *doctor*, one of their own. I could see it on their faces.

"Meantime, my husband had left me, the divorce had come through, and I'd lost my job. Huh!" She gave a sour smile. "I was a personal trainer. Can you believe it? Look at me now. But I couldn't work anymore because of the pain. I could hardly get up most mornings. I got the house after the divorce, but I got the mortgage with it. And I had nothing left, didn't know where the next monthly payment was going to come from. Then *he* called me, offered to settle."

"Trotteur?"

"The same. He offered me a settlement to shut up and go away, signing a contract waiving my rights ever to institute any claim — professional, criminal or civil — against him."

"You took it?"

"I took it. I was penniless and desperate and it seemed the only way I could keep the roof over my head. So, I withdrew the complaint. But" — she looked at Megan with fierce eyes — "not a day has gone by since when I haven't regretted it. I sold myself. I sold bits of my body. I sold my sexuality, my fertility, my marriage, my self-respect. And not even for very much. And now you come and I find out I've sold out other women, too."

"They might not have decided in your favour anyway," Megan said, "even if you had refused the settlement and pursued the case."

"That's what I tell myself at night, when I can't sleep. Funny thing, though, it's not as comforting as a bottle of red."

19

SACRIFICES

Megan was still thinking about Stacey Cole as she drove around a sunny Johannesburg and onto the Golden Highway that would take her just south of the city to Lenasia — to the address of the complainant whose telephone number had been discontinued.

During her training and internship, she'd been to clinics and training sessions in community halls in Lenasia on a couple of occasions, but the area was still largely foreign to her. Ridiculous how when you lived in this city, you only lived in certain parts of it. The directions on Google Maps lead her past the enormous Trade Route Mall, and she looked around her with interest — at the schools, banks and B&B's, the lampposts covered in posters for the latest Bollywood extravaganza, and at the clusters of robed men in animated discussions outside madrassas and mosques.

A gang of young men — some no more than boys, to judge from the soft fuzz on their cheeks — slouched in low-slung jeans, hoodies and unlaced hi-top sneakers outside a corner takeaway eatery whose windows advertised *samoosas, curry and rice, bunny chows* and *Russian & chips*. As Megan slowed to take the corner, one of them — a tall, round-shouldered boy wearing a T-shirt emblazoned with an Andy Warhol-style print of Osama Bin Laden — crooked his right hand into the shape of a gun, pointed it at her sideways, gangster-style, and fired off an imaginary round. She looked away quickly, but not before she caught his sneer.

Eventually, she pulled her Renault up outside what she hoped was Nirvana Reddy's house. The house was small, made of yellow brick and topped by a red corrugated iron roof. A path led from the pedestrian gate to the front door, bisecting a garden blazing with the vivid pinks, oranges and yellows of blooming dahlias, and a white Nissan sedan was parked in the driveway. It looked exactly like a child's drawing of a little house — apart from the high palisade fencing, and the metal sign attached to it depicting a snarling German Shepherd along with the cautions: *Danger! Gevaar! Ingozi!*

Megan checked that her car was locked and then pressed the buzzer next to the pedestrian gate.

"Can I help you?" came a woman's voice, soft and polite.

"Is this the Reddy household?"

"Who wants to know, please?"

"My name is Megan Wright. I'm a psychologist from Acacia Clinic, and I'd like to speak to Nirvana Reddy, if she lives here."

"Nirvana?"

"Yes, Nirvana Reddy."

There was a long silence. Megan saw a net curtain twitch at

one of the front windows, then a man's voice spoke through the intercom.

"I think you'd better come in."

The gate buzzed. Megan pushed it open and walked up the path, keeping a wary eye open for the guard dog. The front door swung open just as she reached it. A man and a woman, both probably in their fifties, stood aside to let her in.

"Please, come this way," said the man, leading her into a small sitting room.

Megan was aware of gleaming, ornately-carved wooden furniture with plush red upholstery crested by crocheted antimacassars. A newspaper lay folded on the marble-topped table between the couches.

"Please, have a seat," said the man. "I am Prashant Reddy and this is my wife, Priyanka."

Mr Reddy was slightly built and balding. He wore a pair of pressed navy trousers and the face above his crisp white shirt seemed to have settled into lines of resigned suffering.

Megan shook their hands and sat down.

"May I offer you some refreshment?" Mrs Reddy said in a soft voice. Even smaller than her husband, and with finer features, she wore a sari of a plain deep blue, and a red sindoor dot on her forehead.

"Just a glass of water, thank you."

The woman left, taking small quick steps, and Megan looked around the room. A brightly patterned carpet was soft under her feet, and colourful, brass-framed pictures of deities hung on the walls.

In a walled alcove at one end of the room was a small shrine.

A deity that Megan thought might be Krishna, was depicted in a carved wooden panel. The god wore an ornate, gilded headdress and was playing what looked like a flute, one leg casually resting in front of the other. He appeared to be looking down at the offering of fruit and rice placed on the shelf at his feet.

Megan's eye was caught by what might have been another shrine, set up on a low table in a corner of the room. Water bubbled and trickled over pebbles in a small water feature behind which was angled a large, framed photograph of a lovely young woman. Candles placed on either side of the frame lit up a face with high cheeks, full lips, a soft smile and deep brown, sloe eyes.

"That is our daughter, Nirvana," said Mr Reddy, following Megan's gaze.

"Nirvana is …" began Megan, unsure of how to ask what she was beginning to suspect, to dread.

A fly buzzed behind her, trapped between the net curtain and the window, randomly butting against the glass in futile attempts to get free. Mr Reddy got up, walked over and opened one of the windows wider, setting the fly free just as Mrs Reddy came silently into the room, bearing a glass of water on a silver tray. She placed the glass carefully onto a white lace doily on the coffee table, then sat down alongside her husband on the couch opposite.

"Thank you." Megan took a grateful sip.

Her mouth was dry, and the water was very cold. Beads of moisture collected into tears on the outside of the glass. Megan's eyes again moved to the portrait of their daughter.

"You have come to see Nirvana, Dr Wright," said Mr Reddy.

"It's Ms Wright — I'm not a doctor. And yes, I came to see Nirvana."

"I regret to tell you that she passed away, almost a year ago now."

Megan swallowed, searched again through the inadequate words, and could only come up with, "I'm very sorry for your loss. I never met her, but she looks like such a beautiful, vibrant young woman."

"She was," said Mrs Reddy in a voice that was little more than a whisper. "She was so very beautiful. And so full of life."

"She was going to be a lawyer, you know. She had finished her degree, and had just started her articles," Mr Reddy said.

"Such a waste. Such a waste of a life." Mrs Reddy's fingers were busy in her lap, folding pleats into the fabric of her sari.

Mr Reddy stared at the photograph of his daughter. "Her whole life was ahead of her."

Beyond the silence which settled on them like a shroud, Megan could hear the water bubbling in the corner, a clock ticking relentlessly on a shelf. A car with a souped-up engine and growling exhausts roared up the road outside.

"May I ask how she died?" Megan had no desire to intrude on their grief, but she needed more information.

"It was an accident — a car. She was just coming out of her place of work."

"She had a car accident on the way home?"

"No, no," said Mr Reddy, seeming to return from some distant place. "She didn't have a car. We couldn't afford to give her one. No, she was walking to the taxi rank, crossing the road, when she was hit."

"A car knocked her over?"

"May he rot in hell," interjected Mrs Reddy, bitterness vying with the grief that suffused her face.

"Priyanka," Mr Reddy chided.

"Don't you Priyanka me. She was young, clever, beautiful — inside and out. She was truly good, a gift to this world. A gift!" she said, turning to Megan. "You say you're a psychologist? Well explain it to me, then. What is the meaning of it all? What is the point? You try and try to have a baby. You pray to the gods, make sacrifices, and eventually you are graced with such a blessing. And you love and care for her, from the day she is born. From before! You feed her only what is good for her, hold her when she is sick, rock her when she cries. You plait her hair and brush her teeth and guide her to say her prayers. You help her with her homework and console her when she is teased. And always, always, you try to shield her from danger. A thousand, thousand times you teach her, 'Look right, then left, then right again.' And then one day she is an adult. Finally, she is mature, wise, strong. And you think it is safe to relax just a fraction, to let go just a mite. And then, bang!" Mrs Reddy slammed her hand down on the armrest of the couch. "She is snatched away from you. What is the point? What was it all for?"

She subsided into sobs of pain and rage. Her husband gently pulled her to him, and she wept into his neck.

"We loved our daughter very much, Ms Wright," he said simply.

"Yes," said Megan. "The loss of a child is a grief beyond words."

Her own hands longed to move across her body and cover her belly, as if by doing so she could protect the life within from the world outside. She had no answers for Mrs Reddy. Every day she heard about cruelty, abuse and unkindness, bore witness to pain. Better than most, she knew just how arbitrarily brutal life could be between its rare moments of beauty. Was she mad to want to keep her baby, to bring it into this world?

Mr Reddy stroked his wife's hand with infinite tenderness, then said, "Forgive me, but I am still not clear as to the purpose of your visit."

"I'm sorry, I haven't yet explained. I'm here because I want to find out more about Nirvana's treatment with Dr Trotteur."

Mrs Reddy's head jerked up off her husband's shoulder.

"I believe that Nirvana instituted a complaint against him with the Health Professions Council," Megan continued. "I currently have a client, also a patient of his, who intends doing the same because of what happened to her. And I want to get more information from other patients who might have suffered at his hands."

"He is a monster," said Mrs Reddy, sitting up and dabbing at her eyes with a corner of her sari.

"If it's not too hard for you, could you tell me what happened to Nirvana?"

"I can do that," said Mrs Reddy.

"Will you please excuse me," said Mr Reddy. "I think I'll go make myself a cup of tea." He left the room and Megan could soon hear the chink of china from somewhere down the passage.

"He doesn't like to talk about women's business," explained Mrs Reddy.

"Do you know why Nirvana consulted Dr Trotteur?"

"Oh yes, I knew. For many years my daughter suffered from endometriosis."

"Endometriosis — that's when the lining of the uterus grows outside it?"

"That's right. It caused her great pain in her pelvis and lower back, and when she had her period, she was in agony. She was worried that one day it would interfere with her fertility. Not that Nirvana was married — she wanted to finish her studies first before she settled down. She was very modern." Mrs Reddy sighed, then continued, "For years our family doctor had just treated her with painkillers and anti-inflammatories, but Nirvana decided she wanted to get it sorted, once and for all. I thought she would go to our local clinic here, the LenMed, but she was a girl who always wanted the best and she said the best in Jo'burg was to be found in the northern suburbs. Anyway, the Acacia was closer to her work, so she went there."

"How did she choose Dr Trotteur? Was she referred to him by someone?"

"No, but he was the only one who had an appointment available on the day she could get off from work." Mrs Reddy paused. Grimness hardened her features. "It was just chance, random."

"And the treatment didn't go well?" Megan prompted after a moment's silence.

"No, it was a disaster. The doctor said he couldn't properly diagnose the condition from an ultrasound. He said she needed to have a laparoscopy. They make a small hole, you know, at the belly-button and then put in a miniature camera so they can see what's going on inside. So, she scheduled one of those at the clinic. He said that if there were cysts or scars from previous cysts, then he could remove them at the same time, also with the keyhole surgery, because she would already be under the general anaesthetic."

"And, what happened?"

"When she woke up, she found he had cut her right open." Mrs Reddy gestured with a slashing movement across her lower abdomen. "And he had given her a total hysterectomy. Removed her whole womb and both her ovaries. He told her the endometriosis was too severe to remove and she would never conceive anyway, and so he just took everything out!"

Megan sat listening in quiet horror as Mrs Reddy continued, "She was young. she still wanted children! Afterwards she was devastated. She told me she felt like she wasn't a real woman anymore. She had such problems with her hormones, she had to go on hormone replacement therapy. And her pain was worse than ever. I don't understand why he did it. Why would someone intentionally maim and destroy someone who had done them no harm?"

There were answers to that one — textbooks and journals and studies full of them — but none which would satisfy a grieving mother.

"I have a question that you may find strange, Mrs Reddy. Did Nirvana mention whether he, Dr Trotteur, said anything to her before she went under the anaesthetic?"

"Oh yes, he did. She told me what he said. It was something

about not worrying her pretty little head. That he'd remove all the stinking bits. As if she was a rotten piece of meat! I remember the last part exactly. She said he told her, 'Trust me, doctor knows best'."

Mrs Reddy looked sharply at Megan, and asked, "Do you believe in evil, Miss Wright?"

"My field deals with health and illness, not good and evil," Megan hedged, but Mrs Reddy didn't appear to be listening anyway.

"I do," said Mrs Reddy. "I do believe in evil. I find it easier, these days, to believe in evil than good."

Megan could find nothing to say to that. In the quiet, she heard the buzzing of the fly again. It had returned and was bouncing against the large windowpane. Mrs Reddy took a section of newspaper from the table and, rolling it up, walked over to the window, lifted the netting and swatted the fly. The buzzing stopped abruptly. She tore off a corner of paper, wiped up the remains of the fly, and dropped it into a small dustbin.

"Prashant may not hurt a fly, Miss Wright, but I am beyond caring about them. 'As flies to wanton boys are we to the gods, they kill us for their sport'. That is what Shakespeare says. I used to spare flies, and observe prayers, and make sacrifices." She gestured to the gifts of food at Krishna's feet. "But none of it made a difference in the end. I don't make sacrifices to the gods anymore. They've taken enough from me."

Mr Reddy came back into the room, carrying two cups of tea. He handed one to his wife and sipped at the other.

"Did Nirvana want to take the matter further?" Megan asked.

Mr Reddy nodded. "We are simple people. I am a teacher of mathematics and my wife teaches English at the local high school. But Nirvana was a law student. She believed in justice, due process, in charges and hearings and verdicts. I'm afraid I tend to believe that doctors stick together and protect one another. The old boys' club, they call it. I thought it was futile. But she was a fighter." He gave his wife's hand a squeeze. "Well, I don't know how it all would have turned out, if she hadn't passed over."

"And the complaint against Dr Trotteur, the one she instituted at the Council — that fell away with her death?"

"What was the point in continuing? Besides, we couldn't face that, we were ... broken," said Mrs Reddy.

"I understand. And there was probably the other legal stuff still to get through."

Mrs Reddy frowned her confusion. "I'm sorry, I don't follow."

"I thought, I mean — wasn't there some kind of case against the driver who hit Nirvana? Manslaughter or something?"

"There might have been, if our dear police service had been of any use."

Now it was Megan's turn to be confused. "I'm not sure I understand."

"We never knew who the driver was, Miss Wright. Nirvana was killed in a hit-and-run."

20
SNOOPING

"**Y**ou owe me for this."

"You did promise to be the fairy godfather," Megan reminded Wade.

"Yes, but there are limits."

They shuffled along in the queue to register for a tour of Acacia Clinic's obstetrics and maternity unit. Most of the women ahead and behind them were obviously pregnant. Megan was beginning to get used to the sensation of bellies, surprisingly hard, nudging against her back.

"Name?" asked the woman behind the registration desk.

She wore a skirt and jacket in the clinic's official maroon and navy, her grey hair was swept into a smooth chignon, and pinned on her lapel was a badge that read "Louise Kelly, Client Liaison Officer".

"Wright. Megan Wright."

"Hi Megan, I'm Louise. Here you go," said the woman, handing Megan a security badge on a lanyard and a nametag which read, "Mrs Wright".

Megan pulled the lanyard over her head, and attached the name tag to the white jacket which she wore over a navy shirt and white linen trousers. She'd chosen her outfit carefully.

"And you must be Mr Wright." Louise smiled brightly when she handed Wade his badge and tag.

"So they tell me," Wade said, running his fingers through his already tousled chestnut hair and winking at her. "But you've spelt it wrong. Here, let me just …"

He took the pen out of her surprised hand, scratched the W out, and pinned the tag to his chest. A look of confusion briefly disturbed the woman's face, but she rapidly recovered her poise.

"Do please help yourselves to some tea or coffee while you wait."

Wade eyed the bowls of instant coffee powder and the cartons of long-life milk with distaste, but Megan made herself a cup of weak black tea.

"Thank you all for coming," Louise said loudly when she'd registered all the visitors, and called in vain — twice — for the Fowlers. "I hope you'll enjoy today's tour of our wonderful obstetric and maternity unit. Please feel free to ask any questions you may have at any time. Here at Acacia, we have a holistic approach to women's health and I'm sure you'll be impressed by our state-of-the-art facilities and patient-centred services. We're committed to giving you the best, safest birthing experience possible.

"We'll start our tour with a peep at the obstetric wards for both pre- and post-delivery, then we'll stop by our neonatal ICU unit, and finally we'll end with everyone's favourite — a visit to the nursery. Please would you all put your cell phones on silent and put them away. Calls and photographs are not permitted on this tour. And please may I ask, for the sake of our patients' security and privacy, that the group stay together at all times."

Megan could feel Wade's sideways glance at her as she stowed her phone in her bag.

Louise clapped her hands twice, like a cheerleader about to begin a routine. "This way please," she said, leading the way through the security doors into the unit. Megan and Wade lagged behind, allowing the excited mothers and fathers-to-be to jostle for prime position immediately behind the guide.

"Here we have our private rooms, each with its own television, en-suite bathroom and wall-safe."

One by one, the visitors peered inside the rooms. Apart from the drip stands and the mobile plastic cots standing alongside the beds, they looked more like plush hotel rooms than hospital wards.

"Of course, we allow — encourage, even — rooming-in of infants because we pride ourselves on offering family-centred maternity care."

"Do you have family rooms where fathers and siblings can sleep over?" asked an eager-looking father.

"Not at this time," said Louise, still smiling brightly. "We find that mommies who have just given birth need their rest. But please note our stringent security," she chirruped, waving a manicured hand at the CCTV cameras mounted high on the pale lilac walls at regular intervals. "Not only will you and your little one be safe here, but we will strive to make your delivery an unforgettable experience."

"In a good way, I hope," Wade said out of the corner of his mouth, while Megan wondered how the birth of your baby could possibly ever be anything *but* unforgettable.

"We at Acacia know that every birth is special and we make every effort to accommodate each mother's unique birthing needs."

"Can we bring in private midwives for an active birth? Or have a water birth?" asked a tall woman in a yellow dress.

"Not at this time, but I can assure you that *our* midwives are more than competent. Here, let me introduce you to the lady who heads up the team." Louise beckoned over a stout woman in a nurse's uniform. "This is Matron Mabuza."

"Ooh, look at all the yummy mummies. You are going to have nice babies here," Matron Mabuza said, rubbing her hands together, as if eager to get started delivering them.

"Now on your left, are the shared obstetric wards, for mothers who have already delivered," Louise continued.

Megan peeked in. There were six beds, four of which were occupied by pyjamaed women, holding or feeding babies. One woman in a floral-patterned gown was walking slowly and carefully, as if in great pain, across the ward. Without exception, they all looked exhausted and shell-shocked — nothing like the glowing icons of maternity in Dr Weinberg's pregnancy magazines.

"Rather you than me, friend," muttered Wade.

"The wards to your right are for our gynaecological surgery patients, fertility treatments and, sadly, miscarriages." Louise tilted her head as she said this, and a sympathetic little moue momentarily displaced her smile.

"The yeas" — Wade gestured to the left — "and the nays." He pointed to the right.

Megan elbowed him in the ribs.

"If we're lucky, we'll catch a glimpse of the *doctors.*" Louise Kelly sounded almost reverential. "They should be on their rounds soon."

"The gods are descending, the gods are descending," Wade said in a dramatic whisper, waving his hands in the air, but keeping himself hidden behind the tall woman in yellow. Megan stuck her hand in the air, attracted their guide's attention, and asked, "What's Dr Trotteur like?"

Louise Kelly looked momentarily disconcerted. She exchanged the briefest of glances with Matron Mabuza, and then said brightly, "All of our gynaecologists are top-notch."

Beside her, Megan heard Wade inhale deeply. "Aahh, the smell of medics closing ranks in the morning," he murmured.

"Let's move on, shall we? This way please."

Megan nodded at Wade, who pushed his way to the front of the group, linked his arm through the guide's and asked, "What is your policy on breastfeeding?" He spun her around and they set off down the corridor, the crocodile of visitors trailing behind.

Megan peeled off from the group and slipped into one of the rooms on the right-hand side of the corridor. There were eight beds in this ward, six of which were occupied. In the bed closest to the door, a thin-faced woman lay silently staring at the ceiling, tears running down her face. Squashing her immediate impulse to go over and try to help or comfort her, Megan scanned the room.

At the foot of each bed hung a slim wire basket which held that patient's file. X-rays, charts and curling rolls of labels poked out of the folders. A small whiteboard was stuck on the wall at the head of each bed, on which was written the name of the patient and — Megan was pleased to see — the name of the patient's attending doctor.

Dr Weinberg, Dr Gebhardt, Dr Maseko — Megan read the names off the boards above the occupied beds on one side of the ward, then walked down the other. At the second-last bed, the board read: *Mrs Marshall (Dr Trotteur)*. Megan walked over to the bed and, picking up the medical file as if she had a perfect right to inspect it, spoke softly.

"Hello, Mrs Marshall. And how are you doing today?"

From what she could understand from the file, it seemed to Megan that Mrs Marshall had been hospitalised for a threatened pre-term labour. A drip was attached to her arm, but otherwise she looked the picture of pregnant health as she read a magazine with a pouting Angelina Jolie on the cover. Mrs Marshall looked up, a little surprised and obviously trying to place Megan in the rotating succession of doctors, nurses and other hospital staff who typically popped in and out of the ward over the course of a day.

Megan whipped a pen out of an inner pocket of her white jacket, and feigned an entry in the chart. "How are things going, mmh?"

"Okay, I suppose," said Mrs Marshall, lowering Angelina onto the bedclothes. "They've managed to stall the labour."

"Excellent, excellent," Megan said. "And I see that your gynae is Dr Trotteur. Are you satisfied with him? Any problems?"

"Why do you ask?" Mrs Marshall sat up straighter, frowning.

"No particular reason. We just, er, strive to monitor customer satisfaction in our quest for … continuous improvement here at Acacia, so I like to pop in from time to time and check all is well," Megan said breezily. "So — Dr Trotteur?"

"He seems fine. But I've only met him the once. They just assigned me to him when I was admitted. My gynae is actually Dr Williams, but she's on accouchement leave herself, now."

Disappointed, Megan turned and was slipping the file back into the wire basket when a movement in her peripheral vision — a brief flash of white at the door to the ward — caught her eye. But when she looked up, the doorway was empty. She turned back to the patient.

"I see. And has Dr Trotteur been okay, er, so far?" she pressed.

Mrs Marshall shrugged. "So far, so good."

"Humph." The derisive grunt came from behind Megan. The nurse who had arrived at Mrs Marshall's bedside, brushed past Megan and stuck an infrared thermometer into her patient's ear.

"Do you —" Megan began to ask the nurse, but just then a white-coated male doctor entered the ward.

Megan held her breath and stared hard. Could this be him?

The doctor headed for the bed next to Mrs Marshall's and the woman lying there pushed herself up on her pillows and said, "Good morning, Dr Gebhardt," just as Megan read the board above her bed: *Mrs Naicker (Dr Gebhardt)*.

Megan could not completely suppress a short sigh of frustration. She was getting nowhere fast. The nurse, meanwhile, noted Mrs Marshall's temperature on her chart and left the ward. Megan decided to follow her and find out what opinions lay behind that grunt.

She'd only taken a step when another white-coated man stepped into the ward. Astonished, Megan stared into the face of Dr Arthur Smith. He stopped dead in his tracks as soon as he saw her. It was always an awkward moment, bumping into a client outside of the isolated, protected space of her consulting room. The rule for psychologists was to take their lead from the client. Greet only if you are greeted, so as not to blow the confidentiality of the client who prefers that others not know that he is a client. Dr Smith's face remained blank, but Megan thought she saw a glint of anger — or was it fear? — in his ice-blue eyes. He gave no hint of acknowledgement, merely spun on his heels and walked out of the ward.

Megan's mind was racing. Why had he been in this ward? Was he a gynaecologist, then? She didn't remember his name being on Patience's list of the clinic's specialists. She was sure, in fact, that it hadn't been. Was his name even Smith? She remembered how he'd insisted on paying with cash. Had he snatched away his credit card to prevent her seeing the name on it?

"Good luck then, all the best," she said to Mrs Marshall and hurried out of the ward after "Dr Smith".

The corridor, however, was deserted except for an orderly pushing a noisy tea-trolley, and a nurse sitting behind the desk at the nurse's station located midway along the corridor. When Megan saw that it was the same woman who'd attended to Mrs Marshall, she made a beeline for her.

She greeted the nurse first, then said, "It seemed, back there" — Megan inclined her head in the direction of the ward — "that you … I mean, I wondered what you could tell me about Dr Trotteur."

"You just missed him, he was here just now," said the nurse.

"He was?" Megan looked both ways down the corridors, but saw no one. Even the orderly with the tea-trolley had disappeared. "What do you think of him?" Megan asked, her voice barely above a whisper.

The nurse looked at Megan suspiciously. "Who are you?" she asked.

Megan hesitated, then said, "I work here, at the clinic. But not *for* the clinic. I'm trying to help women who have been hurt by him."

The nurse looked at Megan for a long moment, seeming to assess her. She glanced around to check that no one was near, then picked up a clipboard and, with her head down as if reading it, muttered softly, "He is rude. Arrogant to the nurses. The midwives don't trust him."

"How is he with the patients?"

"Sometimes his work is perfect. But there are stories about the other times."

"Stories? What stories?"

Megan strained to hear as the nurse's voice dropped even lower. "Sometimes … sometimes he doesn't wait for the results of the biopsies. He just cuts. He is rough with the patients when they are unconscious."

"But why don't the nurses speak up? Complain about him?"

"They are scared. He shouts at them, complains. They say that once he even —"

"Mrs Wright?" A determinedly cheerful voice rang loudly down the corridor. Megan cursed under her breath, stuck a smile on her face and turned to face Louise Kelly.

"I wondered where you had got to. I must please insist that you stay with the group."

"Sorry, sorry." Megan lifted her hands placatingly. "I was desperate for the loo — you know how it is when you're pregnant. And when I came out, you'd all disappeared and I couldn't find you again. I was just asking the kind nurse here if she knew which way you'd gone, when you appeared."

"Come this way, we're just finishing off at the nursery, looking at all the beautiful babies." The guide seemed appeased by Megan's explanation, but she nevertheless watched Megan like a hawk for the rest of the tour, giving her no chance to question any of the other staff.

Wade was waiting with the rest of the group outside the large glass window between the new-born nursery and a small visitor's viewing area. He gave Megan a questioning glance when Louise returned her to the flock.

Megan shrugged. What had she found out, really? Nothing definite — just whispers and rumours and silence.

Louise rabbited on about complimentary mother and baby goodie bags filled with freebies such as nappies, breast pads and cream for cracked nipples. Wade looked mildly appalled. He and Megan stared through the glass pane at the swaddled infants lying like small pink and brown sausages in their blue plastic cribs.

"They look like monkeys," Wade said. "Or toothless old men."

"They do not," Megan said, gazing at the tiny shell-like ears, the fingers waving aimlessly like the tentacles of sea anemones, the scrunched faces and the searching mouths.

The crib closest to the window held two babies lying face-to-face, one wrapped in a pink and the other in a blue baby blanket. They each had a shock of red hair and seemed impossibly small.

"Our latest twins," Louise announced proudly, looking for all the world as if she'd personally pushed them out into the world.

The twin in blue turned his face from side to side. When his lips brushed the tip of his sister's button nose, he instantly clamped his gums down and began sucking fervently. The infant in pink opened her mouth wide and began yelling — a hearty wail which tugged oddly somewhere in the region of Megan's breasts. Both twins were now bawling and turning purple with the effort of their loud protests. Louise Kelly reached out a hand and turned down the volume on the intercom that connected the nursery to the viewing area.

Wade threw an arm around Megan's shoulders, and gave her an encouraging squeeze.

"Let's hope yours also comes with a mute button," he said.

21
PAPERWEIGHTS

I t is her hair that strikes one first — thick, russet and lustrous. It is burning copper where the sunlight strikes it, impossibly hot next to the cool of her eyes. Are they more blue or more grey? He must pay better attention during his next session. Because he has decided that he will have another session. Maybe many. It will be fun getting to know Ms Megan Wright, he thinks, as he sits in his darkening office, watching the night steal away the last light of the day.

Of course, what struck him *immediately after* the contrast of fire and ice was the dent high in her left cheekbone. A small hollow which dimples when she smiles and which attracts his critical eye repeatedly. An indentation poses a challenge. It is not easily fixed; it cannot merely be excised and incinerated.

How frustrating that it is the therapist who gets to ask the questions, how irksome that he cannot simply ask her, "What caused that flaw in your cheek? Why have you not had it filled in?" Or other, more interesting questions: "Where else are you not even? What else needs fixing?"

She thinks she can fix him. Ha! She has no idea, no clue as to what she's dealing with. She thinks she's so clever, listening and diagnosing, plotting how to change him — the him he has presented her with. But he's had a lifetime of perfecting how to hide, lie and pretend. She doesn't stand a chance, doesn't know that it will be he who is studying her.

After his conversation with Weinberg, he found her easily enough — a female, with a practice at the clinic, who refers patients to doctors and calls patients "clients". Had to be a psychologist, he reasoned. Proper doctors used the term "patients." Only shrinks called their patients "clients". There were two psychologists with practices at the clinic, and only one of them was female. Voila!

A thought intrudes, a question which must be answered. He rubs at his chin, feels the scar. What was she doing in the maternity unit? When he saw her, he could hardly contain the shock. Could she possibly have been snooping around about him, or might she in fact be pregnant? What a delicious thought. How he would like to have her on a steel table, in his hands, under his scalpel — her blood oozing red pearls when he slices into her pale flesh. His fingers running through her burgundy curls and parting her lips.

To his surprise, he feels himself hardening. He is not usually aroused by correcting the patients who pass beneath his hands. It is a task that must be completed to relieve the pressure, not a desire that must be satisfied to appease the appetite. But this tumescent throbbing is a pleasurable, unexpected bonus.

He adjusts himself, turns his thoughts from the flesh of Megan Wright, fingers his paperweight. He almost laughs when he thinks of hers — a pretty, frivolous thing stuffed with an ephemeral dandelion clock. His is better. It is a reminder of his sacred work, of what can be improved, removed. He places the paperweight, with its sensuously rounded dome, on top of tomorrow's files — a ritual he follows most nights. Sometimes he likes to keep it in his pocket, where he can fondle its cool, smooth curves. Tomorrow morning, he will again store it in its secret place in the drawer, away from unenlightened eyes, just as he will hide his true self before letting the world in to see the good doctor.

He feels a tickle along the silver scar on his chin. Could it be growing?

No.

He must stop these thoughts. They are from a time long past. It has been many, many years since he allowed others to see Attie.

But perhaps he will give Megan a glimpse. Perhaps.

Some ungrateful bitch has clearly been whining about his improvements to her. He will need to figure out a way to see his therapist's files. What is she planning? And — something that tickles his curiosity more than his concern — what has she been writing so assiduously about him in those notes of hers?

22
DEBATES

"You have … three … new messages."

Megan pressed "1" for her messages, as directed by the automated voice, and as she listened, moved around her office, plumping up the cushions distraught clients had mangled, sweeping crumpled tissues into the waste-bin, and filing notes from her last sessions.

Wade's voice, at cheerful top speed, spoke into her ear: "Okay, I thought chilled baby marrow and cucumber soup to start — keeping it light and fresh. And then, keeping it easy, roast rosemary chicken with boiled baby potatoes and a salad on the side. And, keeping it delish, a mango and strawberry pavlova for dessert. If you have any objections, shout quickly, else my apron and I will be at your place at five."

"God bless you, Wade," Megan said fervently, deleting the message.

The only thing worse than having her family over to dinner, was having to cook for them. When Wade had volunteered to do the honours, Megan had accepted with alacrity. It would be great to have him there for moral support, too. She had an inkling that it was going to be a difficult evening.

Next up came her mother's voice. "Just confirming that we'll be there by six-thirty tonight. Well, Cayley and I will. Your father will be working late, as usual, but he said he'd try for eight o'clock. So don't cater specially for him. But do make an effort to cater for Cayley, please dear. For my sake if not for hers. Nothing too heavy or rich — you know she either won't eat it at all or she'll … do the other. Maybe some fruit, or a salad. She's being quite good about her eating at the moment. I think working with food is helping her. Please Megan, I don't think I could handle another —"

But the voicemail time limit ran out at this point, cutting off Moira Wright's plea.

"Me neither," Megan said to the phone, and began shuffling through the files and paper on her desk.

"It's me!" rang out Cayley's high voice. "Just checking if I can bring anything for tonight — you know I'm a better cook. No? Sure? Well, if you insist. Oh, and while I think of it, don't mention my new job or ask about it in front of mommy dearest. Bit of a drama there. See you later."

Megan sighed, deleted the message and called out, "Patience? You there?"

"Where else?" came the response from the front office.

"What is this pile of files on my desk about?"

Patience came into the office. She was banging the top of her head hard with the flat of her hand.

"Why are you doing that?" asked Megan, distracted.

"New weave. It's too tight."

"And hitting your head helps? Isn't it painful?"

Patience shrugged and sighed in a way that suggested a woman's martyrdom to the dictates and discomforts of fashion could neither be denied nor resisted.

"You said something about files?"

"Oh, right. What are these for?" Megan pointed at the six files stacked on a corner of the desk.

"Monday."

"Monday?"

Patience poked at her head with the sharp end of a pencil. "Yes, those are the client files for your Monday appointments."

"Today's Friday. So, you took them out and put them on my desk today because …?"

"I'm efficient," said Patience, her face suggesting the innocence of angels.

Megan wasn't fooled. "And also because …?"

"Because I might be late Monday morning."

"Thank you for your 'efficiency'," Megan said with a lopsided smile that dimpled the dent in her cheek.

She took a quick look at the names on the files to see what, apart from the absence of a receptionist, awaited her on Monday. The name on the last file startled her.

"*He* made another appointment?" She held up the file so that Patience could read the name.

"Dr Smith? *Yebo*, last appointment of the day."

"I really didn't think he'd come back. I'm not sure I *want* him back. And I definitely don't want him scheduled at the end of the day again. Hmmm …"

Megan pondered her options. Her gut was telling her to

steer clear, to make some excuse not to see him, but she wasn't sure she should trust her gut. She, better than most, knew that people could act weirdly, even scarily, out of pain.

"Call him back to reschedule, will you? Make it a midmorning slot on a day and at a time when you're sure you *will* be here."

Patience sniffed a little defensively. "Why?"

"Because he's one of these." Megan drew a pair of round-framed spectacles on the top right-hand corner of the file.

Patience peered at the small sketch, obviously puzzled. "Harry Potter?"

"No, it means *watch out!*"

Patience strolled out with the file and Megan heard her greeting someone in the front office. In a moment, she was back again.

"Mr Thomas is here."

"Send him in."

Megan switched her cell phone to silent mode, placed it on the desk beside her paperweight, and stood up to greet a smiling Tony Thomas. He wore khaki chinos with a pale blue shirt, and seemed to have picked up a tan. It looked good on him, emphasizing the sherry glint in his eyes and the white of his smile.

She began the session by outlining for him the various elements of theory, practice and skills-training they'd have to cover in anger management counselling, but before she got very far, Tony interrupted.

"I'm sorry, Megan, I can see you've done a fair bit of preparation for today's session. It's just that so have I."

"That's great, tell me more."

"I've done some reading. I bought the *Anger Management Workbook* as well as *Taming the Tiger Within*, and I'm working steadily through them. They have lots of practical exercises and suggestions."

"I see. And are you finding them useful?"

"Reasonably. I mean — breathe deeply and count to ten, visualise yourself lying on a deserted beach — it's not rocket science, is it?"

"I guess not. So, you've decided to do the work by yourself?"

"No, no — that's not what I meant," said Tony, holding his hands up in a reassuring gesture.

Megan noticed that his fingers were long and slender — pianist's hands, they used to be called.

"I still need you, definitely. But not for the basic stuff, you know? That I can do on my own. I need help with the deeper stuff, the hard bits that I can't access without your expert assistance."

Megan was aware that she felt flattered, and dutifully made a counter-transference annotation in her notes.

"The deeper stuff?" she asked.

"I was thinking it might help to know the source of my anger. Where does it stem from?"

"Insight is always valuable, but I should warn you that it doesn't automatically lead to behaviour change. Knowing why we feel, think and behave the way we do is one thing. Changing it is quite another."

"So, I shouldn't put away the workbooks yet?" Tony said, running a hand through his thick hair.

"Not just yet." Megan returned his smile. "All that breathing and counting can come in useful. But I do think it would be useful to talk about the origins of your anger; doing so might even release some of the rage. And, if necessary, we could also consider doing hypnosis at some stage." She braced herself for the usual protests, but Tony merely looked interested. "There are some wonderfully creative and safe ways of discharging anger in trance. And it's also a great way to learn how to relax."

"Sounds good," said Tony, rubbing his hands along the length of his thighs. "Right then, tell me why I sometimes get so angry?"

"Okay, well firstly, anger is always a secondary emotion. It comes after — and usually in response to — some primary emotion, usually sadness or fear. When we're hurt or threatened, we immediately and automatically convert those scary feelings to anger. We feel more comfortable showing the world our anger because anger has an energy to it, a power and some impetus. Sadness and fear, on the other hand, tend to make us feel vulnerable and helpless. To know why you're full of anger — so full that it spills over when you're bumped — we need to know about the times in your life when you were badly hurt, or frightened. Or when you experienced some kind of trauma."

Tony thought for a few moments, then said, "I was in an armed robbery a few years back. And I had a car accident."

"Would you say you've been this angry only since then? Or, if you think carefully about it, were you already angry?"

"I guess it's not new," he admitted.

"Then we're probably looking at your childhood. Should we start with your family?" Tony nodded a little reluctantly, and she continued, "Tell me about your parents."

He grinned widely. "You want to know about my mother — I should have guessed. It reminds me of a joke I heard. A patient's been in psychotherapy for years. One day he says to his therapist, 'You know, I thought I'd been completely analysed, but yesterday I experienced the most remarkable Freudian slip'. The therapist nods and waits to hear more, and the patient says, 'I was having dinner with my mother, and I meant to say: Please pass the butter, but instead I said: You miserable bitch, you've ruined my life!'." Tony laughed with abandon.

Megan gave a slight smile. "Is that true of your mother? Tell me about her."

"You're a believer in nurture, then?" He folded his long arms across his chest.

Megan lifted her eyebrows in query.

"It's the old nature versus nurture debate, biology and genetics versus learning and experience. You clearly believe in the importance of the family experience."

"You sound like you've studied the subject."

"That's me busted. I did do a year of psychology back in my university days, and some reading since. I find it a fascinating subject, and it's great to have someone knowledgeable that I can debate these concepts with."

"Okay, good. So, where were we?"

"You were about to tell me about the critical importance of nurture in shaping who we are."

"I think it's important, yes, but not that it's the sole determinant of how we turn out," Megan said, wondering why she felt like she was defending her beliefs, why she was talking about them at all. Usually her own views were opaque to her clients. The people who came to see her were typically so focused on sharing their personal experiences and defending their own beliefs that they hardly spared a thought for hers. She needed to shift the focus back onto the client, where it belonged. "Where would you locate yourself on the nature/nurture continuum?" she asked.

"I suppose at the deterministic end." He said it almost contritely, and with a wry smile that charmed even as it apologised. "Biology is destiny — isn't that what your guru, Freud, said?"

"I think his actual words were 'anatomy is destiny', but it probably amounts to the same thing," Megan said, resisting the temptation to add that Freud was most certainly not her guru. Instead, in true analytic tradition, she replied to his question with one of her own. "It seems that *you* believe that your genetics, your biological make-up decides your character, and therefore your life path?"

"I believe that many of our choices are already decided for us by a combination of our DNA and necessity."

"Necessity? Would that perhaps be a necessity of circumstance, of life experience, of *nurture*?"

"You won't trap me so easily," he said, wagging a playful finger at her. "We cause, we bring about certain 'necessities of circumstance', to use your phrase, as a direct or indirect consequence of who we are and how we behave, surely? And that, in turn, is biologically determined. Look around you." He encompassed the room with a sweeping gesture. "Could that painting have been created by someone with only athletic ability?" He twisted around on the couch to look at her desk and the shelves behind it. "Could those books have been read or understood by someone lacking a superior IQ? And those seeds" — he pointed to the paperweight — "could only ever become dandelions, no matter how much they longed to rise above being weeds. It's like developing photographs. The latent image is always the one that will come to the fore. A photo of a landscape can never become a portrait. We are what we are."

"You don't believe in individual free will?"

"Not really. But I can see that you do."

"Did I say that?" Megan challenged.

"You didn't need to — your passion shines through. But I'm more cynical. Perhaps it seems strange to you that I'm even here, willing to place myself in your therapeutic hands, given that I'm not convinced therapy works, that it can change what is hard-wired in the individual."

"Therapy *can* help individuals become the best, strongest and healthiest they can be. It can empower them to choose to change." Now Megan felt she was defending the whole profession of psychology, not just herself.

"That's one way of bringing about change, perhaps — to strengthen the good. I'm not convinced that it works very well."

"You think there's another way? A better way?"

"A quicker way, certainly, would be to weaken the bad, to reduce the unhealthy, destroy the destructive and thereby allow the healthy to flourish."

"By becoming destructive in your own right?" Megan argued.

His argument reminded her of a piece of graffiti scrawled behind one of the doors in a toilet cubicle at university: "Fighting for peace is like fucking for chastity." But she could hardly say that to a client, no matter how provoked she felt.

"Couldn't it be argued, Tony," she said, "that we are what we *do*? If I choose to break down, to destroy, then I am a destroyer, not a healer."

"Even if the ends justify the means? Even if it helps the individual or serves the needs of the broader society?"

"Even so."

Tony leaned back in his seat, cricked his neck and stretched his long legs out in front of him. "Well, I can see that I've come to the right place. I have a therapist who not only believes that change is possible, but who is ready to begin changing me in a non-destructive way."

Was that what the whole debate had been about? Had he only been playing devil's advocate — testing her to check whether she believed it was possible for him to change under her guidance?

"You're right about the first part, but not the second. Only you can change yourself. Are you ready to begin, or do you want to carry on with theoretical debates?"

"We're out of time for today," said Tony, looking at the clock and grinning mischievously at Megan. "Sorry, I know that's supposed to be your line. Should we start with my mother in the next session?"

She couldn't help grinning back. "Yes, let's do that."

23
FAMILY WAY

The dinner party, Megan reflected afterwards as she brushed her teeth and rubbed vitamin E oil onto a belly that was still disappointingly flat, had not been as bad as it could have been.

It had been worse.

Wade had arrived early and cooked a feast of food in his inimitable style. When he heard the doorbell ring, he poured a large whiskey into a nearby measuring cup.

"Is that for the chicken?" Megan asked.

"Nope, it's for the Dutch courage."

"I can't drink."

"It isn't for you. You forget how well I know your family," Wade said dryly, and downed the drink in one gulp.

Oedipus made a general nuisance of himself — leaping up against Megan's mother when she arrived, begging for scraps, and drinking from the toilet bowl in the guest loo before laying his head on everyone's lap in turn, leaving behind spots of drool. Or possibly toilet water.

"Oedipus Rex! Kitchen!" Megan ordered when he began his second circuit.

The dog tucked his tail between his legs and retreated, sending doleful looks back at her.

Cayley, as usual, was preoccupied with the food. First, she asked if there was any cream in the soup and on hearing that there was, she pushed it aside. Next, she peeled the skin off her chicken breast with the delicacy of a surgeon exposing an organ for surgery — an image which, given her current preoccupations with Trotteur, did nothing to improve Megan's own appetite. Megan was happily surprised to see, a little later, that all of Cayley's chicken was finished, but then the ecstatic beating of a furry tail under the table indicated where it had gone. She got up, caught Oedipus by the collar and dragged him back to the kitchen, shutting the door behind her.

Cayley nibbled on a few lettuce leaves (no dressing) and then proceeded carefully to wipe cream off two strawberries and a slice of mango with her serviette, before eating them very slowly. She left the decadently chewy meringue untouched on her plate, a silent witness to her own self-discipline and Megan's thoughtlessness.

Moira Wright, wearing a flowing dress more suited to a royal wedding than a casual family dinner, alternated between pleading and cajoling Cayley to eat, and bemoaning her husband's absence, breaking stride only to berate Megan's lack of decorating ability.

"This place looks no better than the day you moved in. You've probably still got some unpacked boxes stashed somewhere. And those curtains are dreadful, dear, way too short."

Although Cayley herself was ominously silent on the subject of her new job at the catering company, Moira bragged happily that she'd received glowing reports on her daughter's performance. When Wade, trying to be polite, asked Cayley to tell him more about the new job, Megan kicked him under the table and shook her head meaningfully.

Moira spent much of the evening complaining about her husband, how hard he worked at Mathews, Madonsela and Gaines where he was an audit partner, how he was never home, and how much she missed him. But once Richard Wright arrived, she placed his plate of food down in front of him with an injured air, and then set about studiously ignoring him.

Wade tried valiantly to keep the conversation flowing and made an effort to engage Megan's father in a discussion about the latest revelations of corruption in big audit firms, but Richard Wright was clearly uncomfortable with Wade and said very little beyond praising the Shiraz and downing several glasses of it.

When Megan cleared the plates from the main course to the kitchen, tossing a few scraps to a mournful-looking Oedipus, she checked her phone for messages. There was a missed call from Mike, the first in several days. Perhaps he was really beginning to miss her, to rethink his attitude to the baby. When she listened to the voicemail message, however, Megan knew that she'd been mistaken, perhaps even deluded. True, he did say that he missed her, but he made no mention of the pregnancy. He sounded cheerfully drunk and there were loud voices and music in the background. A woman's voice kept calling, "Come back here, Mikey."

Mikey?

Ignoring the burning behind her eyes, Megan deleted the message with a savage stab at the screen, chucked her phone into the breadbin, and carried the coffee pot into the dining-room. Oedipus trotted hopefully behind her.

Eventually, realising that there would be no contentedly quiet moment in which to tell her news without fuss, Megan tapped a fork against her water glass and announced that she had something important to tell her family.

"You're getting married to Mike!" exclaimed her mother gleefully.

"You're getting married to Mike," said Cayley, without a trace of enthusiasm.

Megan took a deep breath. "No, I'm having a baby."

"So you *will* be getting married!" her mother trilled.

"So you *will* be getting married," her father said flatly. It sounded like an instruction, or perhaps a threat.

Cayley's eyes grew rounder and wider. "You're getting married and you're having a baby?"

"No. I *am* having a baby. I am not getting married. I may not even be staying together with Mike."

"But what about a wedding? What about —" her mother began.

"Now, Megan," her father interrupted, "bringing a child into this world is a serious business. To do it single-handedly is irresponsible. This needs to be thought through properly."

It was like he thought she was nineteen, rather than twenty-nine.

"I have thought it through, Dad. I know I want this baby,

but — even if Mike had asked me, which he hasn't — I'm not going to compound an already difficult situation by marrying when I'm not one hundred per cent sure about it."

"Do you mean to tell me that that fellow hasn't even done the decent thing?" her father said, outraged.

"Can I be your birthing partner? Can I?" Cayley asked, bouncing in her chair with excitement.

"Shut up, Cayley," Moira snapped.

Cayley looked flabbergasted.

"Wade is going to be there with me at the birth," Megan said.

"Don't be ridiculous, Megan, that needs to be the child's father, it needs to be Mike," Moira insisted.

"It needs to be a midwife or a nurse." Richard Wright eyed Wade. "One cannot be too safe."

"What exactly do you mean by that, Mr Wright?" Wade asked, and Megan felt her own hackles rising.

"But *I* want to do it," said Cayley, like a petulant child.

"Want doesn't always get, Cayley. If you haven't already learned that, then now's a good time to do so," Megan said. "I have asked Wade to be my doula."

"Wade is going to be your doo-fucking-la? *Wade*? I'm your sister!"

"And I'm your mother!"

"And who's going to be her husband and the child's father? That's what I'd like to know," Richard demanded.

"Look, if it makes you happier, I'll gladly —" Wade began.

"Shut up!" said Cayley and her father in unison.

"Hey! Don't talk to Wade like that," Megan snapped. "He's my oldest and dearest friend."

"Oh, defend *him,* why don't you. Take his side, hold his hand while you give birth to *my* niece or nephew. I suppose I don't matter at all, I'm not important."

"Cayley, of course you matter," Megan soothed, though her palms itched to slap her sister.

"Pregnant!" Cayley cried.

She stood up, toppling over her chair, and ran to the nearby guest toilet. Soon loud, retching noises carried over to where the rest of them sat silently.

"Hope it wasn't my cooking," Wade said.

24
HIDDEN

Megan settled herself at her desk, pulled her hair back into a ponytail, and opened Dr Arthur Smith's file. She pressed the *play* button on the digital recorder in front of her, fitted the small ear buds into her ears, and adjusted the volume.

"So, how have you been since we last met?" she heard her own voice ask.

"Fine thanks, how are you," came Dr Smith's reply.

"You know, Arthur —"

"Art," he corrected her.

She would have to make a concerted effort to remember to call him that. It didn't come naturally because the name didn't seem to fit him. It was too casual, too American ad-exec for this compulsively neat and tightly-wound man.

"You know, *Art*, this is the one place you don't have to answer 'Fine, thanks,' when asked how you are. Here, with me, you can check inside and then tell me how you really feel."

"I'm fine. I'm just worried."

In her internship, Megan and her fellow interns had joked that FINE was an acronym for "fucking incapable of normal emotions". In that sense, maybe Arthur (Art!) *was* fine, but in the normal sense of the word he'd looked anything but. He seemed thinner and behaved even more agitatedly, shuffling about in his seat, flicking his gaze repeatedly to her cushions, and tapping his hands on the armrests of the chair. He'd arrived precisely on time for their appointment, hardly pausing in reception before hurrying into her office.

Reminded of something, Megan stopped the playback, unplugged herself from the headphones, and went into the front room where Patience was busy with invoices.

"I meant to ask about Arthur Smith. Did you —"

"Art," Patience said. She pronounced it Att, so Megan didn't immediately understand what she was saying.

"What?"

"Art, he likes to be called Art Smith."

"Oh, Arrt," Megan said.

"Yes, Arrrt." Patience elongated the r-sound and muttered under her breath, "*Mlungu.*"

"Whatever. Did you make a copy of Dr Smith's medical aid card when he was here yesterday?"

Patience's face creased into apologetic folds. "I forgot. Sorry for that. He came in so quickly. Then, after, he was hopping and tapping so much I forgot."

"Hopping and tapping? What do you mean?"

"He was hopping from one foot to the other foot all the time he was standing here, and tapping on my basket, now this side, then that side." Patience demonstrated on the sweet basket while frowning at the impudence of the behaviour.

"Did he make another appointment?" Megan was half expecting, given the nature of the session, that he might just have fled.

"*Yebo.*"

"Please make a note to get his card copied next time. And his identity book or driver's licence. I want to check his identity with the medical aid."

"Good idea — that man is strange."

Megan didn't respond to this unscientific diagnosis, but privately she concurred. Arthur Smith's unnerving behaviour not only made her want to confirm his true name and identity, it had also driven her to record his session. She found his near constant fidgeting and fretful mannerisms so distracting that she battled to focus on what he was saying, and had thought a review of his words might prove useful. Also, if she was being honest with herself, the fact that there would be a recording of the session had made her feel somehow safer. If he jumped up and knocked her about with an even number of blows on either side of her head, then at least the police would know who to arrest. Guiltily, she chided herself for being ridiculous.

Her room was already set up for audio recording. She occasionally recorded sessions when doing hypnosis with a client where childhood sexual abuse was suspected — she had no desire to be accused by some "false memory" apologist of implanting memories with leading questions or suggestions.

Wade, who was a fair handyman, had fashioned a metal bracket large enough to house the small digital recording device she'd purchased, and screwed this under one of the side tables in the office. The small, super-sensitive, wireless microphone nestled in an arrangement of dried flowers which sat on top of the table.

It wasn't that she tried to hide the recording device from her clients — indeed, they always signed permission forms before she ever recorded them — but experience had taught her that when clients could *see* the device, they became all too aware that they were being recorded. They wound up focused on the recorder, started speaking self-consciously, and censored their stories. It was easier just to have the whole setup out of sight and out of mind — that way they spoke much more freely.

Yesterday, though, she'd been grateful that the equipment was set up and hidden. For her session with Arthur Smith, she'd checked that the recorder was fully charged and had lots of room on the memory chip, before slotting it into the bracket under the table. Two minutes before the session was due to begin, she switched on and hit the record button.

It might be considered unethical to record a patient without his knowledge and explicit consent, but she'd decided to go ahead and do it anyway. She'd been sure that Arthur Smith would react adversely — have what Cayley would call "a major freak-out" — if she'd suggested the idea of recording him. She consoled her conscience with the thought that he'd signed the intake form which granted her permission to use "any necessary techniques".

Now, back at her desk a day after the session, she resumed listening to the recording.

"What are you worried about?" she heard herself ask.

"I'm worried about seeing you, almost bumping into you,

in the labour ward." He sounded nervous, even scared.

"Yes, I was surprised to see you there, too, Art. Are you a gynaecologist?"

"Why are you so concerned about my speciality?"

"Why are you so concerned about my finding out about it?"

As she listened to the recording, Megan stared at a miniature Zen garden on her desk — a gift from Mike at a time when, presumably, he'd still cared about whether she was stressed or calm. It was a square, black-lacquered, shallow tray filled with fine white sand and three miniature "rocks". She picked up the tiny rake and began dragging it lightly through the sand, leaving curved parallel lines in its wake. The activity and the creation of balanced natural perfection was meant to be soothing, and she could use all the soothing she could get while listening to Arthur Smith's increasing agitation.

"I work here, at Acacia," his voice said. "People know me. And I don't want anyone to find out I'm seeing you. That's why I wanted to come at the end of the day, when there are fewer people about. Now your receptionist tells me there are only mid-morning slots available. When I saw you in that ward, I thought you might say something, that others might find out that I'm your patient."

"Art, I'm ethically bound to keep all aspects of your treatment confidential, even the fact that you're seeing me at all. But what would be so dreadful about others knowing? What's your fear?"

"They'll find out that I'm …"

"That you're …?"

"Nuts!" he almost shouted the word. "Mad! I'm going off

my rocker and it's getting worse. I can't do anything without … It's beginning to affect my work, and I can't stand it anymore."

Megan set down the rake and shoved the inane Zen garden aside; it wasn't helping. She rewound and listened to his outburst one more time, to be sure. She felt again what she'd felt in the session — a strong sense that Arthur Smith was a man balanced precariously on a knife-edge, one small push away from falling into uncontained panic.

She heard her own voice respond with calm, slow, comforting words, using empathic responses to contain Art's emotions. With another client, she might have amplified the feelings, encouraged the release and the relief of catharsis, but not with him.

"You're afraid of what you're thinking. You're feeling out of control and you're worried about what's happening to you."

"Yes, I am. Very worried."

She could hear the slight relief in his voice, the rising panic temporarily checked by the unusual validation of feeling understood.

"Will you keep it confidential — that I'm your client? You won't tell anyone what I tell you, or greet me in public?"

As she listened to this section of the recording, where she'd tried to set Art's mind at rest about confidentiality, Megan's eye was caught by the potted cyclamen on her desk. Its deep red flowers looked healthy enough, but the plant had several brown and desiccated leaves. Had she watered it too much, or not enough? Unsure as to whether it was diseased or perfectly healthy, she extracted a pair of scissors from her desk drawer and began snipping off the dead leaves. They crumbled into dust in her hands. From there, she wandered about her office, the recorder tucked under one arm and headphones in her ears, pruning and clipping all her neglected office plants. They were in a pitiful state. She could only hope that she had greener thumbs with her clients than with her plants.

When the recording arrived at the place she especially wanted to listen to, she went back to her seat at the desk and picked up a pen. She stared at the last notation she'd made in the session notes.

Anxiety (Obsessive-Compulsive Disorder)? Or Personality Disorder?

Sitting still, she focused intently on the audio playback, trying to assess whether she was listening to anxious obsessional fantasising, or real and destructive intent.

"Art, what are you worried will happen? Are you scared something will happen *to* you, or is it that you're worried you'll *do* something?"

"How did you know that?"

"I'm a therapist, it's my business to know this stuff. What are you worried you might do?"

His answer came in a gabbled rush. "I'm scared I'll do something bad — threaten someone, or ride them over, or hurt them. I have access to drugs, you know, some of them can be toxic. Maybe I'll do something very bad. The thought keeps coming into my head that I'll hurt someone. What if I can't control it? The thoughts I have, the things I imagine doing — they're really bad. And are they just thoughts, or are they really memories? What if I've already done something bad? Have I done anything to you?"

"No, Art, you haven't harmed me."

"But what if I have? It's like a voice whispering inside my head. My throat gets tight so I can't swallow, and it feels like there's a vice around my chest. Every day it gets tighter. I can't breathe. And I know that something bad is going to happen to me, or to my family. Or I'll do something, something terrible, unless … unless I …"

"Unless you what?"

"Unless I make things right. Even. Balanced. And unless I check that I haven't hurt anyone. Have I hurt you? Oh, there I go again!" His voice was rough with self-disgust. "I know I've asked you that already, and I know I haven't hurt you. You just told me that yourself. I know it's insane to think this way, but I still worry."

He groaned and there was the sound of several blows. That was when he'd slapped the side of his head.

"Don't do that, Art. You definitely have not hurt me. But I need to know … in your checking, have you discovered that you've hurt anyone else?"

"No, of course not. But then again, what if I didn't really check — what if I only thought I did? Or what if I didn't check properly and I need to do it again? And again. And again. Over and over and over!"

Megan could hear, even on the recording, that his agitation was rising.

"Arthur, Art! Focus on me, now, Art. What did you mean about needing to make things even?"

"Huh? Oh. They must be even, the same on the left and the right. And even numbers."

185

"What must?"

She heard the long silence on the tape, remembered how he'd tapped on the arms of the chair with his hands and looked at her, as if evaluating whether he could trust her with his truths. Eventually he replied — speaking softly, sounding embarrassed.

"Shoelaces, toothbrush strokes, steps ... lift buttons." He'd smiled bleakly at her when he said the last words. "I'll do something bad unless I go back and check, unless I go back and do it right. Evenly. Twice."

Megan clicked the stop button and let out a slow breath. Listening to the recording of the session had confirmed what she'd thought at the time. On the bottom of the session notes she wrote:

Diagnosis: Obsessive Compulsive Anxiety Disorder

(obsessions: symmetry, order, harming others; compulsions: checking; symmetrical behaviours, e.g. tapping & counting)

Next session: education on disorder, discuss meds, set treatment plan.

She underlined her diagnosis. Arthur Smith was harmless. He caused pain only to himself and posed no real threat to others. She wasn't wrong — she was sure of it.

A knock at the door made her jump.

Patience came in. "I'm going now. Are you still working?"

"Just reviewing some cases before I knock off," said Megan, kneading a knot in the back of her neck. "Cheers, Patience, have a good evening."

Patience rolled her eyes. "Thulani's mother and sister are

coming up from Newcastle to visit. I don't need a *sangoma* to throw the bones to know it's not going to be a good evening. Better thing *you* have a good evening. Women in your condition need lots of rest."

"What do you mean — women in my condition?" Megan blustered.

She hadn't yet told Patience about the pregnancy. But her receptionist just smiled knowingly and went off with a little wave of her fingers.

25
NAUGHTY

The following day started with Lindi Nyoka's final session. She'd recovered well from her trauma and promised to call Megan if she felt she wasn't coping. Next up was Tony Thomas. Megan realised she was looking forward to seeing him again, but only — she told herself sternly — because he was an intelligent and interesting client.

Once again, he arrived five minutes late for his appointment. She wondered if he was generally careless with time or if he deliberately came late to avoid bumping into the previous client.

"Sorry I'm late. I was mucking about with images of the Mona Lisa in my studio, and I lost track of the time."

Megan had intended to start the session with a thorough history-taking, beginning with his family as it had existed before he was even born, but somehow she and Tony wound up talking about whether parents should or shouldn't be unconditionally accepting towards their children. Once more, he surprised her with his unorthodox views.

"Do you really think, Megan, that conditional acceptance is a bad thing?" he asked.

"Don't you?"

"No."

"Are we talking about the same thing?" Megan said. "I'm referring to the type of relationship between a parent and a child where the parent sets conditions — standards of achievement, behaviour or appearance — that must be met by the child if it is to receive love, acceptance and approval. A relationship where the parent directly or indirectly communicates that they love the child so long as he gets straight A's, or is obedient, but not when he fails, or is unpopular or fat, for example. Is that what you understand by the concept, Tony?"

"Pretty much," he said, nodding.

"And you don't think that it's dysfunctional or unhealthy to set conditions like that for a child?"

"I think it's impossible not to."

"Tell me more about that."

"Unconditional acceptance — that's the dream you psychologists pedal, isn't it? But we're kidding ourselves if we think we can accept another person on the planet, let alone annoying little nippers, without wanting to change them in some way so that it's easier and more comfortable for ourselves. Why should we accept or love someone who messes our house, steals from us, wets the bed, or embarrasses us in public? How *can* we approve of that? It's the same for you, really."

"For me?" Megan said, surprised.

"Yes. How can you unconditionally accept a patient whose

attitudes or behaviour disgusts you?"

"Don't you think it's possible to disapprove of the *behaviour*, while still loving and accepting the *person*?" she countered, trying to keep the discussion off herself.

"I think that's specious nonsense, idealistic psychobabble claptrap!" He reached out a long arm and brushed at the air, as though sweeping away cobwebs, but his smile took the sting out of the words.

"Really?" Megan was taken aback by the vehemence of his argument and wondered if he really believed what he was saying, or if he was merely playing devil's advocate again.

"How is it possible to separate the person from his actions? Wasn't it you who was telling me just the other day that we are what we do?"

He'd got her there, she thought, backed her nicely into a tight philosophical corner of her own making. It was high time she got the discussion off generalities of abstract theory and delved instead into the real world of lived, personal experience. *His* world of experience.

"You have no children," she said.

"No," he said, looking surprised at the turn in the conversation.

"Then you must be talking from the experience of having *been* a child."

"Must everything stem from one's childhood?"

This time, Megan merely smiled at the attempt to deflect her back into a debate on psychological theory. "Did your parents accept and love you unconditionally?

"Hardly," he snorted. "But who could blame them? I was a

naughty kid — I probably deserved most of what they sent my way."

This was interesting. Perhaps they'd uncover some important contributors to his anger in the session after all.

He was blaming himself, of course, as children often did. The adults in their lives usually told their kids that their problems were their own fault and, too young to know better, the kids usually believed it. Paradoxically, blaming themselves also gave victims some sense of control in a situation in which they were largely powerless. If you behaved badly, you could tell yourself that your mother or father rejected you for what you'd done, rather than for who you suspected you were at your core — unworthy, unlovable, contemptible.

Choosing her words carefully, Megan said, "It sounds like your parents labelled you a naughty boy, and told you that you deserved what you got. Does the adult you still think that? That the things you did were unacceptable?"

"Oh, yes," he said in an offhand tone.

"What did you do?"

His face grew serious. "What do you mean?"

"What did you do that was so bad, that was unacceptable?"

"Stuff. Naughty things. Well" — he laughed uncomfortably — "don't all kids get up to mischief?"

"We're not talking about everyone, Tony. We're talking about you. What did *you* do?"

He blew out an irritated sigh. "I'd make a mess in my room, or the bathroom. Or I'd tease the cat. Once I started a fire behind the garden shed."

Megan nodded, held the silence.

"I stole from my mother's purse."

"That's significant. Stealing from a parent is often the child's attempt to even the score when he feels short-changed on the parent's love, time or attention. He steals from her because he wants something more from her, but doesn't know exactly what it is, or how to get it."

His expression, as he listened, was sober, thoughtful. Perhaps she'd touched a nerve.

"How did your parents respond when you did those things?" she asked.

"The usual way. Yelling and shouting. 'We brought you into this world and we can take you out again!' That kind of thing. And hidings, or leaving me in a cold bath when I messed the bathroom. Once, my father banged my arm in the car door."

"On purpose?" Megan asked, inwardly flinching in horror. Outwardly she maintained her neutral game-face, determined not to shut down his confidences by displaying shock or judgement.

"He slammed the door on it three times. Bang-bang-bang" — Tony mimed the action — "so I hardly think it was accidental. I remember him. I must have been about nine years old."

"Tony, it sounds like abuse." She spoke gently, but it needed to be said.

"Does it? Hmmm. It wasn't always the physical stuff I found hardest. My parents when I was —" He cut himself off. Perhaps it was getting difficult for him to continue. He was dry-eyed, and speaking in a completely calm voice, but those emotions had to be building up inside him.

"When I was twelve, my parents drove me to a rubbish dump on the other side of town. I can still see it in my mind's eye, still smell it. It's the kind of smell that sticks on you, you know? It gets into your hair and your clothes. Anyway, they said I was rubbish, so I belonged on the rubbish dump. They dragged me out of the car — I was screaming, hanging onto the seat belts, the door handle — and put me inside a skip. Then they drove off. Left me there. All I could think was … what if they never came back?" His eyes were out of focus now, staring off into the distant but still vivid memory. One of his hands rubbed along his thigh.

"I guess they probably just drove around the block, but it felt like I was in there forever, among the bags of stinking rot." He shuddered. "One of the workers at the dump peered over the top of the skip and laughed at me. Cackled. He had only two teeth left in his head, both of them here." He tapped one side of his face. "I was so scared, I almost wet my pants, but I was too scared to make more of a mess because what if they did come back? And good thing I didn't, because they did return. Asked me if I'd learned my lesson, if I'd be a good, neat, clean boy from then on."

"Tony, you're describing all kinds of abuse," Megan said. "That pain, the rejection and abandonment, the message that unless you were perfect, you were worthless — that would definitely have left you with feelings of deep fear and rage. And you wouldn't have been able to express your anger for fear of provoking more abuse. The damage would just have lain there, banked in your subconscious, collecting interest."

"Ah, look, they weren't all bad. I don't want to give you the wrong impression. There were good times, too, laughs and fun. It got easier as I got older, and learned how the world worked. My parents — when I was older — we got on better. They left me to my own devices a lot of the time."

"Was that because you were different, because you'd learned how to act good? Or do you think it was because they found it easier to cope with an older child?"

"Maybe a bit of both."

"It's quite a turnaround, though, going from beating you and abandoning you at rubbish dumps, to letting you get on with your own thing," she commented.

"It's like they were a completely different set of parents," he said, with a weak attempt at a smile. "And here I am, sitting before you today. I survived." He clasped his hands in the air in mock celebration of the grand feat.

"*Surviving* shouldn't be the best we can say of our childhoods, Tony. We should be raised in conditions in which we can thrive."

"Could've, would've, should've," he said dismissively. "When it comes down to it, are any of us really raised in a perfect environment?"

Megan saw the question for what it was — an attempt to back off the personal and retreat to the impersonal safety of theoretical debate. Reasoning that he'd probably had enough deep-work for one day, she allowed him to draw her back into an emotionless discussion of healthy ways to raise a child. It was best practice, anyway, to ensure that clients were anchored in the cognitive domain, and had their protective defences back in place before returning them to the world.

Although the session had been emotionally demanding as well as thought-provoking, Megan felt they'd made real progress. Next time they'd explore the long-term impact of his childhood experiences, and discuss using trauma techniques or hypnosis to help him heal the old wounds and build a better self-concept than the one he'd presumably been left with.

A gap between his intense session and the next client gave Megan a chance to catch her breath, have a cup of raspberry tea (good for strengthening uterine muscles, according to the pregnancy books), and to return some calls. One of these was to Mike. He sounded so sweet, and asked so tenderly how she was doing (as close as he had yet come to asking her how the pregnancy was going), that a sharp pang of longing pulsed through her, misting her eyes and causing her throat to ache.

The last session of the day was with Alta Cronjé. It was heartening to see how much better she was doing — her relationship with Johan had improved, sex was mostly back on track, she was full of plans for the future, and she was more determined than ever to press ahead with charges against Dr Trotteur. Megan related a summarised account of her visits to Stacey Cole and the Reddys. Alta was saddened for the women and their families, but also understandably disappointed because of the implications for the case against Trotteur.

"One dead and one who can't testify — that's not much help to us. It's still just my word against his. We've got no proof, no witnesses."

"I know," Megan conceded, "but I'm making a plan to get more information."

"What plan?" Alta asked, her eyes gleaming in anticipation.

"Ask me no questions and I'll tell you no lies," Megan said. She was only half kidding.

26
LOCKED OUT

Two things were clear to Megan: one, she needed more information and two, she wasn't going to get it by politely asking Trotteur to hand it over.

Surely, in amongst all his cases, there were other patients who had been badly treated? If she could just lay her hands on his records and contact his patients, then she'd be able to amass more evidence, enough to sway a jury of his peers at the medical board.

She knew *what* she wanted. The *how* of going about getting it was the tricky part. She looked down at the spidery mind-map of ideas on the paper in front of her and experienced a moment of surreal disbelief. A brainstorm of ideas for stealing confidential information — that was what it amounted to. It hardly seemed possible that she was contemplating it. She, who never so much as parked in a handicapped bay or cheated on her tax return, was now spending her Friday night in her office, considering various ways of breaking into and entering a medical colleague's consulting rooms.

Tapping her front teeth with the end of a pencil, she evaluated each of the options she'd mapped out in turn.

Steal keys from Trotteur's receptionist/nurse.

She discarded this idea almost immediately. It just wasn't practical. Trotteur no doubt had a receptionist, but Megan had no idea who the woman was, where she kept the office keys, or even if she had a set at all — Trotteur might well do his own opening and closing.

Bamboozle a night cleaner.

Tempting. This seemed like a workable option at first consideration. On the odd occasion when she'd worked very late, Megan had seen the army of navy-clad cleaners sweep through the clinic's office suites, emptying bins, dusting, polishing and vacuuming.

How hard could it be to slip on a white coat, clip on her clinic ID, and walk confidently into Trotteur's office as if it was her own while the cleaner was busy there? But the more carefully she thought about it, the more potential problems she could envision with this plan. What if the cleaner checked her ID, compared it to the name on the door and rumbled her that way? Or there might be a policy that cleaners were not to admit anyone into the offices without a security officer being present. Where had this idea sprung from — had she read it in some internal memo? Also, there was the chance that she might get the poor cleaner into trouble. She scratched a line through the idea.

Force door open with crowbar.

The simplicity of this plan appealed immediately. It could be done easily and quickly, and no one else needed to be involved. At least, she *thought* she would be able to do it herself. The main problem was that breaking the door open would tip Trotteur off that the office had been entered. There was nothing of great value to steal in the suites — the reason why the sum total of each office's security amounted to a single lock on the sliding door — so burglary would seem an unlikely motive for the break-in, especially when nothing was taken. Trotteur would surely begin to wonder why his was the only office broken into and what the real reason might have been. She had no wish to put him on his guard, but how to get into his office in a way that left no traces?

She sighed and pushed back from the desk. Breaking into places always looked so easy in the movies — a simple matter of sliding a credit card between door and frame, or picking the lock with a hairpin. She doubted it would be so simple in real life.

But why not try?

On a sudden impulse, she extracted her credit card from her wallet and rooted about in her desk drawer for a hairpin. Armed with these felonious tools, she went into the empty corridor outside her rooms and slid the glass door closed. If she could open her own door without a key, she would be able to open Trotteur's, because all the offices had the same metal-framed sliding glass doors with similar locks.

It took mere seconds to discover that there was no way a credit card would work — the door slid at least a centimetre into the frame when it closed, leaving no room for a card to slide between lock and frame.

Glancing left and right to check that she was still alone, she stuck the hairpin into the keyhole. Now what? Wiggling it about hopefully in a random way, she realised that she had no clue as to the inner structure or workings of locks. Just as she was about to give up on the whole absurd process — she was a shrink for crying out loud, not a cat burglar — the pin hooked into the lock. She pressed her ear against the door as she'd seen countless criminals do on TV, even though she had a vague idea that listening for the tumble of locks was something you did when cracking safes, not picking locks. Carefully, she turned the hairpin, straining her ears to hear some click which might signal success.

She heard and felt nothing. She turned the hairpin still further, and then saw that she'd merely been twisting the thin metal over itself, so that the protruding part resembled a corkscrew.

"I give up," she muttered to herself in irritation.

She yanked the twisted hairpin out of the lock at the same moment as she realised that the door was locked and her keys were in her handbag on the desk inside her office.

"Dammit."

She kicked the obstinate door and cursed again before setting off in the direction of the clinic's main security office. Half an hour later, she was back at her desk crossing out the crowbar and lock-picking options and noting, for the record, that there would also be no way to beg, borrow or steal a set of keys from the guards in the security office. They'd seemed polite and patient but, sadly, not stupid — verifying her identity carefully before escorting her back to her rooms and opening the door with a key extracted from a safe in their own office.

Bribe the building manager.

She rejected this idea immediately. There was no way it was likely to work. The manager would be more likely to report her to the clinic's authorities than to aid and abet her efforts.

Which left only one more idea on the list.

27
AFTER HOURS

The white-coated figure waited outside the main entrance to the Acacia Clinic, eyes scanning the parking lot and coming to settle on a tall man who stood, cradling his bleeding arm, outside the adjacent Emergency unit. He wore an orange tank top over black jeans and, at first glance, it seemed that the spray of dark red spots might be a pattern on the stretched fabric. He was enormous, his head too small for the thick neck which triangled down to the steroid-pumped muscles bulging in his arms and shoulders.

A woman, eyes wild and lipstick smeared, limped out of the unit on towering heels. She walked up to the man, slapped what she could reach of his face and screeched, "I'll kill you, Benny, you bastard! If he dies, I'll kill you!"

She beat her small fists against his chest. The man bowed his head, held his injured arm out to the side away from the woman. A steady tick of blood dripped down to form a small puddle beside his booted feet.

"I'll kill you, Benny, I swear I'll kill you," she sobbed, her arms flailing uselessly against the wall of his chest.

He pulled her closer with his massive arm, held her tight against him, and brushed his lips with infinite gentleness against the top of her head.

"Are you the doctor?" a nearby voice said.

A man, short, dishevelled-looking and carrying a battered tan briefcase, stood at the clinic's entrance.

"That's me. Are you Joe?"

"Uh-huh. So, which way?"

"Follow me."

They moved through the silently sliding automatic doors.

"Thanks for coming out so late at night."

"No problems. Part of the job, hey," said Joe, looking around and giving the plush and gleaming interior of the clinic an appreciative whistle.

The foyer was quiet this late, stripped of the hubbub of the daily hustle. A single intake clerk dozed at admissions, his head resting on the back of the chair, his arms folded across his chest. A cleaner's head bounced rhythmically as he buffed the floor with a rotary floor-polisher, the headphones plugged into his ears leading a red vein to some device deep in his pocket. The coffee shop was closed. A few desperate souls, their faces tight with worry and pale with exhaustion, clung to plastic cups of coffee from the vending machine. An orderly pushed a wheelchair across the foyer to park it alongside the row which already waited, empty and expectant, for the next day's burdens.

They took the stairs, Joe Cohen explaining he never rode in lifts if he could avoid it.

"Only last year I was stuck in one for three hours. Three hours between floors there in the Carlton Centre in the middle of town. Funny, hey — me stuck and not able to get out?"

The corridor was dimly lit after the fluorescent brightness of the stairwell. They walked past the darkened rooms on either side until they stood outside the right office.

"This is it."

Joe looked at the door, cocking his head like a parrot eyeing a treat. He set his briefcase on the tiles, crouched down on his haunches and peered at the lock.

"So, can you do it?"

"This? No problems." His voice sounded scornful. "Piece of cake."

Joe opened his briefcase, revealing a shamble of tools, keys, a small drill and a few screwdrivers. His hand hovered, then selected two instruments. One was a thin metal implement, shorter than a pen, with a bent, pointed hook, and the other had an end which had been beaten flat then bent into a curved wiggle.

With small, delicate fingers, he inserted first one pick and then the other into the lock. He manoeuvred for mere seconds before announcing, "There's it."

He extracted the picks and pushed the door open along its tracks.

"That was quick." It had taken mere seconds.

"*Ja*, these locks are a joke, man. You pay me for my travel time more than my work time. And speaking of ..." He looked up expectantly, tossing the tools back into the case and closing it with a twist of wire.

"Sure. Here you go."

Joe took the cash, stashed it in a pocket of his jeans and said, "Don't lock yourself out of your office again, doc," then strolled off to the stairs at the end of the corridor.

"Don't worry," she said. "I won't."

28
Taken in

Megan waited until the stairwell door swung shut behind Joe before she slipped into Dr Trotteur's rooms. It had been much easier than expected. She'd simply called an all-hours locksmith, told him she was a doctor who'd locked herself out of her office and that she urgently needed to get in. She'd concocted a cock-and-bull story about the security office being closed until Monday, unless she wanted to call out the manager on his weekend off, but the locksmith had asked nothing more than the address and where to meet her, warned her of nothing more than his extortionate call-out fee.

She slid the door to Trotteur's rooms closed behind her, activated the flashlight on her cell phone, and swept the beam briefly around the office to get a general idea of the layout.

The door to the doctor's office plus a high-ledged reception counter backed by filing cabinets lay to her left, and the waiting room — its walls hung with certificates, framed black and white pictures, and a portrait at the rear — was on her right.

Aiming the light towards the floor, she stepped around to the back of the reception counter.

A typist's chair faced the computer monitor which sat, with mouse and keyboard, on the desk. Rows of lever-arch files, index books and an internal phone directory were stacked neatly on the desk. A small wooden frame held a snapshot of a grey-haired woman with a baby and a toddler perched on her lap.

Megan sat in the chair, and nudged the mouse on the off-chance that the PC was merely in standby mode, but the screen remained dead. She shone her light under the desk to find the computer's main box and pressed the power button. In less than a minute, it had booted up. On the screen was the familiar Microsoft sign-in box. A name was already set as default in the user name field: Beth Finch.

"Hello, Beth," Megan murmured to the woman in the photograph. "Now what would your password be?" Maybe she would get lucky. Perhaps Beth, like many older folk, would be unenthusiastic about technology, unsophisticated about security.

Megan tried the system default *1 2 3 4,* then *1 2 3 4 5, password* and *qwerty* without any luck. She thought about the woman's name for a moment, and tried *Elizabeth, Elizabeth Finch, Beth, Beth Finch,* then tried again, with and without spaces, with and without capital letters — all without success.

She drummed her fingers impatiently on the desk, running through various possibilities. Then she grabbed the small photo frame and flipped it over, bending back the tiny metal catches to release the backing and extract the photograph.

Yes! On the back of the photograph was written: "Rachel and Jared, Dec 2012".

Deleting her last try in the password field, Megan entered every permutation and combination of the names she could think of. But every time, the machine obstinately beeped its refusal and displayed the error message.

She checked her watch. She'd been in the office for almost fifteen minutes and was no closer to accessing the records she'd come for; perhaps a more low-tech approach was called for. Shining the light on the two filing cabinets behind her, she tugged at the drawers. Locked. A rummage through Beth Finch's desk drawers turned up pens, paper clips, a banana, a tube of hand cream and some headache tablets, but no keys to the cabinets and no handy aide-mémoire of passwords. She searched in and under the pen holder, behind the files, felt under the counter. Nothing. Damn.

A new idea raised its head above her racing thoughts. Back at the computer, she cleared both sign-on fields, and into the username field, she typed an *A*. Nothing. She deleted it and typed a *B*, then repeated the process with *C*. She'd go through the whole alphabet if necessary, in the hopes of cueing an automatic completion of the username. But as soon as she typed *D*, the field auto-filled with *DR TROTTEUR*. So he was a user on this PC, too. The password field remained empty. Once again, Megan went through the process of trying different possibilities, and again she struck out.

It occurred to her that there might be some clue in his office — on his desk or shelves. Perhaps she'd find the filing cabinet keys in one of his drawers or, if Beth was as efficient as Patience, there might be a stack of patient files waiting on his desk. Getting to check a few records would be better than nothing.

The door to Trotteur's office was ajar, beckoning her into the dark room beyond. Her hand reached automatically for the light switch beside the door, then hesitated. Although the lights to this inner office might not be visible from the corridor, they *would* be visible to anyone — a patrolling security guard perhaps — in the parking lot. Unlikely as it was that anyone would be staring up at this office at this late hour, it was wiser not to take the chance.

The sweep of the phone's light revealed an office far more luxurious than her own. A thick Persian carpet covered most of the floor, two comfortable armchairs faced an enormous dark wood desk behind which was a tall-backed, black leather chair as big as a throne. Windows ran the length of one wall, low bookshelves the other. On the wall above these, box frames displayed a collection of what looked like antique medical instruments.

She swung the beam back to the desk. The light flashed and reflected off an object resting on top of some papers in the centre of the desk. It was a perfect half-globe of what looked like glass, about the size of a tennis ball. She stepped closer, reached out a hand, picked up the glittering object and shone the light onto it.

With an involuntary shudder and a cry of revulsion, she dropped it at once. It landed on the desk with a soft thunk. Her heart kicked deep inside her chest, her stomach heaved, her mind refused to believe what her eyes had registered. Preserved for eternity inside the dense glass was a small ovoid organ, cream-coloured with tiny red veins marbling its slightly lumpy surface. Attached to it, running over one side of its surface was a slender fleshy-pink curve of some kind of tube or ligament.

Ovary, fallopian tube — a rational corner of her brain supplied the labels. The rest of her mind was spinning. A shiver rippled over her scalp. Her head turned, pulling her eyes away from the macabre thing on the desk to stare back over her shoulder at what she'd seen, but not fully taken in when she'd first entered Trotteur's rooms. Dazed, she walked back to the reception room, raised the phone, which now felt heavy in her hand, and shone the light on the walls.

Black and white pictures — photographic prints — of people-less landscapes were arranged, perfectly straight and at absolutely even intervals along one wall. The bottom-right corner of each print was dated and signed with the initials *ATT*.

"Photography … I do mostly landscapes …"

Her feet walked her to the back of the room where a coloured print of a portrait hung on the wall, the gestalt of it instantly recognisable by the low, wide neckline, the folded hands, the long dark hair. But the muted greens and browns of the background were now the backdrop to a face strangely unfamiliar, perfectly symmetrical — the features of one side duplicated and flipped over to make the other. The smile was uniform, lacking even a semblance of mystery, and the hands seemed oddly placed.

"I was mucking about with images of the Mona Lisa …"

Blood pounded in Megan's ears. Her breaths were shallow. She swung the beam to the wall with the framed certificates, knowing what she would see. The degrees were conferred on the inductee Anthony Thomas Trotteur. *Anthony Thomas* Trotteur.

"Please, call me Tony …"

She switched off the light.

29
RATTLED

For a full minute, Megan stood still, trying to slow her rapid breathing, struggling to absorb the blow that had set her reeling. This butcher who had hacked into and out of woman after woman and called it *improvement*, this misogynistic monster who'd tortured vulnerable women's minds with his whispers, who'd maimed their bodies and devastated their futures, this man was *her client* — charming, urbane, intelligent, *attractive* Tony Thomas.

She felt sickened, and livid with herself. Just what kind of a psychologist was she not to have suspected anything? She was supposed to be an expert but he'd so easily fooled her with his façade of normality. My God, he'd sat in her room debating free will and determinism, told her jokes and heart-wrenching stories of his parents. Was any of it true?

Anger vied with shock. And won. She would get what she'd come for, and make sure he got what he deserved. She headed back to the receptionist's computer and held her trembling hands poised over the keyboard.

Think! She knew things about this man, she reminded herself, things he'd told her and things she'd learned from others. She tried another succession of words as potential passwords: *perfect, cut, extra, just right,* even — in desperation — *Ihatewomen* and *I hate women.* Each tap of the enter key was answered by the beep of the error message.

She tried to recall what he'd told his patients — Alta, Stacey and Nirvana — the women he "improved". A thrill of premonition tingled through her. Carefully she typed: *Drknowsbest.* It didn't work, but perhaps abbreviations were not impeccable enough for Anthony I'll-make-you-perfect Trotteur. Holding her breath, she typed *Doctorknowsbest* and hit enter.

Got you, you bastard! The log on screen vanished and the main screen materialised before her eyes. The creepily symmetrical Mona Lisa was its wallpaper.

Working quickly, she examined the icons on the desktop, and accessed MS Word. Scanning the document directory and opening some likely-looking files, she found some letters, a few reports, but nothing that looked like it would be helpful, until she opened a document named *clientrecords_master.doc.* Bingo.

It was a list of clients, together with their contact details (telephonic, postal and email) and the date of last visit. Checking the file properties, she saw that it had last been updated two days previously. She retrieved a memory stick from her bag, inserted it into the flash drive and copied the file, then exited the program and opened the MedBillings application. It was the same software that she, along with most of the practitioners in the clinic, used.

It would take a while and a whack of memory to copy all the patient statements across. She needed to extract the records of those patients who'd had surgery performed on them by Trotteur. It was possible in the program, she knew, to sort the records according to their ICD-10's — the diagnostic and treatment codes which had to appear on every patient statement. She herself ran extracts on her own records based on psychological diagnoses from time to time. Off the top of her head, she could have quoted the codes for major depression, adjustment disorder, victim of crime, stressful life events and a dozen other conditions, but she had no idea what the codes were for gynaecology and obstetrics.

She scanned the desk again. Surely the efficient Ms Finch ... There! In the dull glow of the screen, Megan could see a plastic sleeve stuck on the inside of the counter. Inside was a list of codes and their explanation — these must be the ICD-10's most commonly used in the practice which Beth Finch had typed up for easy reference.

Megan checked the list and then ran a sort on the records using the codes for gynaecological procedures: cryosurgery; pelvic laparoscopy; cervical and uterine biopsies; endometrial ablation; tubal ligations; vulvectomy and vulval excisions. She chucked in anything that ended in –ectomy, on the basis that it was probably the removal of something in the way a hysterectomy was the removal of the uterus. She copied the records to the memory stick, then repeated the sort, extract and copy process using the codes for obstetric procedures: delivery, caesarean section, episiotomy, dilation and curettage.

She was just about to eject the memory stick when she heard

voices from the corridor outside. Cursing, she fumbled for the monitor's power switch, killed the screen's glow, and ducked behind the counter. If it was the cleaners, though, she was about to be discovered anyway. The door rattled. A bright beam of light flashed through the office then disappeared. Cautiously, she peered around the side of the counter, just in time to see a security guard walking past, already shining his flashlight into the next office along the corridor.

Megan sagged with relief against the counter. It was obviously just a routine security patrol — something else she hadn't factored into her plans for this night-time reconnaissance mission. It was time to get out of here. At any minute, the cleaners might well appear. She removed the memory stick, powered the computer down, pushed the chair back under the desk and made sure everything looked just as it had before she'd arrived.

Back in Trotteur's office, a quick check showed her that only the vile paperweight was out of place. Every part of her being was repelled by the idea of touching it again, but she forced herself to pick it up and place it back in the exact centre of the pile of papers on the desk. As she did so, the letterhead of the top paper caught her eye.

It was a letter — of commendation and thanks, no less — from the Chief Superintendent of Johannesburg Central Hospital. He wanted to express his sincere gratitude and appreciation to Dr Trotteur for volunteering his services at the Obstetrics and Gynaecology Unit. It was the civic-minded generosity of private practitioners such as the esteemed Dr Trotteur that helped cash-strapped government facilities supplement their limited resources to the greater benefit of the community at large, he enthused.

Acid rose in Megan's throat at the irony, at the vast gap between the polished, benevolent face Trotteur presented to the public — the same face he'd presented to her — and the unspeakable malevolence of what he was no doubt doing to the never-ending stream of vulnerable patients at the government hospital.

He had to be stopped.

30
Trapped

"*oxie?* Is that even a word?" Megan asked, staring
sceptically at the Scrabble board which lay on
the carpet between them.

"I'm wounded," Wade said. "Of course it's a word — I
found it in WhackyWords.com."

"The most reliable of sources."

"It means verve or vigour, or pep. As in, 'It seems to me,
Megan, that you have recently lost much of your moxie'."

"Yeah, well …"

"And that's a triple letter on the X and a double word score,
so that makes it forty-eight for me." Wade wrote the score on
the pad of paper beside the board before glancing at her in
concern. "How's it going, friend? Spill the beans."

Megan sipped at her cup of raspberry tea, picked out five
tiles from her rack of letters and, using the E of *moxie*, arranged
the word *absent*. It seemed appropriate.

"Did you want the spilled beans on the AWOL boyfriend,
the unplanned pregnancy, the situation at work, or the

dysfunctional family?" she asked.

Wade snorted. "That *was* some dinner party."

"If I tell you that's been the highlight of my last month, would that give you a clue as to why my moxie's been minimised? No, Oedipus!" Megan pushed the dog away from the plate of shortbread towards which he'd been inching stealthily.

"That bad?" Wade snapped a finger of shortbread in two, popped one half into his mouth and tossed the other to Oedipus, who snatched it from the air and swallowed it in a single gulp.

"You shouldn't do that. He's fat enough as it is."

"Meh," Wade said, gently blowing crumbs off the board and arranging pale tiles to form the word *romance*. "Fifteen for me — not my best." Tapping a finger on the word, he gave her a significant look and asked, "So, how *is* it going?"

"Let's just say that if I had the letters, I'd make *moribund*. If you allowed slang, I could make *crap*. But since you're a purist, I'll have to make do with *bad*."

"Six points. Impressive."

It's more than I've been scoring with Mike," Megan said, tallying the scores and noting with disgust that Wade was already ninety-seven points ahead.

"He's still in Cape Town?"

"Yep. It's as far away as he can get from the baby without setting sail for Antarctica."

"Weak," Wade said.

"It is, isn't it? And cowardly and immature and plain bloody pathetic!"

"No, Megs, I mean that's my word — *weak*. Twenty-two

points. But of course," he said quickly, seeing her glare, "he's weak, too. And plain and pathetic and everything else you said. So … are you going to end it?"

"I keep hoping this is just a passing panic, that he'll come to his senses and come back home — to both of us." She touched her still unrounded abdomen.

"Do you *want* him back?" Wade asked mildly.

"I know, I know. You're going to say that he's just a good-time-Charlie who's been fine as long as things went his way, but that he'll duck as soon as there's a drama. That *is* what you're thinking, isn't it?"

"It's obviously what you're thinking. Project much?"

Megan threw a piece of shortbread at him. Oedipus caught it mid-air and swallowed it.

"And the baby?"

"It's going well, I suppose. It's a bit weird, though. I don't really feel pregnant."

"Still your turn, Megs. You think maybe you're scared to bond with it — the baby, I mean? That your life is so hectic and your relationship with Mike too uncertain to really accept what's happening?"

"You know you've been hanging around a shrink too much when you start speaking like one, Wade." Megan stared hopelessly from her rack of useless letters to the board, then reached for the bag of tiles and slid all of them back into it. "I give up. Your turn."

She shook the bag and was fishing out new letters when Oedipus gave a sudden bark and ran across the board, sending tiles skittering in all directions. She and Wade groaned at the mess, but the dog was already at the window, sniffing and pawing at one of the curtains. Megan saw that a small gecko was clinging to the fabric just out of Oedipus's reach.

"No, Oedipus!" she shouted. "Down! Sit!"

Tearing the top sheet of paper off the scoring pad, she headed over to where Oedipus was whining in excitement. She folded the paper in half lengthwise and tried to ease it under the small reptile. It was tricky because the creature's claws were entangled in the fabric, but Megan was reluctant to prise it loose with her fingers in case she hurt it. It looked so fragile: the tiny bones were visible ridges under the wrinkled skin, and she could see a rapid, panicked pulse at the sides of its throat. She carefully manoeuvred the paper between the gecko and the curtain, and gently pulled back.

"There you go, little one," she said.

Suddenly free, the gecko made a mad scramble across the paper and slid off the edge. Oedipus pounced, snapped it up in his jaws and chewed with apparent relish.

"Eeuww," Wade said, pulling a disgusted face.

"Idiot dog!" Megan yelled, and promptly burst into tears.

Wade took her hand and led her back to the carpet, where they sat, leaning up against the couch. Oedipus tried to lie alongside Megan, but she shoved him away.

"Here." Wade handed her a serviette and pulled her head onto his shoulder. "Tell me what's wrong. You're not crying for the lizard, are you?"

"No, I'm not crying for the freaking lizard! My life's a mess. And I've gotten myself into such trouble. I don't know what to do."

"Tell me," he urged.

"I can't. It's confidential."

"You don't have to tell me the names. And you know I'll never tell a soul. What's happened?"

"I've fucked up, that's what's happened. There's no other word for it. And I don't know what to do to get out of it. I'm trapped." Megan blotted at her eyes with the serviette. "You remember I mentioned a client that was maybe hurt by a doctor at the clinic?"

Wade rubbed a comforting hand along her arm. "I remember."

"Well, it turns out that it *did* happen. And not just to her. To other women, too. He butchers his patients in the most dreadful ways. He leaves them mutilated and sterile and damaged in every kind of way."

"But why hasn't he been stopped? Haven't they complained or reported him?"

"They have. At least, some have. But it's hard to report because it's so private and intimate. They're embarrassed. Plus, it's difficult to prove that he did it negligently, let alone intentionally. It's just their word against his and he's a respected member of the medical fraternity and they're 'traumatised hysterical women'. Two women got as far as bringing cases against him at the Board, but one died in a car accident before the hearing and he paid off the other — and she's still a bloody wreck, I've seen her. Every day he operates on more women. I found out he even volunteers at Jo'burg Central. God knows what he's doing to those poor women."

"But surely you can get more women to speak up? You could ask his patients."

"I thought of that, too, and I am going to contact them — at least, I think I am — but Wade, the way I got his records, his *confidential* patient records, was by breaking into his office, going into his computer and stealing them." This admission brought on a fresh round of tears.

"You did what?" Wade's hand had stopped its rubbing.

"I know. But how else was I supposed to get the information?"

"You, Mega-Uptight-Wright, broke into a doctor's office, hacked his computer and stole his records?" Wade sounded both amused and impressed.

"It's not funny!" Megan said, pushing herself off his shoulder and blowing her nose.

"No," he said, immediately wiping the grin off his face.

"And you haven't even heard the worst part."

"It gets worse?"

"Yes. He … he's my patient."

"What? Who is?" Wade's face was blank with incomprehension.

"The doctor. When I was snooping in his office, I found … stuff. I discovered who he really is. And who he is, is one of my existing patients."

Wade's mouth fell open.

"He's been using his middle name as a surname, so I didn't realise. And I must be the worst, the most freaking incompetent, useless excuse for a psych not to have noticed that there was something seriously wrong with this man. *Anger issues!*" She made a sound of disgust. "He's been toying with me. I suppose he discovered that I was sniffing about, so he came to check me out. And it was a very clever move, because whatever he tells me in sessions is confidential. I'm ethically bound not to tell anyone."

"But he hasn't told you about hurting the women, has he?"

"No, not yet. But even if he had, I couldn't tell, do you see? I couldn't testify against him because he's a patient." Megan began picking up the Scrabble pieces, stacking them into little towers in her hands. "So, I either have to let *her* down, abandon my support for her case, or I have to testify against another client, which is a breach of ethics and confidentiality. I don't think they'd even allow my testimony — I'm pretty sure he could argue that as he's my client and so is she, it would be a complete conflict of interest."

Wade took the letter tiles from her and dropped them into the cloth bag. "But you could stop seeing him and then he wouldn't be a client anymore. Problem solved, surely?"

Megan shook her head, grimacing. "No. My duty of confidentiality doesn't end when the therapy does, I'd still be bound as tightly as I am now. Besides, I'm not even sure I *can* terminate therapy with him."

"You can't possibly carry on seeing him, knowing what you know. He's dangerous!"

"I know that. But you can't just stop seeing clients because you don't like what they tell you, or despise who and what they are. You're obliged to go through a whole termination process — several more sessions of closing off issues, building them up and then referring them to someone else. And who the hell would I refer him to? How could I send him to a colleague if I suspect he's still dangerous? And," she said, retrieving a stray tile and tracing a finger over the letter, "what reason would I give him for terminating? I can't tell him that I'm already seeing a patient of his and have now found myself in a dual role conflict — that would tell him that I know who he really is, that I've been snooping, in other words. Plus, it would compromise *her* confidentiality. He might well put two and two together and figure out who she is. It could put her in danger."

"But —"

"And, anyway, you're not allowed to refuse to see a patient, even for good reason, if they say they're in crisis and need to continue treatment with you — that's clearly stated in the Code. And Wade, this bastard has read the regulations, I'm sure of it. He'd like nothing better than to report *me*, to bring a case against me, so as to discredit anything I may have to say in the future.

"If I'm investigated for an ethical breach — not to mention the breaking and entering, and info-theft — and get a verdict against me, I can get suspended or even permanently erased from the register. This is my job, Wade, the only way I know how to make a living. He's got me well and truly stuck, and I bet he knows it. I bet he's getting his rocks off on it." She shoved a handful of tiles into the bag.

"But isn't there *any* way you could report him?"

"No one's going to take an anonymous letter or phone call seriously, if that's what you're thinking. Certainly not the Board — they have very set procedures for complaints."

"The police?"

"You want me to make an anonymous tip-off about bad surgery to the South African Police Force? Are you kidding me?"

They both knew how overwhelmed, short-staffed and

unenthusiastic the cops were. Most times, they couldn't even be persuaded to open a case for attempted hijacking. An anonymous tip about medical malpractice would only be ignored.

"There must be limits to the confidentiality thing, Megan, exceptions?" Wade was beginning to sound as desperate as she felt.

"There are a few exceptions. You can disclose confidential information if the client seriously intends committing suicide — fat chance with this narcissist — or if he intends clear harm to someone else."

"Well, there you are!"

"No, there I *aren't*. It's got to be specific. You have to know who the intended victim is, what the perpetrator's plan is — how, when, where — so that you can alert that person, and the authorities if necessary. It's not enough that you think he's hurt women in the past and your gut instinct and intuition tells you he'll do it again — sometime, to an unknown someone. And this guy is way, way too clever to tell me those sorts of details." Megan dropped the last of the letter tiles into the bag and yanked the drawstring closed. "No, the only way I could disclose information against him is if I'm compelled by law — subpoenaed or something, and even that's not a clear black-and-white situation. How do you get someone to subpoena you when you're not allowed to tell them who your client is or that there's something they ought to know about him? And if you do, if you have testified against a client and it's been smeared across every newspaper, radio, TV and social website — and it would be in this case, the gruesome details are just too salacious to ignore — how much do you think other existing or potential future clients will ever trust you? It's a bloody disaster."

Hiccupping into silence, Megan folded the Scrabble board and packed it into the box, tossing the tile bag and the racks on top of it. Wade stared at her with a horrified expression on his handsome face.

"I don't know what to say, Megan. It sounds like the most insane profession in the world. Like the inmates are running the asylum."

Megan just nodded. She had no more energy, even for tears.

"So, what do you think you'll do?"

"I'll have to see him." She sighed. "I'll try to get him to spill details of what he's already done, just in case I am subpoenaed one day. And I'll try to trick or manipulate him into letting slip any plans he might have for the future. And maybe, just maybe, I can try to help: do or say something that will make a difference, get him to stop. That's supposed to be the point of therapy, isn't it? To heal and help?"

"Do you really think you can fix this person?" Wade put the lid on the Scrabble set and tapped it down.

Megan shook her head slowly. "Honestly? No, I don't. For one thing, he's got to be seriously disturbed and this is not my area of expertise. For another, I can't confront him with what I know without breaking my other client's identity and confidentiality. I can't even reveal that I know his true identity. And how the hell am I going to sit in that office, alone with him, and pretend to be all empathic and unconditionally accepting? Ugh," she said, remembering her debate with 'Tony Thomas' on that exact subject. How he must have laughed at her ridiculous idealism and naiveté. "Just the thought of it makes me feel physically sick."

"Anything I can do?"

"Another hug would be really good," she said.

Wade embraced her tightly and Oedipus, seizing his opportunity, trotted over and gobbled the last of the shortbread.

31
CONFRONTATION

Megan studied the man sitting across from her, noticed how he dodged questions, answered only indirectly, gave nothing away. She, too, would have liked to avoid and delay and sink into dreamy denial. Most of all, she would have liked to have run far away, to be lying on a beach somewhere, or safely strapped into an airbus headed for outer Mongolia, rather than sitting here, watching this man duck and dive her questions, and reject her interpretations.

But there would be no more escape for him than for her. "Wherever you go, that's where you are." Someone wise had once said it, the Buddha maybe, or perhaps Confucius. Megan knew it to be true. It was time to confront.

"Arthur … *Art*," she said, interrupting a complicated tapping ritual involving both his hands, the arms of the chair and the laces of his polished black shoes. "You're in therapy, presumably, to confront your problems, to deal with them. And that's not going to happen while you're avoiding the vital questions. So, starting here and starting now, we're going to get to grips with this. And we're beginning with what you've most consistently avoided."

Art Smith looked up. There was panic in his gaze — the look of a small boy considering what would happen if he yanked up the coverlet, and checked precisely what lurked beneath his bed.

Megan leaned forward in her chair, staring at him intently. "I'm talking about your work. What is it that you actually do? What were you doing in that ward?"

"I was seeing a patient."

"You said you weren't a Gynaecologist."

Arthur rubbed fretfully at a temple with one hand, then duplicated the gesture identically on the other side. Megan wanted to grab those hands, make him sit on them or something — anything to still their continual fluttering, tapping and picking. How could she ever have considered him potentially dangerous? He was clearly riddled with fear, rigid with anxiety, and suffering wretchedly.

"I'm not. I was seeing a patient who'd been operated on. Her cervix was … I'm … I'm an oncologist."

Megan slumped back in her seat. "An oncologist?"

"It's a cancer specialist."

"I know what an oncologist is, Art. What I don't understand is why you've been hiding it. Why you say it like you're confessing to being a serial killer."

"Because that's what it feels like — like I'm a killer. They come and see me, and then they die. Old and young, male and female, rich and … well, I don't see the poor — not here —

but the rich and the not so rich. And all of them busy rotting alive on the inside!" He paused, seemed to consider what he'd said for a moment, then continued, "And some on the outside — the melanomas."

He took a deep breath and began speaking. Out it poured, all the toxic pain and horror that had been poisoning his heart and mind, and filling his soul with despair. It was like she'd lanced some purulent psychic boil. Once he began speaking, he seemed unable to stop describing his daily work: a grim carousel of death and disease, of blackened lungs, corrupted bowels and cannibalistic blood. The wasted old men riddled with metastases, the children whose brains hosted tumours like malevolent parasites, the women who would never bear children. The few who snatched uncertain remission against the odds; the many who signed up for treatment which left them ill, impaired, wearing wigs, padded bras or colostomy bags. Those who died no matter what you did. And the families who remained — the shocked wives, husbands and children grieving their lives around the gaping hole left by death. Worst of all were the parents who railed at God, the world, themselves, and at him, Arthur Smith, for the sheer bloody unfairness of life and death.

Megan let the outpouring wash over her, tried not to let it stick on her and failed. It felt like he was transmitting his personal and professional demons directly into her. Did they lose potency *en route*? That was the theory.

"It's like passing a hot potato," one supervisor had told her years back, "they pass it to you in therapy, you pass it on in supervision, and so on. It gets cooler as it passes from self to self."

It didn't feel that way now. She could see the dead and soon-to-be-dead in her mind's eye as Arthur described them: a never-ending line of misery and defeat leavened with cruel hope. She preferred the words of her one-time therapy lecturer: "If they can live it, you can hear it." That, at least, was honest.

She listened to Arthur's feelings of complete powerlessness against the enemy called cancer, his fear that nothing he did made any difference. She helped him connect the dots between his increasing sense of helplessness at work and his futile attempts to control what *could* be controlled — the number of steps, the evenness of shoelaces, the straightness of cushions — in a vain attempt to gain some slim sense of mastery in his world, and to distract from the voracious leviathan at the centre of his life which was beyond taming, beyond conquering.

At the end of the hour, she felt crushed, as if the cushions of cartilage between her vertebrae had been compressed flat by the weight of her client's pain. Conversely, Arthur left looking a little lighter; he even forgot to tap the doorframe on his way out. She had no idea, as she sat, pressed into the stuffing of her seat, where she would find the energy to move, or the will to see the rest of the day's clients, especially Trotteur, who loomed like her own personal black cancer in the remains of the day.

By the time his appointment began, she still felt utterly unprepared for what she would have to do, who she would have to pretend to be.

"So, where were we? Or should it be you asking that?" said the man she'd known as Tony Thomas.

He sat in front of her, his lips twisted in amusement. How could she have imagined that smile to be self-deprecating? It was not. It was arrogant and condescending. His charm was shallow, a mere trick of camouflage for the beast within. She was silenced, paralysed by the magnitude of what she knew about him.

Playing for time to pull herself together, Megan opened his file and looked down at the top paper inside. "Um, we spoke last time about conditional acceptance, and about your parents."

"Ah yes, which ones?" he said.

"You had more than one set of parents?"

One minute into the session and already he had her on the back foot. She was sure she'd sketched a genogram in the first session, she always did. She rifled back through the notes with hands made clumsy by nervousness. The file slipped to the floor, the loose papers slid out and spread into a fan. Instantly, he kneeled to gather them up. She was sure that he was trying to read them as he placed them in a tidy pile and handed them to her. She took the papers from him, careful not to touch his hand.

"Are you okay, Megan? You seem a little flustered."

He looked concerned, but she was no longer sure that anything about this man was genuine. The way the irises of his eyes, dark as aged port today, floated above his lower lids no longer intrigued her. Now they merely looked creepy.

"Here it is." Megan gazed down at the first session's notes: mother, father (both deceased), Tony — an only child, unmarried, no children of his own. It was as simple a genogram as you could get. "I have only the one set of parents listed. What have I missed?"

"Oh, there were many parents, many homes — in addition to *The Home*," he said, emphasising the last two words.

"*The* home?"

"Yes, I was a Home-boy, removed from the custody of my parents at the ripe old age of four, and brought to a child welfare house with a house-mother — no house-fathers: too much opportunity for hanky-panky with the onsite fledglings — and a bunch of other little boy and girl rejects." It was the first time she'd heard bitterness in his voice.

"You were abandoned there?"

"Oh yes, there and other places. I was abandoned many times." He rubbed at his chin where the faint silver line of a scar was just visible. "If we were to *reframe* my childhood — that is what you call it, isn't it, your profession's brand of spin-doctoring? You see how I have done my reading like a good boy, Megan! Then we could say that I am an expert in the processes of abandonment and rejection."

"How many foster parents did you have?"

This was information-seeking, not therapy. She'd have to be careful, throw in the odd reflection or interpretation so he didn't get suspicious.

"I stopped counting after five. It gets too fatiguing, you see: the desire, the determined, desperate faith struggling to exist in the face of real, lived experience. The hope that this time things will be different, that this time they'll want you. Then the honeymoon period when you're all they ever dreamed of, trying so hard to be what they want, trying to be *perfect*. The love, the affection, the acceptance, the mothering … Bliss!"

His face wore an ecstatic smile. As she watched, it was

replaced by a grim expression which set his features in hard lines.

"And then the creeping disappointment with you as the reality of your imperfection sets in, the realisation that you're not a doll to play with, not malleable, not — somehow — quite right. And then, inevitably, the return-to-sender. And those were just the good ones." He gave her a humourless smile. "The ones who wanted to keep you as a toy for their own pleasure, their smacks and caresses — those were the truly bent ones, Megan, the ones you *begged* to be taken away from."

Megan swallowed. She could imagine those experiences only too well.

"And all the while your file grows thicker with the reports on your flaws and faults: the little theft here, the odd experiment with the cat there, the unpredictable temper, the inability to keep friends. And the complaints that you're too moody, too strange, once even 'too intelligent'. All the deficiencies and defects that make it impossible for you to be adopted, to be kept or loved."

Megan had no idea what to say. Compassion and empathy for the child he'd been warred with abhorrence for the man he'd become. Her therapist-self felt moved to help, her logical-self ordered her to stay detached, and to think carefully before she said anything.

Once, during her post-graduate studies, Megan and her fellow students had been assigned an unsettling and difficult exercise to challenge their preconceptions about therapy. Each student had been asked to identify their own personal nightmare of a client: the type of person who would make their flesh crawl, their negative judgements rise, their empathy dissolve — the kind of person they would *have* to refer because they simply could not imagine working with him or her.

The nature of the invented "clients" had been revealing: an unrepentant paedophile (Megan's choice); a campus rapist (suggested by a young female intern); a government minister who beat his wife (the product of a mature female student's fear); a lesbian couple contemplating adoption (a conservative Christian male had suggested that one). As always, the imagined revealed the denied. At the time, Megan had wondered if the exercise was just one big projective test concocted by a nosey lecturer.

Each of them then had to volunteer to play one of the hypothetical clients, so that every intern got the opportunity to role-play a therapy session with the very client whom they could not ever envision counselling. Being the client was surprisingly easy; one person's bogeyman behind the door, it turned out, was another's dressing gown on the hook. Megan had no problem playing the lesbian who wanted to be a mother, but she'd been amazed that the men in the group seemed unfazed at the idea of playing the role of a rapist or wife-beater.

No one had much wanted to play the paedophile, but one young student had eventually stepped up, sat in the chair opposite Megan and told her "his story". He described how he had himself been abused as a child, explained his deep need to belong in a world where he was a despised misfit, confessed his longing for a non-threatening kind of love. To her amazement — and a little to her horror — Megan had felt understanding and empathy growing inside her. He really was just like any other client: wounded and suffering, floundering through his life, and using harmful ways of trying to ease or disguise the pain. And she'd found herself to be capable of counselling the unacceptable client.

The exercise had stood her in good stead in the years since. Amid the majority of truly good and likeable clients who instantly evoked her compassion and admiration, she still had to listen to the (thankfully few) clients who expressed vile feelings, confessed revolting or unspeakably stupid acts, and expounded indefensible ideologies. And always, every single time, she'd been able to connect to that deep inner swell of empathy which lifted her above petty judgements and into understanding.

She could allow that empathy to rise now, for this man who had suffered so much in his childhood. She could sympathise, understand, and try to help. Or she could attempt to get more information out of him, try to entrap and thwart him. She just wasn't sure she could do both at once: be both his therapist and his enemy, his therapist and his opponent. How do you do counsel a man when your goal is no longer to aid, but to deceive and to trick him into his own downfall?

Nothing she'd ever learned, in theory or in practice, had prepared her for this.

32
DOUBLE AGENDA

Megan gave herself an inner shake and turned her full attention back to the repellent, pathetic and dangerous man in front of her.

"So many rejections, so many abandonments," she said at last.

"Eventually we found a good fit, though — that's what they call it, a *fit*. As if they were trying on jeans, rather than children. Well, I suppose the whole process was a lot like child-shopping. Eventually, I was placed with a pair of older parents who left me alone much of the time and didn't want to know too much about what I was up to. Those are the parents in your little picture, Megan." He pointed at her notes. "A good fit: no pets, no other children, not too many expectations — those were requirements listed in my file by then."

"How old were you at the time?"

"I must have been twelve, because I remember my thirteenth birthday was with them. They gave me a microscope set as a present, and I got given a pack of modelling clay by my 'uncle' Brian — he was a dodgy one, too. It —"

"What do you mean?" Megan interrupted.

"It was terracotta clay, the sort that you could model and then leave out to dry so that it got hard. It felt so good between my fingers. Soft, pliable, malleable. I could turn it into anything. Anything! I could make it just how I wanted." His long fingers moved with the tactile memory of sculpting, and he smiled at Megan. "I can still smell that clay."

"Your uncle?" she prompted. "The dodgy one. What did he —"

"He's not the important part of what I'm trying to tell you!" he snapped.

His face contorted briefly into a grimace and Megan watched, fascinated, as it rearranged itself into the usual benign expression within seconds.

"I'm trying to tell you about the modelling I did with clay. Please pay attention. I began with making little figures of animals — cows, ducks, snakes, that sort of thing. But soon I moved onto making human figurines. I was good, too."

"You were an artistic child?"

"No, I was *exact*. Precise and meticulous. My figurines were models of accuracy. I read up on the ratios of the body, and made sure my little people complied. Did you know, for example, that the length of the forearm between the wrist and the inner bend of the elbow is the same as the length of the foot? No? Well I did. I made little mommies and little daddies and little kiddies and babies, and my picture-perfect families were in great demand, I can tell you."

His face was more animated than she'd yet seen it — lit by an inner excitement which made his eyes sparkle and a muscle in his cheek twitch.

"You finally had the perfect family," she said.

"I started selling them on the playground, and soon everybody wanted them. Well, the girls and their mothers, mostly. There was this craze at the time — printers' trays. Do you remember them? People hung them on the wall and put all sorts of knick-knacks and miniatures in the little compartments. Well, everyone wanted my miniature people for their trays. They were excellently done, very detailed. They were even anatomically correct — under their clothing. What a shock the mothers would've got if they'd pulled down the little pants!"

"Did the boys want any of the figurines?"

"Some did. They wanted little soldiers mostly. But not for show, they wanted them to play with — soldiers and cops-and-robbers, drivel like that. They always wound up breaking heads and arms off. It made me angry."

"You didn't like their games? You didn't play with them?"

"Megan, if you're trying to assess whether I was socially integrated, there's no need to pry so subtly. Just ask."

"Okay then, did you have friends or were you a bit of a loner?"

"I was alone — not a 'loner', mark you — by choice. I've always been discriminating."

"What might you have missed out on by not having friends?"

"Nothing, nothing at all. Those children were idiots, *cretins* — and I mean that word in the technical, psychological sense. They were far below me intellectually, and as ignorant as pigs. When they weren't squealing on the playground, they were clustered around the arcade games in the corner cafés. Space Invaders! Pacman!" He almost spat the words out, so deep was his contempt. "Puerile idiocy. War and shoot-'em-up games which didn't even look real."

"You would have preferred that the violence in the games was more realistic?" She needed to steer him to the subject of violence. Violence and women.

"Naturally. Though the goals of the games — destruction and devastation — would still have been contemptible. It is so easy, Megan, to destroy and damage. It's much harder to improve, to enhance and, ultimately, to perfect." He paused, looked down at his slender hands and seemed to be thinking for a few moments. "These days, of course, they have excellent computer games."

"You play computer games?"

"That surprises you, does it? It shouldn't. I've told you I like to make things functional and perfect. I started with the SIMS games when they came out, but there's such a range now. You can craft your own avatars, build a virtual second life with your own perfect people in lives of your own creation, under your own control."

"You like control and perfection."

"They are the only goals really worth pursuing!" He leaned forward and looked so roused that for a moment, Megan thought he would stand up, but then he settled himself back on the couch.

"I still have them, you know, the perfect ones — the ones that I made right."

Megan frowned in confusion. "You've lost me."

"The figurines, the clay figures! I only ever sold the imperfect ones, the ones with flaws. The faultless ones I kept for myself. I still have them," he almost sang in obvious delight. "And do you know the really funny thing? Those morons never even noticed that the ones they bought were inferior, substandard failures. They never even looked closely, just accepted the second-rate. Most people are like that." He shook his head in contemptuous disbelief.

"Maybe they preferred them that way."

"What on earth do you mean?"

"I think perhaps it's the oddities and the idiosyncrasies that separate great art from machine-made, mass-produced tat. We love, and therefore we value — or maybe it's the other way around: we value and therefore we love — the imperfection of a hand-carved mask, the deliberate fault in the hand-knotted Persian that makes it unique" — she took a quick breath — "the mysterious beauty of the Mona Lisa's crooked smile."

"In my office, I have a rather special print of the Mona Lisa, Megan, which is truly beautiful — quite an improvement, really." This time his smile was unmistakably sly, almost as if he knew.

Making an effort to keep her face expressionless, she asked, "An *improved* Mona Lisa?"

"Oh yes. You'll have to come see it sometime."

Did he suspect that she already had?

"What's it like, Tony, valuing perfection so highly, believing that you were rejected *because* of your imperfections, and yet having to live in a world filled with the imperfect and the unfixable?"

He said nothing for several moments, merely rubbed at his chin. Eventually, he said, "One does what one can."

"How?"

Would he take the bait?

"In one's little corner of the world, with the tools at one's disposal, one does what one can to make things a little more perfect."

The way he said it told her she would get nothing further from him in what remained of the session.

33
ASKING QUESTIONS

Patience came into the office wearing a caftan of dazzling purple and pink, and set a cup of tea down on Megan's desk.

She eyed Megan intently. "No more clients until two o'clock. Now it's time for tea."

"Is this *rooibos*?" Megan pointed at the pale amber liquid.

"Yebo."

"I don't drink *rooibos*."

"Expecting mothers must not have so much caffeine." Ignoring Megan's tsk of exasperation, Patience continued, "When is your next check-up with Dr Weinberg?"

"What do you mean?" Megan avoided meeting Patience's sharp gaze.

"I mean you must go see him again. Get him to check you out. To me, you don't look pregnant."

"I never told you I was!"

"Mn-mn-mn! If I knew only what I was told, then I would know less than a virgin on her wedding night. I'll make the appointment for you," she said, and sailed magisterially out of the office.

Megan got up and closed the door, hoping Patience would get the hint, then returned her attention to her computer and to the new cell phone lying on her desk. On the screen of her PC was the anonymous Gmail account which she'd just set up for MRSI — Medical Research Services International. Its inbox was pristinely empty, apart from the welcome messages from Google.

She'd compiled an email, starting with an introductory spiel about MRSI having been commissioned to conduct a research project on women's experience of gynaecological surgery and subsequent psychological outcomes. Two thousand women around the country, it stated, had been randomly chosen from hospital records to participate in the survey. Their anonymity was guaranteed, and they would be contributing to the development of women's health services by taking a few minutes to complete the attached questionnaire.

Here Megan had drafted questions asking if the participant had received gynaecological or obstetric surgery in the last year, and if so whether she'd been satisfied with her experience. Did she feel any of the procedures had been unnecessary? Was she satisfied that she'd given informed consent for every procedure? Had she had any negative, frightening or traumatic experiences in hospital?

At the end of the questionnaire, Megan included an open section for any comments that the participant might want to add, and then, in bold capital letters — highlighted for good measure — she'd typed the instruction: *Please return completed email questionnaire to sender's email address by using the 'reply' feature. Under no circumstances should the questionnaire be sent to your doctor.*

Then she sent the mailer to every patient with an email address on the lists she'd copied from Trotteur's records. It had taken her the better part of a morning in which she'd only had two clients, but at least it felt as if she was doing something.

The new cell phone was a pay-as-you-go cheapie, possessing only the most basic functionality under its bling pink and silver casing. She checked the voicemail which she'd set up with a message recorded in her calmest and most encouraging voice, urging the caller to leave their name and contact details.

"You have ... no ... new messages."

Megan was disappointed but not too surprised. It was only a day since she'd pinned the notice on the board at the hospital.

Attention female patients, it read. *Have you been badly treated by your doctor? If you have been operated on without good reason, or had surgery done without your permission, or if you have been traumatised and left with pain, then please call me. I want to help you.*

At the bottom of the page, she'd made a fringe of vertical cuts, and written the new cell phone number sideways on each strip of paper. Back in her university days, they'd used notices like this to advertise vac jobs, second-hand textbooks for sale, and invitations to raves. Now she was hoping that one or more of the women waiting in the chaos of disorganisation and desperation that was the Obstetrics and Gynaecology Unit at Johannesburg Central Government Hospital would read the notice, tear off a slip, and call her with some information that she could add to her thin dossier of evidence against Trotteur.

Talking to the nurses, trying to winkle information out of them, had proved the difficulty of her mission. They were no more interested in listening to her explanation and request than they were in listening to the pleading cries of their patients.

At an intellectual level, Megan knew that the health workers at Jo'burg Central Hospital were burned out, leached of impulses to compassion by a healthcare system which left them overwhelmed by the challenges, by the sheer bloody impossibility of providing a competent service to the needy millions, while thwarted at every turn by the impediments of bureaucracy, underfunding, corruption, inferior equipment and inadequate staffing.

She comprehended that the apathy, callousness and cruelty were both products of and protections against the helplessness of the untenable, yet unchanging, working conditions. She realised that to walk these littered corridors, to pass trolleys and cribs carrying the overflow of patients from overcrowded wards, to climb the six flights of stairs to the unit because the lifts were continually out of order, would sap the will and crush the spirit of anyone.

She knew. In theory, she even understood. Yet she'd still been shocked at their attitude. Ahead of her, in the long queue at the nurses' station, had been a man in blue overalls, with a woman — obviously in advanced labour — leaning heavily on his arm. When he begged for her to be admitted, helped, given a bed, the three nurses sitting and chatting behind the counter ignored him at first. Then one of the three, a male nurse, said to him, "Can't you see we're very busy here. Also, we are hungry and need to have our lunch. Where's our KFC, brother? When we are hungry, we can't deliver babies."

The man gently lowered the woman to the floor where she sat panting, leaning against the pale green wall, then he disappeared down the corridor, presumably in search of the deep-fried bribe.

Megan was about to take her turn when she heard a groan from behind her. Turning, she saw a girl, shockingly young and clutching a swollen abdomen, next in the line. Megan stepped back and allowed the youngster to go first.

"Please," the girl said to the nurses who were studiously avoiding eye contact, "the baby is coming and it's too soon. And the pain —" She gasped and bowed over her belly as another contraction hit. A whimper escaped between her clenched teeth.

"These girls," said one of the nurses to the others, rolling her eyes in contempt as she spoke. "These girls who can't keep their legs together. They come here, and gasp and moan at us." She turned hard eyes to the girl and said, "You panted and screamed enough when you were making this baby. Now you must shut up. Here you are no one special. Go and sit."

"But my baby is coming and it's too soon. It won't live! You must stop the labour."

"Let it come. One less baby in this world is not such a bad thing. Go and sit." The nurse motioned at the rows of waiting patients, partners and squirming babies on one of the benches, and they shuffled up to make a small gap. "And don't make my bench or my floor dirty with your mess. When you feel it coming, you must go sit on the toilet."

By the time Megan stepped up, shaken by the callousness she'd witnessed, she knew her quest was futile. When she enquired about Dr Trotteur — how they found him as a doctor, whether they had any complaints — they merely turned blank stares at her.

"What are you doing here? You think because you are white you can come ask questions and cause trouble?" said the male nurse.

"No! I just —"

"Just nothing! Go away. We don't work for you, *madam*."

They all laughed. Megan felt her face flame.

"I know you don't work for me. You don't work for *anyone*. You don't work at all," she snapped.

She spun on her heel and walked away from the desk, stepping carefully between patients sitting on the dirty floor. Out of sight of the nurses, she took the fringed notice from her bag and stuck it to an old, cork noticeboard on which were pinned cautions about AIDS, exhortations to abstain from sex, and a large poster of white, sandy beaches and palm trees, advertising a travel package to Mauritius departing in 1997. There were not enough drawing pins to hold the existing notices in place — some of them hung askew from a single pin — so Megan rummaged in her handbag and eventually found an old paperclip lying in the bottom. She bent it open, then used it to pin her appeal to the noticeboard.

A few of the women waiting on a broken bench opposite the board watched her with dull eyes, but nobody seemed interested enough to get up and read the notice. She was just leaving what was beginning to seem to her like one of Dante's circles of hell, when she heard a soft voice call, "*Sisi*."

A thin, birdlike nurse stood in an adjacent corridor, beckoning with a crooked finger. Megan approached her, curiosity surging.

"This way," whispered the nurse.

She clutched Megan's upper arm with a surprisingly firm grasp and steered her down the corridor. Bundles of soiled bedding and bloodied surgical scrubs were piled up against walls painted in the pale green of cheap primer. Perhaps Megan's face showed something of her dismay, because the nurse said defensively, "The laundry is on strike."

Just then the lights went out, leaving the corridor dimly illumined by the weak light that fought its way through the grimy windows.

"Power failure. They probably didn't pay the bill again."

"Aren't there generators?"

"Only for some of the operating theatres and ICU's, not for here." The nurse pulled Megan into an alcove off the corridor. "My name is Pumla."

"I'm Megan." They shook hands.

Pumla checked the corridor, and then spoke softly and quickly. "I heard you — asking the others about Dr Trotteur."

"Yes. Do you know him?"

Pumla's face was pinched with anxiety. "We all know him."

Megan waited, holding the silence.

"He hurts the patients," Pumla said eventually.

"Hurts them how?"

The other woman didn't reply.

"Please," Megan said. "He's hurt a woman I'm trying to help. I've found out that he has hurt many other women, done terrible things to them. I'm sure he must have done it here, too, to these poor women. We want to report him, to stop him, but we need witnesses."

"I can't testify. I won't be a witness," Pumla said quickly, looking alarmed. "But I will tell you this: he excises before he has results. Okay, in this place it can take weeks to get biopsy results, so he says he is playing it safe by cutting at the same time. He says the patient might not return, might not get the chance for another operation. And that is maybe true, because there is a backlog for surgery. But even so, the other doctors don't do it."

"What does he cut?"

"Their genitals. He removes the vulva, tightens the vagina. He does hysterectomies — too many. He does sterilisations but when you check the charts, there is no consent from the patients. And" — she flashed a distressed glance at Megan — "sometimes, when he does deliveries, he uses the forceps very hard. I think he must damage the babies. One was bleeding from the ear afterwards. He never uses the suction cup, for the head, you know?"

Megan nodded.

"Sometimes he says the patient doesn't need anaesthetic, so the woman suffers. And twice, *twice* I have seen him pull the baby out. Once it was breech and he pulled it by the feet, like this" — she braced one foot high against the wall and simulated yanking back forcefully — "and pulled hard! That baby's hips were dislocated, and it is very hard on the mothers."

"Don't any of the women complain — the patients, I mean?" Megan asked.

Pumla stepped out of the alcove for a moment, checked both ways, then stepped back.

"What do they know? They are poor and ignorant, they believe what the doctor tells them. Besides, you have seen how it is here: no one will listen even if she complains."

"Please, *please* won't you consider testifying?" pleaded Megan, but the nurse shook her head adamantly.

"No. He will get me fired. I have children to feed, a family back in KwaZulu to support. I am the only breadwinner in my house. I cannot be unemployed."

"I understand," Megan said. She *did* understand, but still, she was bitterly disappointed. "Here is my card. Please, call me if you think of anything else or if you change your mind."

"I hope you catch him." Pumla grasped Megan's hand tightly for a moment and whispered, "I will pray for you, *Sisi*."

Then she turned and walked rapidly away down the shadowy corridor.

34
BREEDING

"Last time we spoke about how you enjoyed making perfect figurine families," Megan said.

"We did."

"Beautiful, intact families, unlike your own. Perfect little families with perfect little children who weren't rejected or abandoned."

Tony rubbed at his chin, but didn't respond. Well, she was no longer here to do therapy anyway, thought Megan, and changed tack.

"I wonder, do you ever wish you could perfect real people?"

"It's tempting, but hardly possible."

"Meaning?"

"I never told you, did I, what I do for a living?" said Tony with a slow smile.

This was something she wasn't supposed to know. Was he testing her, or simply getting ready to tell her?

"You said you were a photographer."

"I am a photographer — I like to create images. But what I do for a living is medicine."

"You're a doctor?" She injected her voice with a note of surprise.

"I am indeed."

"But why didn't you tell me that?"

"I had to know I could trust you, that I could rely on your confidentiality, your ethics. Now that I know I can, I can tell you everything."

"Everything?"

This might be the moment when he finally began to talk about what he'd done.

"There's so much to learn about me, Megan. 'I contain multitudes'."

"Walt Whitman."

"Very good, I'm impressed. Do you know the full quote?"

"Isn't it something like: 'Do I contradict myself? Very well then, I contradict myself. I contain multitudes'."

"'I am large. I contain multitudes'," he corrected. "From his *Song of Myself*."

"Are *you* large, Tony? Tell me about your multitudes. The song of you."

He paused for a long moment, looking at the afternoon light streaming through her window and reflecting off the glass paperweight on the desk. "There's so much to learn about me," he said again. "For example, don't you want to know where I work?"

Was he fishing to see what she knew?

"Sure."

"Here, Megan. I work right here at Acacia."

"Goodness! It's amazing that we've never bumped into each

other or cross-referred. I didn't even know that there was a Dr Thomas working here." Two could play this game.

"Ah … time for another confession."

Megan raised an interrogatory eyebrow.

"I only told you part of my name."

"*What?*" Megan tried to force as much astonishment into her voice as she could.

"My name *is* Tony Thomas." He reached into a pocket and extracted a slim, silver business card case. "But my full name is —"

Megan took the card he handed her and read the name aloud as though she'd never heard it before, deliberately mispronouncing the surname. "Anthony Thomas Trotter?"

"Not Trotter!" His nostrils flared slightly and she saw his hand clench on the arm of the couch. "That's a pig's name. It's Trot*teur*. It's from the old French word *trotier*, meaning a messenger."

"And are you? A messenger?"

"Nominative determinism, now? I thought you believed in free will."

Megan ignored this. Looking up from the note she'd just made, she said, "We need to update the personal details on your intake form after today's session. Tell me, was there a reason why you didn't use your real name?"

"My *full* name," he corrected.

"Your full name. Is there a reason why you didn't want me to know who you actually are?"

"Think I'm paranoid, do you? You know what the bumper sticker says: just because you're paranoid doesn't mean they *aren't* out to get you!" He laughed uproariously.

"Why would they be out to get you? Have you done something wrong?"

"That was a joke, Megan. I think they must have cut your sense of humour out of you when they trained you. Did it used to be here?" He tapped his own left cheekbone, while staring at the indentation in hers. "Is that what caused the depression in your cheek?"

She waited, but he said nothing further, just looked at her with that infuriating faint smile twisting his lips. She read his card again.

"So, you're an Obstetrician Gynaecologist. That surprises me. I would have thought plastic surgery would be the chosen field for someone who values perfection as much as you do."

"A perceptive observation. But by giving the brood mare the best care, one can maximise the odds of the perfect offspring being born, you know. Make sure that mothers have only the babies they want, and will keep, and take proper care of."

Brood mare! His misogyny was staggering and his urbane, civilised mask was slipping. Hopefully he'd reveal information she could use against him.

He gave a short sigh, as though mildly annoyed. "Though, full disclosure, I did start specialising in plastic surgery. I had a full scholarship for academic excellence and underprivileged origins — the poor little foster child experience was useful for something, you see — so I could afford to specialise. But I found plastic surgery limiting. I could only improve appearance, seldom function. And plastic surgery only changes the surface appearance, it doesn't go deep inside, where I longed to be."

Megan repressed a shudder. "You longed to work inside people? To do surgery?"

"It upset me, I admit, that a perfect face, or a face capable of being made perfect, could sit atop someone imperfect on the inside. Dirty and rotten." He spoke the last three words in a higher, rougher voice, then continued in his usual smooth cadences, "So, no, ultimately I decided against plastic surgery. Besides, so many people were so ugly and deformed that they would never be flawless anyway. Many were damaged by their genes, their incubation and births. There are some people, Megan" — he looked at her intently, as if he really wanted her to grasp his point — "who simply ought not to breed."

This time, she could not keep the incredulity out of her voice. "Tony, do you really, seriously believe what you're saying?"

"Absolutely. There is enough ugliness in the world. We should be eliminating it, not adding to it."

"But to prevent people from 'breeding', as you call it, based on something as superficial as appearance!"

"Oh, you're wrong there, my dear. It's not superficial at all. Oddities of appearance are often the outward benign congenital anomalies which are correlated with serious, deeper pathology. The same genetic mutations, teratogens or abnormal development processes which lead to deformities of appearance also cause deformities of development and function. Witness the hooded eyes and webbed fingers of the Mongol —"

"The *Mongol?*"

"— the flattened lip of the foetal alcohol syndrome baby,

the haemangiomas and furrowed tongues of the schizophrenic, the sandal-gap toes, facial asymmetry and increased distance between the eye sockets of the autistic." He spoke rapidly and passionately, and there was an almost zealous glitter in his dark eyes.

"You think these people should not be born," Megan said, trying — and failing — to keep the horrified revulsion out of her voice.

"What is their purpose?" he challenged. "What do such sub-normals contribute to the improvement of form and function in this world? Answer me that, if you can."

She took a deep breath, and tried to corral her racing thoughts. "You speak, Tony, like a disciple of eugenics. The logical extension of your beliefs are policies of racial hygiene and ethnic cleansing, the horrors of Nazism."

"They knew a thing or two, those men. They spoke the truths that we in this politically correct age are too cowardly to voice."

Megan was speechless with disgust.

"Oh, I've shocked you again." He gave a small, high giggle. "But this time I'm only kidding. I'm just trying to rattle your cage, Megan. I've been playing devil's advocate because you know how I like a good debate. Of course I don't really believe all that perfect specimen nonsense." He waved a dismissive hand. She must have looked dubious, because he continued, "I don't! I'm a doctor for God's sake. I have the stethoscope and framed Hippocratic Oath to prove it. Honestly, would I work at helping and healing if I really thought that way?"

"No, that's true. If you thought that way, your work

wouldn't be that of helping and healing. It would be something very different indeed."

The look he flashed her was alert, perhaps even suspicious. She needed to be careful. She must not allow her disturbed feelings to betray her, and she would surely show her hand if she asked again whether he'd ever tried making real people perfect.

She saw, now, that they were playing a game, like two equally-matched chess players moving their pieces around the board, neither gaining an advantage over the other. Unless she could break the *impasse,* they would dance about the truth interminably, because she would never get any real facts out of him while his guard was up. Perhaps if his guard was down, though ...

"I have an idea, Tony, something I want to suggest to you. For our next session."

"Oh, yes?"

"We've explored, a little, how your early experiences of being abandoned, abused and rejected might be the root of your issues."

"My *issues?*"

"Your anger and your unrealistic expectations. That *is* why you came to see me, isn't it?"

For a moment he, too, had looked rattled. But now his complacent smile returned. "Oh yes, of course. Why else?"

"I've often dealt with clients who have anger — old, deep-seated rage — and I find that the conventional approach of "talk therapy" is of limited benefit to them. It brings about understanding and insight in the rational mind, of course, but no real release or change — because the heart and the mind are not one. The conscious mind trundles along nicely in therapy, but the subconscious holds onto its primal fear and rage. Talk therapy doesn't reach the core" — Megan pressed a hand against her solar plexus — "the primitive emotions, the damaged inner child."

"What are you proposing?"

"How would you feel about a session of hypnosis?" She'd hardly finished the sentence before he started laughing derisively.

"Hear me out," she said. "We could use it as a way to reclaim, re-parent and heal that abandoned, wounded inner child, that rejected little Home boy deep inside you who thinks perfection is a precondition for love and acceptance."

He was rubbing his chin again, his fingers feeling along the almost invisible silver line.

"Or, if you prefer, we could use the trance state to do some work with rage-containment and a safe, controlled-release of pain for the wounded part of you who is angry at himself for being contemptibly less than perfect, and enraged with the flawed, rejecting world?"

He paused for a moment and seemed to be studying her carefully, assessing something.

"Which?" he said. "The hurt child or the angry man?"

"Either. Both." She shrugged. "We can see what your subconscious wants us to do, and go along with that."

"It's an interesting idea, Megan. I can't say it doesn't intrigue me a little. But" — he shook his head — "it won't work. You'd never be able to hypnotise me. *I* wouldn't go into a trance. That only works on those with a weak will and inferior mindpower."

"You're probably right," Megan said.

She thought carefully about her next words, tailoring her usual double bind to fit his views on "sub-normals" and "mindpower".

"But in my experience, the only individuals who struggle to achieve trance are those who have rather dull imaginations or lower, concrete intelligence. They're too limited: they can't achieve the necessary levels of abstract thought, can't work with the symbolism of the subconscious mind." She leaned forward slightly towards him and gave a conspiratorial smile. "But at the very least you'd have a wonderfully restful session in which you learned the technique of progressive relaxation, which is a great method that you can use to reduce stress and manage anger in your day-to-day life."

He looked at her for a long moment, the dark, floating irises of his eyes unreadable. "I suppose it might be revealing. Right then, let's do it!"

35
YEA AND NAY

It had been a really long and a *really* bad day — possibly the worst of her life, thought Megan as she flung her handbag aside, kicked off her shoes, placed a tall glass of wine on her bedside table, and flopped onto her bed. Oedipus immediately leapt up beside her and licked her face until she buried it in the pillow. He turned his attentions to her feet, licking squelchily between her toes with his warm tongue; it felt both revolting and strangely comforting.

The day had started out well with two relatively easy sessions with long-term clients. When she checked the new cell phone, she was delighted to find a text message from Pumla Phahlane. She had, she said, reconsidered and would be willing to submit a statement about what she'd witnessed of Trotteur's brutal and abusive practices at Johannesburg Central Hospital. There was more good news waiting in Megan's Gmail inbox: a returned questionnaire to the fake survey intimating complaints about Dr Trotteur. Then, mid-morning, an elated Alta Cronjé had arrived for her appointment. She was smiling broadly and in her hand she waved a piece of paper like a medal of triumph.

She'd hardly taken her seat in the consulting room before she was telling Megan all about it. The letter was from the Health Professions Council — a response to the complaint that she, with Megan's help, had compiled and sent to the Medical Board. It confirmed that they had received and logged her complaint, and would be scheduling a hearing to deal with the matter.

"They say that they'll 'treat the matter as expeditiously as possible, given the extremely serious nature of the allegations'!" Alta read aloud from the letter. "As soon as they've set a date, they'll notify me and 'the accused' — nice ring to it, hey? The *accuuused.*"

"That's such good news, Alta. How are you feeling?"

"Great! It's finally happening, you know? It's coming to an end, and then all this will be over and I can just rest and be peaceful. It's going to feel so good to stop him, too. To make sure he gets what he deserves. Bu-ut," she drew out the word, and her smile widened still further, "that's not all my good news."

"There's more?"

"I'm expecting."

"Expecting what?"

"I'm preggers! I'm so happy, and Johan is over the moon."

"Congratulations! May I give you a hug?"

"Of course," Alta said and they embraced tightly.

There seemed to be a lot of unsaid things in the hug, and both had bright eyes when they sat back down.

Megan had wanted to tell Alta that she, too, was pregnant, but the sharing of that kind of personal news — and the fact that she would be away from the practice for several months — had to be communicated to clients very carefully. Some took affront and felt abandoned, others seized on the opportunity to divert therapy from their own difficult issues and focused instead on the therapist, some began to resist deep work in anticipation of the day when she would not be there to see them. For all these reasons, she was planning to tell clients only much later, perhaps around the five- or six-month mark when hiding the pregnancy would become difficult anyway.

Alta's delight, and Megan's joy for her, made what happened later in the morning that much more unreal and painful.

Megan had gone for her scheduled check-up with Dr Weinberg but, looking around at the burgeoning bodies of the other women in the waiting room, she still didn't feel like she belonged. When Weinberg asked how she was, Megan replied honestly.

"I feel fine. I don't even feel nauseous anymore. But I also don't feel pregnant."

"Would you like me to show you?" Weinberg asked, smiling in the knowing and gentle way of those whose daily work involved miracles invisible to the naked eye.

"Yes! Please."

She went through the ritual undressing in the examination room and then Weinberg, accompanied by his ever-smiling nurse, entered, dimmed the light to reduce the glare on the ultrasound screen, and started the scan.

"It will need to be an internal ultrasound, I'm afraid," said Weinberg, slipping a condom over a phallic-shaped probe and knotting it so that it wouldn't slip off. "An external ultrasound this early wouldn't give a very good picture. Now just relax … There we go. In just a moment you'll see the little foetus with its tiny heart beating away, and then you'll be convinced that it's real."

Dr Weinberg wiggled the probe this way and that, fiddled with the controls on the machine and its monitor, and subsided into ominous quiet. Behind him, also staring at the screen, the nurse cleared her throat but said nothing. She was no longer smiling.

Was something the matter? Where was the heartbeat? Why wasn't the doctor saying anything? Megan wanted to shout her terror at him, but she didn't want to hear his response, his confirmation of what she already knew — something must be very wrong.

Weinberg sent her to the radiology department for another scan, explaining that their machines were more sensitive and powerful than his. Clutching the referral note, she walked down to the clinic's busy radiology department, filled out the ubiquitous forms, and was given a glass and a large jug of water.

"Drink it all, fast as you can without making yourself sick. Do *not* go to the toilet — we need a full bladder to get the best image," the assistant behind the counter said.

Megan focused on the way the woman's plucked, arched eyebrows moved as she spoke; it helped her not to think. Then she took the only available seat in the waiting area, between a man coughing relentlessly and a grey-faced teenage boy clutching a wrist bent at an odd angle, and tried not to think about what was happening. She drank glass after glass of water while she stared at a sign which said, "NB!!!! If you are pregnant, please inform the radiologist and/or technician!"

Her bladder was close to bursting when her name was eventually called. Again, the darkened room, again the probe — doubly uncomfortable now because of her full bladder. Again, nothing pulsed in the image on the screen. The radiographer said nothing, except, as she left the room, "I'm sorry. I'll do your report straight away and you can take it back to Dr Weinberg."

"It's a molar pregnancy, I'm afraid — or a blighted ovum, in the old terminology," Weinberg said, his face grave and his voice grim.

It wasn't a viable pregnancy, he explained, it would not have gone much longer without a spontaneous abortion occurring — that was what he called it, "a spontaneous abortion". Her body had only been fooled into thinking it was pregnant, and secreted hCG hormones, causing the symptoms she'd experienced.

"It's important that we evacuate the uterus completely. Any uncontrolled growth is not desirable and we don't want to take a risk of a hydatidiform tumour developing. We need to do it as soon as possible. That means tomorrow, I'm afraid, otherwise my next surgery is next Wednesday and that's leaving it longer than I would like."

The words washed over Megan: *blighted, not viable, fooled, evacuate, tumour. Tomorrow.* She felt dazed, numb with shock. Her puzzled brain seemed to be working very slowly, at complete odds with her racing heart. All she could take in was that she wasn't pregnant — maybe never had been — and that she had to have surgery.

Dr Weinberg handed her over to his nurse. "Mrs Wright needs a D&C, let's do it first thing tomorrow. You'll need to move Mrs Cele down the list. Tell Mrs Wright when and where to report tomorrow, please, then call down to confirm the theatre is booked and get her name onto the surgery board."

Only one word of this penetrated the dull fog enveloping Megan.

"I'm not Mrs," she said to the nurse. It seemed important to get this right.

"I understand. Is there someone I can call to come fetch you, now?"

"What? No, no, I … I need to go back to my office and get organised. I need to cancel my clients for tomorrow."

"I suggest you cancel them for a good week. Give yourself time to recover, dear, physically and emotionally you're going to take a bit of a bruising. Here is the information you'll need," she said, handing Megan some printed sheets. "You'll need someone to collect you afterwards — tomorrow, I mean. You won't be in a fit state to drive yourself home."

Back at her office, dry-eyed but trembling, she told Patience everything. It was only when the woman wordlessly hugged her tightly against her massive bosom that Megan felt the tears and the wracking sobs come.

Patience would organise the practice, cancel all the clients — except for one — for rest of the day, and for the whole of the next week, but there were calls which Megan needed to make herself. She went to the bathroom, washing her face and fixing her make-up while she debated whom to call first. She needed to tell Mike, and Wade, and her family. Her family! She could not face her mother and Cayley. If she spoke to them now, she wouldn't be able to get through the single therapy session that remained that day, and that she could not — would not — cancel.

She decided to call Wade, tell him no sympathy was permitted yet — it would only set her off again, and there would be time enough for tea and tears afterwards, after tomorrow. She would ask *him* to call her family, tell them not to call her until tonight.

She must get through this last session. She'd prepared so carefully for it, scripted almost every word of the hypnotic induction she intended using on Trotteur. Bugger reparenting the inner child. She needed to stop him from hurting more women. She had no idea if it would work, but she had to try.

Back in her office, she did a quick visualisation exercise on herself, imagining packing the fact of the blighted pregnancy, together with all the grief and fear that went with it, into an old-fashioned trunk, which she closed, locked and stowed on a shelf labelled "later". She focused on clearing her mind, then reoriented herself to the present and opened her eyes.

Composing her features into what she hoped was a convincing semblance of friendliness, she buzzed through to Patience to send in "Tony". Once he'd greeted her and sat down, she pulled out the small footstool she kept for the purpose and slid it under his feet. Then she began.

36
MONSTER

"**T**here you are, that will help you be more comfortable and relaxed."

Megan was already beginning to seed her speech with words preparing Trotteur for trance. She would say them as often as she could without alerting him to the repetition.

"How about you pop one of those cushions behind your head so your neck can *relax*. That's right, all *comfortable* now?" She put the slightest stress on the words so that the emphasis would be discernible only to the subconscious mind.

He smirked and said, "Is this when you dangle a pendulum in front of my eyes?"

"Oh no, I've never been *comfortable* with that method. It's not so *ease*-y, you know." This time, she spoke the words she wanted him to register subconsciously just a little more slowly. "Perhaps, though, you might allow yourself to find a spot on the ceiling and just stare at it without blinking ... That's right."

He stared fixedly above him. Was he aware that he was

already doing what she'd told him to do?

"Now, Tony, I'm not at all sure that you'll be able to *relax fully and go into trance.*" Already, she was using subliminal suggestions. "As you told me last time, you don't think anyone would be able to make you *go into trance.* And so you allow yourself to *relax now and go into a deep trance* or perhaps you will prevent yourself from *relax*ing and just sinking into a *comfortable* state. Whatever is best, whatever is most *comfortable* for you, that's what you'll decide."

She guided him through the fixed-eye induction which she normally utilised, and at the usual point, his eyes slowly closed. This was no guarantee that he was in trance, though. He might be faking. Or just relaxing. She took him through several deepeners, the last of which walked him down an imagined flight of stairs with suggestions to relax more deeply on each step.

"… and now step *down* to seven, deeper and deeper, more and more *relaxed* … Soon you may find that your breathing slows right *down*. As you breathe in," she timed the words so that they matched his own inhaled breath, "think about breathing in *rest* and calm and *relax*ation. And allow that to spread through your whole body and mind. And step down to six. Each time you exhale," again, she timed the words to his action, "think about breathing out stress and letting go of all worry and all distractions … Just step *down* to five … More and more and more relaxed, all the way down."

Her voice was slow and rhythmically ponderous now — the sort of voice which would surely make a conscious Trotteur laugh in ridicule. But he merely breathed deeply. His face looked blank and relaxed.

"Four ... and if any distracting sounds or thoughts come into your mind, just notice them ... don't engage with them ... just let them pass through and drift off and away, just *drift off and away.*"

Megan took her time with the induction, using repetition and soothing imagery to instil what she hoped was the deepest possible trance. She studied her subject carefully. It *looked* like he was in trance. He was slumped in the couch cushions and he sat perfectly still, breathing slowly and deeply, the long fingers of his hands limp in his lap. Body paralysis was one of the markers of hypnosis — nobody sat that still when awake — but, still, he might be faking to see what she was up to.

She didn't dare test his depth of trance as she usually did with clients — by telling them that they were so deeply relaxed they couldn't open their eyes, and then asking them to check whether they could. She was afraid such a direct method might alert his conscious mind, make him mindful of the fact that he was in trance (if indeed he was), and that he'd then take it as a challenge to wake himself up.

For the same reason, she wouldn't be able to use direct methods or express suggestions that he stop harming women. He might be in trance, but he wasn't unconscious or asleep, and his conscious mind would hear any suggestion that blatant, and start resisting or waking him up. Moreover, if he caught on to what she was doing, he would immediately know that she'd been investigating him, and was possibly amassing evidence against him. That was something she didn't want him to know until the Board hearing.

She needed to plant her suggestions as subtly and imperceptibly as possible.

"And, take that last step down, to one … Wonderful. So, as you *relax* and just enjoy feeling so calm and so *deeply relaxed*, I would like to tell you a story: a story about a hero who slayed the Anger Monster. Would it be okay for me to tell you the story? You can just answer 'yes' or 'no'."

For a few moments Trotteur said nothing. Megan's mind raced. She wondered if he was thinking it through, looking for the catch, or if he was trying to figure out how he would respond if he truly was hypnotised. Or, was this in fact the typical delayed response of true deep trance?

"Yes." The word was spoken softly, with the bare minimum of lip movement. His voice sounded as if it was coming from a long way away. It certainly looked like trance.

"Well, this story starts with a forest, a deep ancient forest, dark with the shade of old trees," Megan began, using a sing-song, slightly monotonous voice, placing an emphasis of tone, timing or volume on the words she wanted to implant at a subliminal level. "I wonder if you could see the forest in your mind's eye. And when you can see this ancient, primal, dark place, please let one of the fingers on your right hand lift and lower so that I know."

Again, there was a pause, then with an almost imperceptible twitch, the index finger on his right hand rose a few millimetres and then a few more, in small spasmodic movements. Megan was convinced. Trotteur, she was sure, was in a deep trance.

"Okay, that's excellent, now just relax and sleep deeply and perhaps you might find yourself moving into that forest as I tell you this story …"

In Freudian and Jungian symbolism, the forest was often a

metaphor for the primal feminine. It was something, Megan thought, to do with pubic hairs being like undergrowth and the shade representing the unknowable and slightly sinister mysteries of womanhood as perceived by the old analysts.

Normally, Megan didn't set much store by such psychoanalytic symbols and meanings, but today she was willing to try anything and everything. Besides, it was pretty certain that his hatred of women was related at least in part to the abandonment and rejection by his mother and subsequent mother figures. Why was it always the mothers who were blamed? The distracting thought twitched at her thoughts, but she forced it to "drift off and away"; this induction needed to work at many levels and she had to stay sharply focused.

It seemed fitting to return Trotteur, symbolically, to the core mother in the form of the unconscious archetype of the crone. The symbolism would not stop there. Trotteur used a knife of sorts — his scalpel — violently to cut and mutilate women. A Freudian would say this represented a sexual violation of the female, a symbolic rape: the knife being the phallic symbol which penetrated their genitals. Megan also planned to tap into Arthurian legend — she figured Trotteur would fancy himself as special, a king. Plus, she would use associations of trees in gardens and forbidden fruit. Layers upon layers *within* layers of messages — enough to confuse and bypass conscious controls and unconscious defence, the commands hidden inside permissive and tentative language, the suggestions designed to register only in the subconscious mind.

She looked down at the carefully prepared and meticulously

worded hypnotic script she'd written and continued, "Now, Tony, perhaps you can just *relax* and *listen to me* as I tell you about our hero, a powerful, intelligent man, a king who penetrates the thicket of forest, going deeper and deeper on his important quest. There is a monster, you see, which threatens him and his kingdom. An angry monster which breathes fire when crossed or threatened. The whole community is at risk of being destroyed by the angry monster's actions, but especially the women, who have such tender skin that they are more easily burnt, and the monster seems to prefer breathing his fire on them."

Had that been a tiny twitch at the corner of Trotteur's mouth? *Go slowly, deeply and very carefully*; this time the instruction was to herself.

"So, the hero walked along a path laid down years and years and years ago, which led into the heart of the forest, to the deepest place inside, and there he found a witch. Some in the village said she was a wise woman and a healer, and many came to talk to her when their hearts were burdened."

If Trotteur wasn't in as deep a trance as she hoped, then he ought to take this bait and feel more reassured that he could see through her metaphor. He would think that Megan had concocted a story in which she, the wise and healing therapist, was represented in the form of the witch who would send him to slay his own monstrous anger. He would, hopefully, think that it was one of those hypnotic anger reduction techniques she'd spoken of, and he would be right. At one level, this was exactly what she was doing — heaven knew the man could do with a reduction in his rage. But her real message would be more craftily and subtly implanted.

"The hero asked the witch, 'How must I slay this monster of anger that threatens all? Although I am a king, I am but a man, yet the monster is fierce and hot and may destroy me.' The witch replied, 'There is a way, but *you must listen to me* very, very carefully. *You must do as I say* down to the last instruction; if you don't *obey me*, then you will be destroyed by the monster.' The hero took up the challenge. 'I will do it,' he said. And the witch said, 'At the end of the forest, just before where the world ends or perhaps begins…',", Megan said, inserting one of the confusing nonsense phrases that muddled the conscious mind and engaged it in trying to figure out what was meant, leaving the subconscious mind freer to listen to the subliminal suggestion which she was now about to embed, by emphasising only certain words in her script.

"…'there is a tree that the patient women, one after another, have planted to harvest its fruit which they love. Stuck in the base of that tree, which is named the patient tree after the patient women who planted and tend it, in the place where new life begins, is a blade, a sword of great power. You must pull that sword out of the tree, do you hear me? *You must pull the blade out of the patient women*'s tree, and *never put it back, never put the blade back into a patient* fruit or tree. When you have slain the monster, *you must* bring the blade back and *lay the blade down safely next to the patient* tree,' the witch told him. 'I understand,' the hero replied. And the witch said, 'It is important that you remember this instruction in the deepest parts of you so that even when you have forgotten, which you will, *you will remember* this order: *you can pull the blade back out but you cannot put it in,* or something terrible will happen to you. *If you try to cut* the tree or the fruit of *a patient* woman, then you will find you cannot or *something terrible will happen.* When we wound others, we wound ourselves — it is the eternal way,' the witch told him and she spoke the truth. Then she told him to take the magic sword and find the anger monster and slay it."

Tony lay immobile against the cushions, but the second hand of the clock on the wall behind him moved relentlessly on. She needed to move more quickly.

"So just stay deeply relaxed, Tony, deeper and deeper with each breath that you inhale … and exhale … as you focus on that hero who walked deeper into the forest, right to the edge of the trees. And there, just before the place where the world ended and the nothing began, he saw the tree. It did not look like anything special to him, but he wasn't there to see the tree: he was here to claim the blade of majesty and power. He saw the sword stuck deeply into the base of the tree, the part where all life comes from. He grabbed it and pulled it out of the tree. It came out smoothly and easily. It was smaller and plainer than he'd imagined, hardly bigger than his hand, with a steel handle and a wickedly sharp blade," Megan said, trying to conjure the image of a scalpel without mentioning the name of the thing.

"He looked up at the tree. It was not beautiful enough, the branches were not perfectly symmetrical, the arrangement of flowers did not please his eye, parts of the trunk were too thick, or scarred by knotholes or disease. He thought he could improve that tree, prune it into better shape, he thought he knew best. So, he picked up the blade to make a cut, was about to plunge it into the tree, when the words of the wise old crone came back to him. He remembered what she'd told him: *You cannot cut the patient* tree because of the magic power in the blade. She explained it to him when she said, '*If you try to cut a patient* woman's tree or fruit, *something terrible will happen* to you.' He remembered her instruction — it's very important to *remember that instruction* — and pulled back the blade. He ran quickly from the forest to the outskirts of the village where the anger monster was.

"And perhaps you can allow yourself to see it, Tony, just see that monster — so full of anger and rage, so old. It's been there for a long, long time. Can you tell me what it looks like?"

"… stitches … s'in Piggy …"

"It has stitches. Well, well … And piggy, hmmm?" She had no idea what he meant and no time to explore it further. "Well that is interesting, but stitches or no, something needs to happen to this monster to save the hero, and for the hero to save others in the kingdom. What needs to happen, Tony?"

It was rubbish, of course: primal rage could not be cured in a session by slaying a mythical, symbolic monster. But it might help a little, and it would reassure Trotteur by giving him a clear memory of what they had done in the session. She would do her best to ensure it was all he remembered from his time in trance.

"… Must kill it."

"Yes, the anger monster needs to be destroyed. Now the hero slays the monster with his magic blade and perhaps you join in. You may even find that you become the hero, that *you are the hero* in this story, Tony. Allow yourself to puncture the monster. Let the rage leak out like air from a balloon, and let it drift away into the air, until the monster falls — empty and limp and floppy — down to the ground; and you feel so good, so satisfied, you have triumphed in this quest."

She almost smiled at the imagery of turning the erect libidinal urge of the knife into an orgasm of violence against rage itself, and returning Trotteur to a post-climactic stage of replete satisfaction.

"And, Tony, you will remember this part of the story in the front of your mind, very well, clear as a bell as the bell knells in the village." More of the mind-distracting nonsense phrases. "The people cheer, the anger is gone and you feel so proud and so good and it is time to return the knife to the dark forest where it belongs. So sleep, deeply. Keep going deeper as you just *relax* and you go *deeper and deeper* into the forest, walking the path you know well, back to the tree of the women. It's time to *put the blade down safely*, that's what the witch said he must do, or something terrible would happen, *put the blade down safely next to the patient* women's tree.

"On the hero walked," Megan said, using 'you' and 'he' interchangeably now, deepening the association in Trotteur's subconscious mind, hoping that it would hear the instructions to the hero as orders to himself. "And he walked along, feeling relaxed and relieved that the anger was gone, to the edge of the forest. And when he got to the women's tree, he began to *put the blade down safely* next to the tree. But then he saw one of the fruits of the tree. It looked so ripe, juicy and moist, that he was very tempted to cut into its sweet flesh, to stick the knife in and carve it open and let the ruby red juices flow. He picked up that beautiful gleaming knife, felt it in his hand, stronger than it looked, filled with power. He got excited at its power, at *his* power."

On a hunch, Megan snuck a glance at Trotteur's lap. Sure enough, she could see an erection straining against his trousers. Sick pervert. A part of her own mind registered that she seemed to have abandoned the ideal of non-judgemental, unconditional acceptance completely. She hoped it was only for this man.

"He took that knife and made to cut into that delicious, tempting, imperfect flesh, but as he did so, *Tony,*" she called to his subconscious with the use of his name, signalling it to play close attention to what followed, "something terrible happened. Let me tell you what happened."

Then Megan implanted the subliminal suggestion she'd earlier devised, and reinforced it with imagery and repetition. She finished by reiterating: "The tree and the fruit of tree of the *patient women must not and cannot be hurt or cut* according to the magic of this place and the witch. Then, when he saw what he'd done, he came to his senses and he *remember*-ed what the witch said he must do with the knife: that he must *put the blade down safely* beside the women's tree. And he did this, and all was well. And he left the forest. He had slain the anger monster, put down the sword and could now lead a peaceful and happy life, free from anger. He felt no need to return to the witch because he had no more need of her ear or her advice."

Megan hoped his subconscious would heed this suggestion, too, and that he would stay the hell away from her in future.

"Now there are parts of this story, about slaying the monster of anger that you can remember clearly in the top and front of your mind, but you can allow the other parts to sink deeply, so deeply into yourself that you can't consciously remember them and that's okay because your subconscious mind will remember them for you without any effort, so you can just let them sink down deeply now. And the subconscious will remember what the conscious mind has already forgotten."

Satisfied that she'd done what she could, Megan proceeded onto the reawakening and reorientation phase, first bringing him up to a lighter level of trance, encouraging him to begin to be aware of where he was and the sounds he could hear, and suggesting to him that it felt like he'd been at this level of trance all the while. She made deliberately blatant and direct suggestions that he would in future feel much less angry, and then she returned him to full wakefulness.

Trotteur stretched his long frame, blinked several times before opening his eyes, and yawned.

"I must say I feel very relaxed," he said.

"That was the goal," she said, smiling. "I'll be on leave for the week or so, but —"

"Oh, are you going away?"

"— but Patience is already booking for after that, if you want to make another appointment on your way out. Else you can call when you feel you need an ear or some more advice." Which would be never, if the suggestion which she was now reminding his subconscious of, had taken effect.

"I do feel very good, like I've slain that anger monster." He winked at her. "But I don't think I was in trance, Megan, I can remember *everything*."

Megan's mouth went dry. The wink and his words could

mean he'd seen through it all. Or they might mean that he could only remember what he could remember — which felt to him like everything, but wasn't. There was no time to probe further; Trotteur was already moving out of the office.

She squeezed in one last suggestion. "That's how it works, Tony. When you're in trance, you're not unconscious, and afterwards, you're not amnesic. You will remember what you need to remember."

He had left, waving three fingers in greeting, and she'd sat, staring for long minutes into the ethereal heart of her dandelion paperweight, as though herself in trance.

Even now, hours later and lying on her bed, tickling Oedipus softly behind the ears, she had no idea whether it had worked. On balance, she thought probably not. It had been a long-shot — post-hypnotic suggestions were notoriously unreliable, especially if they went against the grain of what the subject truly and deeply wanted to do. It normally took many sessions, direct and indirect suggestions, and loads of reminders and repetitions to plant complex command suggestions. Usually, when clients wanted to change long-held patterns of behaviour — smoking or over-eating or panic reactions — she recorded hypnotic inductions for them, and sent them home with the instruction to listen daily for at least two weeks.

So, she was doubtful about the possibility that one session of indirect and subliminal suggestions would alter Trotteur's behaviour. She may well have achieved nothing, but she had at least tried — done her best to stay his hand for the period before his hearing and while she was out of action — and she felt better for the effort.

If she was honest with herself, perhaps this session had been more about her own issues than his. It had met her desire to feel she was doing something, and her need to distract herself from the grief which threatened to overwhelm her. Moreover, in the hypnosis session, she'd done almost all the talking, which meant she didn't have to listen to him, all the while faking empathy and hiding her revulsion.

Her phone rang and, more from habit than a wish to talk to anyone, she checked the caller display. It was Mike, finally returning the message she'd left on his voicemail that morning, a message which had begged him to call back urgently.

So, there was still one more thing to do before this longest of bad days' work was done. She took a large gulp of wine, and answered the call.

37
PLOTTING

Something will have to be done. Something will have *to be done*, he thinks as he takes the entry logbook from the guard at the gatehouse. Ordinarily, he amuses himself by giving patently false names as a protest against the time-wasting uselessness of this "security" ritual. Since he started therapy, he has been working his way through the emotions. It pleases him that entry logs in office blocks, hospitals and gated communities across this city have documented their visits from Mr R.U. Happy, Mr I.M. Sad, Mr B. Cross.

Who should he be today? Not Mr Happy. No, certainly not that. Perhaps Mr Disappointed, though that seems too mild a word for what he is feeling now.

Mr Calm and Relaxed: that is who he had been after the hour with Megan — at least that part of the session had worked for him. He had felt really rather good as he made his way to the Gehenna that was Johannesburg Central Hospital's gynaecology and maternity unit — until the moment he'd seen the notice. It stood out, new and virgin white against the old posters and yellowing notices on the board. The gap where two slips had been torn off were like missing teeth in an uneven, mocking smile.

As he read it, a wave of ire washed away the lingering relaxed contentment. He ripped the notice off the board and crumpled it in his fist, looking around suspiciously at the staff and patients in the unit. Could this possibly be about him?

Spinning on his heel he stalked back to his car which was parked in the dark, litter-strewn, bowels of the hospital. There he sat for a moment, trying to calm himself. He loosened the collar which was a noose around his throat, and opened a window, but the rage rose through him and flowed hot into his hands. They clenched into fists and hammered again and again and again against the steering wheel. A short woman in too-tight shoes walking past the row of parked cars looked at him with a raised eyebrow.

Useless cretinous bitch, he thought.

Then he screamed it out of the window, "Useless cretinous bitch!"

It soothed him a little to see her jump with fright and trot away from him. He unfolded the paper, smoothing it flat with hands that were not entirely steady. He fiddled with the settings on his phone so that his number would be blocked, and keyed in the number printed on the tear-off slips. The solicitous voice which invited him to leave his details gave no name, but none was necessary. He recognised its tone and cadence.

That voice, which this very afternoon had lulled him into relaxing and listening to stories, now fanned the fury which was burning inside.

What did she know about him? Who had she been asking?

What had she been saying? He needed to shut her up, so that no more treacherous little words could trickle out of that luscious mouth. He had to stop the oozing and the seeping. Had to reign back in the wayward thoughts that were increasingly spinning out away from his control.

It took him the whole drive over to this wretched yuppie squatter-camp to calm himself, to make the connection between the pinned notice at the hospital and the reply to a survey on "the patient's experience of gynaecological services" which had been copied to his email address by Miss Acron, one of his more beautiful and satisfied patients.

His hand is steady now as he waves it in spurious greeting to the guard who lifts the boom, and steers his vehicle along the rows of nearly identical cluster houses, all built to some idiot's idea of a Tuscan village, all bizarrely out of place in the heart of this African metropolis.

He is certainly disappointed. She has gone down in his estimation, despite her fine eyes and burnished hair. Even as a therapist, he has no more respect for her. Slay the anger monster, indeed! Did she really think he was stupid enough to fall for such puerile drivel? She is no better than some charlatan performer in a second-rate theatre. And he is no planted patsy in the audience, paid to play along with her silly games. Games that she has been trying to play inside his head while all the while she is plotting against him.

How dare she?

What he needs to do is arrange a little something to get Miss Wright's focus back where it belongs — off his affairs and squarely back on her own tawdry little life. In his experience, there is nothing like a personal crisis to help one prioritise, to bring home what really matters in life. But he will have to find out more about the interfering Miss Wright, more than the bare bones of information he has gleaned from the clinic's staff directory, the telephone book and a quick internet search. She keeps her life remarkably private, does Miss stick-your-nose-where-it-doesn't-belong Wright.

What does she love? What would she hate to lose?

He drives slowly past a unit with a neglected front garden behind a palisade fence. The kikuyu lawn which comprises most of the front garden is looking parched in this late summer heat. A fat Golden Retriever is energetically digging up one of the few flowering shrubs. Perhaps it is digging for an old buried bone. These obsessions with things long buried ...

The dog's size is evidence of its greed. Really, life can be quite serendipitous on occasion — tossing you the very opportunities you need, like a hunk of meat to a hungry dog.

It is clear now what needs to be done. He leaves the complex and heads back for the clinic, humming an old melody about identical houses made of ticky-tacky. He must check his operating list for tomorrow because he wants to plan the day; he has some shopping to do before he returns here.

38
SOFT AS A BREATH

Megan looked down at the small pills cupped in her hand. "Two? Are you sure?"

"Doctor's orders," the nurse said cheerfully, handing Megan a plastic cup of water. "Swallow this one and pop the other one under your tongue and let it dissolve there. I know it's a difficult day for you, but we'll try to get it over with as quick as we can. Now take your pre-meds."

Megan did as she was directed and lay back against the uncomfortable pillows of her bed. She was in what Wade had called the "nay" ward, along with three other women. Their faces, bare of makeup, looked pale and vulnerable. One of the women, in the bed adjacent to hers, was asleep. The other two each had a man sitting beside them, holding their hands while talking softly. Megan stared down at her own hands — rings off, nails bare of polish, a white plastic bracelet labelled with her details fastened around one wrist.

The chair beside her bed was empty. Mike had said he'd catch the first plane out of Cape Town that morning, but he wasn't here yet. She'd told her family and Wade to stay away until after the operation, thinking it would be easier not to have to deal with them, but now she felt very alone.

The nurse came back a little while later, with two orderlies in tow. They lowered the backrest so that she lay horizontally on the wheeled bed, and set off out of the ward down the corridor which lead to the operating theatres. Megan stared up at the lights passing overhead, but this immediately brought Alta Cronjé's experience to mind and so she made herself look down at the hospital gown she was wearing instead. She felt dizzy. Perhaps the pre-meds were kicking in.

The gown was patterned with little blue birds that reminded her of the Twitter bird.

"What's happening?" the Twitter bird asked in its perpetual blue box.

What's happening is this, she should tweet now, I'm rolling along, rolling along with blue birds on my boobs. No, she couldn't tweet that, couldn't tweet now — how absurd. The medicine must be making her loopy. And drowsy. Her eyes wanted to close just as if she herself was going into a trance. She had to explain something to the orderly walking at her head.

"I'm not going into trance," the word came out *tance*. "I'm going to the theatre, but not for a play. For an operation. S'going to dilate and curett— curat— . . . cure me. Doc Weinberg, not Doc Khumalo. Is a doctor, not a soccer player."

She was battling to speak, her tongue was thick in her mouth, her head was heavy and her mind muddled. It was hard to focus her gaze, even on the little blue birds, so she closed her eyes and floated for a bit.

They opened when she was lifted and transferred to the operating table. She could see the form of a man in green surgical scrubs connecting her to various monitors which beeped and glowed as he switched them on.

"I'm alive then?" she tried to say out loud, but what came was a slurred, "Live'en."

"Oh hello, Mrs Wright, you're awake? I'm Dr Matthee, your anaesthetist. I'm just getting you hooked up so when the doctor comes we can send you straight to lala land." A woman in scrubs and a mask appeared at his side, and handed him a folder which he consulted before continuing, "I see from your chart that you've never had any adverse responses to anaesthetic before, is that right?"

What she wanted to say was that she felt cold and wanted a nice duvet to cover her, but she didn't try to respond; it seemed like too much effort to form the words. Her tongue seemed to be a long way away from her brain.

"Excellent, here he is now. We can begin. The doc will be down at the action end of things, and I'll be sitting behind you here, at the pretty end," said the anaesthetist, rubbing her cheeks with his warm hands.

It felt nice. She allowed her eyes to close again.

"Oh, are you doing this surgery? I thought she was Weinberg's patient?"

"He had some minor emergency — a domestic crisis with a pet, I think. So, when they asked for a substitute, I volunteered to help. She's all mine, now. Aren't you, Megan?"

Megan's eyes opened wide, staring up into the dark sherry-coloured eyes which glittered above the green mask covering his mouth. She opened her mouth wide to scream, but only a muted gargle came out. She struggled to lift herself, but her heavy, leaden body wouldn't obey her brain's commands. With all her might she tried to force the words of protest out as loudly and clearly as she could.

"No. Not him. Not my doc'r!"

"That's right," he said in a voice intended to reassure others even while it terrorised her. "I'm not your usual doctor. But Dr Weinberg couldn't make it and so you'll be in my hands today. But there's no need to worry, I'll do a perfect job, I promise. You'll be as good as new — better actually!" He laughed. "Doctor knows best."

"He can't!" She had to make the nurse and anaesthetist understand, she had to stop this. "He's m'patient!"

"Oh dear, we are a little muddled from the pre-med, aren't we? You're *my* patient, Megan. Now be calm like a good girl while Dr Matthee here sends you to sleep. Sister, you're blocking my light standing over there. Please move to the other side and give me some room over here … A bit further back, please … Thank you."

Megan tried to scream, but she could no longer find her lips on her face. His voice spoke again, from close by to where she screamed and sobbed inside the immobile lump that was her silent, unresponsive body.

"You can go ahead, Martin."

"Her BP seems a bit high. I'll have to keep a close eye on it here."

"Perfect. Sister, see if you can be of any assistance to Dr Matthee. I really have no need of your help."

Megan felt a faint touch at her right ear. Raising her impossibly heavy eyelids a fraction, she saw that he had pulled down his mask and was leaning over to her ear.

"I do like to send my ladies to sleep with a little message, Megan, and now it's time for *you* to listen to *my* words."

"Okay, Mrs Wright," came the loud voice from behind her. "You seem quite out of it already, but I'm going to count you down anyway, okay? I'll count backwards from one-hundred and you see how far you can go before you fall asleep. Here we go: one hundred … ninety-nine …"

She tried to focus her mind on the loud voice which was counting, tried desperately to shut out the dark whisper.

"… ninety-eight … ninety-seven …"

His voice was as soft as a breath, yet she heard his words as clearly as if he'd shouted them. "I'm going to rip out your womb, Megan, because it's as rotten and useless as the rest of you."

"… ninety-"

39
BATTLE OF WORDS

The first thing Megan saw was a small, golden pyramid. She blinked. Sitting on top of the cabinet beside the hospital bed where she lay curled on her side was a triangular plastic box of stacked chocolate balls wrapped in gold foil. There was a large tag attached, with something printed on it. Blinking again, she focused her gaze on the writing.

"Chocolate cures everything, and is cheaper than therapy," it said.

"Hey, friend. Are you back?"

Wade sat beside her bed, holding one of her hands in both of his. She could see she was in a small hospital room, private, from the looks of it.

"Oh Megs, I'm so, so sorry." Cayley was there, too. She leaned over Megan and scooped her up into a tight, bony hug. "It's so horrible for you."

Megan's eyes were hot with tears. Pain ached deep inside her, but another, more urgent awareness intruded. Her racing heart thudded in her chest. Something was wrong.

"What's wrong? What happened?" she asked.

"Don't you remember?" Wade said, frowning.

"You lost the baby, Megs, I'm sorry. They had to do a D&C," said Cayley, now arranging the cushions more comfortably behind Megan's head, and running a cool hand down her cheek.

"I know that." Megan pushed herself up onto her elbows. The haze was clearing from her thoughts now. "But what did he do to me?

She pushed the bedclothes down and felt her belly, sliding her hands over it as if she could tell the damage wrought on the inside by running her hands over the outside.

"What did he do to me?" she pleaded, looking from one to the other of them.

"Are you feeling okay, Megs? Should I call a nurse?"

"Wade, get the chart out of there" — Megan pointed to the wire basket at the foot of the bed — "and tell me what was done to me. Cayley, you need to take a look under the blankets and tell me what you see."

Cayley looked at her blankly for a few moments, and then said, "You want me to check out your vajayjay?"

"Just do it, dammit!"

Wade and Cayley exchanged a glance, but Wade moved to get her chart and Cayley poked her head under the sheet.

"What can you see?" Megan demanded of them both.

"I'm no doctor," Wade began, "but from what I can figure out, they did something called a D&C, and your BP and temperature are fine."

"Cayley?"

Cayley pulled her head out. "Megs, really! I see undies. Ugly ones. And a pad. What else am I supposed to be looking for?"

"Please, Cayley, I need to know that nothing was … cut."

"Okaayy," Cayley said slowly.

She disappeared below the sheet again and Megan pulled her panties down. Wade turned his back on them both and furiously studied the medical chart.

"Right," came Cayley's voice from under the sheet. "Today's vajayjay report: all seems normal in appearance on the outside. I have no information on the inside. Satisfied?"

Not much reassured, Megan asked Wade, "What else? Does the chart say anything else?"

Wade turned a few pages. "Honest, sweets, it's in code. I can't —"

"Give it here." Megan snatched the chart from his hands. She was trying to decipher the notes and figures when a nurse, with the doleful eyes and drooping lids of an old basset hound, came into the room.

"How are you feeling, Mrs Wright?"

"It's Miss. Miss Wright," Megan snapped. Then she took a breath and tried to ask what she needed to know in a calmer voice. "Please, can you just please tell me exactly what happened in the surgery with me?"

"It was a bit of a strange one," said the nurse, attaching a blood pressure cuff to Megan's arm.

"Why, what happened?"

"Well, first of all, Dr Weinberg was supposed to be operating, but he couldn't come. They say his dog was poisoned! Can you believe it? Then he was scared maybe someone wanted to break in to his house, and he didn't want to leave his wife and —"

"So Dr Trotteur operated?" Megan interrupted.

The blood pressure cuff inflated, signalled a reading to the monitor and then deflated again.

"He was supposed to, was all gloved up and he started, but then next thing he was bleeding all over the table and the floor. But not into you," the nurse hurriedly assured Megan as she removed the cuff.

"Oh!"

"Yes, he'd cut himself. His hand must have slipped or something, but he cut his other arm. Quite badly, too. They say he needed loads of stitches. Then, of course, he couldn't do you, so they had to wait until Dr Maseko finished the surgery he was busy on, then he came and did your D&C."

"Is that all he did?"

"Yes, that's all you were scheduled for. It was just a bit of a delay, but everything went fine. Dr Maseko is perfectly competent, you know." She said the last part a bit fiercely.

"And I've still got my … there was no hysterectomy or any other excisions?"

"No, why should there be? It was a routine D&C."

Cayley and the nurse were staring at her as if she was behaving very strangely, but Wade's concerned gaze told her he understood.

"How are you feeling," asked the nurse. "Any pain?"

"I'm fine" Megan blew out a deep breath and felt her shoulders slump in relief. "I'm fine." It was true, she was. Her plan had worked. It had come down to his words against hers, and hers had triumphed. "But I'm very sore. I'll take something for the pain."

The nurse looked confused, but counted a couple of red and green capsules into a medicine cup, and placed it on the bedside table.

"You'll be able to leave this afternoon; we just need Dr Maseko to check and release you." The nurse made a note on the chart, dropped it into the wire basket at the base of the bed, and walked out of the room.

"Want to tell me what that was all about?" Cayley said.

"Later." Megan nodded her chin in the direction of the doorway where Moira Wright was just entering.

"Oh, my dearest, my pretty little girl, how are you?" She leaned over to kiss Megan and enveloped her in a cloud of cloying, spicy perfume.

"Okay. I guess."

"My poor baby. Is there anything I can get you?"

Megan winced at the word "baby", shook her head.

"It's terrible for a mother to see her child suffering. You never stop being a mother, you know, even when your babies are all grown up."

"Mo-om," said Cayley.

Her mother meant well, Megan knew, even if her every word salted the wound.

"Would you like to come home when you're released? I can pop you back in your old bed, in your old bedroom, feed you up and take good care of you?"

"No." God, no. "Thanks."

"Well, at least it's all over now, Megan, it's all behind you and you can just move on with your life." Mrs Wright patted her daughter's shoulder.

"Mom!"

"What?" Mrs Wright asked Cayley, her voice already beginning to sound injured. "I'm sure Megan agrees with me, don't you dear?"

"You think this is a good thing? That it's all worked out for the best? That my baby is dead."

"Well, really! I wouldn't put it quite that way, dear."

"How would you put it?"

There was a loud retching noise from behind Mrs Wright.

"I feel sick, I'm going to puke!" said Cayley.

"What's the matter, baby?" asked Mrs Wright, transferring her attention from Megan to Cayley.

"That salad I had in the canteen. It's making me feel sick. I need to throw up. Where's the bathroom? Mom, help me," said Cayley, gagging exaggeratedly.

"Oh, dear. If it's not one, it's the other. This way, dear. But please don't be sick until we're at a loo."

Mrs Wright took Cayley, who was doubled-over and making retching noises, and hustled her out of the room. At the door, Cayley turned her head and, behind her mother's back, winked at Megan and blew her a kiss, before hauling her mother away. The room was suddenly silent and still.

"Are you okay, Megs?"

"No. Not really," said Megan, and she began to weep.

Wade held her gently, silently handing her tissues, while she bubbled over with the mixture of loss and grief, fear and relief, emptiness and guilt. A pile of crumpled tissues later, as she was shuddering into silence, there was a new voice from the door.

"Uhm, I'm here." Mike stood just inside the room, looking uncomfortable. He held his phone in one hand and a bunch of cellophane-wrapped proteas in the other. Airport kiosk flowers.

"Hi," Megan said.

"Better late than never, I suppose," Wade said.

Mike gave Wade a sour look. "What's that supposed to mean?"

"I'll see you later, Megs," Wade said. With his eyes on Mike, he added, "Press the button if you need help," and left.

"Wanker," Mike muttered.

He put the flowers on top of the bed alongside Megan. She stared at them. They looked a little battered, the ends of the petals were beginning to brown and fold over into dry, sharp points.

Mike walked over to the window and peered out. Then he sat down in the chair beside the bed with a long sigh, as if he'd spent an exhausting day on his feet, and ran a hand through his blonde hair. It was getting long, it needed a cut. He puffed out his cheeks with a breath, looked around the room and put his phone down on the cabinet beside the bed. Buying time.

Eventually he looked directly at Megan. "Well?"

"Excuse me?"

"I mean, what happened?"

"When?"

"Huh?"

"What happened when? What exactly do you want to know? What happened when I was pregnant? What happened

296

when I had a scan and they found no heartbeat? What happened when I went home alone last night and came in alone this morning to have the remains cut out of me? What happened in the op, or after? You'll have to be a bit more specific, Mike, you've missed so much."

"Ah, come on Meggy, don't be like that."

"Like what?"

"All pissed off at me. It's not my fault you miscarried. I didn't do anything."

"Except run away when you found out I was pregnant. And stay away when I decided to keep it. Except for not being here for me the only time I've ever really needed you."

"Meggy …"

"Don't Meggy me!"

"Okay, then, Megan. Happy now? Look, I'm sorry it happened, sorry you had to go through all this shit. But maybe, in a little while, you'll, you know, see that it's for the best that it's … gone."

"It was *not* for the best. And it's not gone, it's dead!"

Megan snatched the pyramid of chocolates and threw it at his head. He deflected it with a raised arm. With a loud crack, golden balls rolled in every direction across the floor.

"I wanted that baby! I. Wanted. It. And I needed you here, with me. But you just headed for the hills." Megan could feel self-pity rising inside, constricting her chest and closing her throat. "You probably even found someone there to comfort you."

It was a shot in the dark. Later, she couldn't even be sure what had made her say it, but the dull flush which coloured his face and the quick flick of his glance to his phone told her she was right.

"Ahh." It was a short cry, an expulsion of breath and pain. "You did, didn't you?"

"Look, you've got to understand, Meggy. It meant nothing, she's no one —"

"That's supposed to make me feel better, is it? That you cheated on me, not for some grand love, but for a nobody who means nothing to you?"

"It was just … I just felt so alone. You were all focused on the pregnancy and I —"

"You're saying it's my fault for neglecting you?" The self-pity was gone now, replaced by anger and contempt. "Do you know, Mike, that until now, until this very moment, I never comprehended the full extent of your narcissism?"

"There you go, therapizing again! Can't you speak plain English?"

"Fair enough. Here it is in plain English: You're a selfish pig! Now bugger off — we're finished."

Mike's face was red, his features thick with anger and resentment. He looked like a spoiled boy thwarted in a game.

"I need to get my stuff from your place."

"Any time. Just call ahead so I can make sure I'm not home. And don't forget to leave your key." She shouted the last words at him as he stalked out of the room. "Bastard," she said.

The word came out softly, almost dispassionately; she thought her rage might be spent. But then she saw his phone on the cabinet beside her. Seizing it, she eased herself off the bed and walked gingerly to the door, her breath hissing with the pain. She stuck her head out into the corridor and yelled, "And you can take your bloody phone with you!" as she hurled the phone after him.

At the sound of her voice, he turned to face her. His hands fumbled to catch the phone, but it slipped through his fingers and hit the floor hard.

It wasn't very mature, Megan knew, not very evolved, but it *was* very satisfying to see him on his hands and knees, groping about on the floor, trying to pick up the pieces of shattered metal, plastic and pride.

40
STUCK PIG

The bitch. The dirty, stinking, filthy bitch!

He stares at the row of neat black stitches which wind down and across his left forearm, creeping through the flesh like some many-legged insect. Reminding him of that other time. That other place.

She did this to him, he knows it. She did something or said something in that wretched session of hypnosis, and it has contaminated him. Infected his mind and subverted his will. When he lifted that scalpel, its blade glinting in the bright light of the overhead lamp, when he brought it down to her tender, rounded flesh just to make a small, satisfying nick — the real cutting and slicing would come later, after his hands had reached inside the core of her — the blade had refused to move closer.

No, that was wrong.

His hand refused to move the blade closer. It stuttered and shook. Baffled, he grabbed his right hand with his left, steadied it, and made to move the blade into her flesh.

And then, unbelievably, impossibly, his own hand turned on him.

It burned like a flame and bled like a stuck pig ... no, not that, never that. It bled like a ... like a river.

He stood like a simpleton, burning and bleeding, staring bewildered at the gaping wound, until Martin Matthee ordered the nurse to lead him away. To be stitched.

To be scarred.

Again.

He had cut his own arm. No. That, too, was incorrect. She had done it. She had done it just as much as if she'd been holding the scalpel. She had made his body revolt against itself with her vile, treacherous words. She had stitched him up.

He'd planned to kill her fat, filthy dog, but when he saw the list of scheduled surgeries, he decided to use the poisoned meat on Dr Weinberg's mongrel instead, and to kindly volunteer to do the surgery of Megan Wright. A clever substitution, a neat plan.

But she'd ruined it. Ruined him.

You could never trust a woman, liars and lie-ers, they were all the same. They said one thing while really their words were doing something else to you. He would like to cut out her tongue. He would like to cut out all their tongues.

What else has she done to him, how much does she know, who else knows, who has she told?

And who has told her? Ah, yes. That's the real question, the mother-lode. A part of his mind registers the bitter irony of the term. His mothers — the first and all the others — had been empty of any value. Empty rotten whores and holes, the lot of them. Just as she was — 'n o-thing, wasn't that what Hamlet called them?

And one, at least one, of the o-things has been tittle-tailing and tattling. So, which little she-dog has been yapping away to Megan

Wright? Which other dirty, stinking girl will he have to silence before he finishes his unfinished business with Miss-fucking-Wrong and terminates his therapy permanently?

41
LITTLE BOXES

Megan stared at the two brown cardboard boxes in front of her — one big and one small, but both, as it turned out, too large for purpose. Oedipus sniffed at the boxes and then flung himself down on the carpet with a deep sigh.

Megan had collected all of Mike's belongings from the townhouse and dumped them unceremoniously into the larger of the two boxes which now contained his toothbrush and comb, a few CDs (Eminem and Radiohead, mostly), several copies of SA Rugby Magazine from the top of the toilet cistern, some underwear, a pair of jeans and a few shirts from the wardrobe in the bedroom, and from under the bed, several dusty socks and a pair of running shoes. There were so few of his things in the townhouse that they barely filled two-thirds of the box. Perhaps that, right there, should've clued her to the fact that Mike had never been committed to her, or to their relationship.

She scanned her bookshelf, extracted two volumes and

tossed them into the box. *The Peter Pan Syndrome: Men Who Never Grow Up*, and *Why is it Always About You? The Seven Deadly Sins of Narcissism* — those should provide him with more edifying reading than a magazine about rugby.

After a moment, she took down a book for herself: *Emotional Vampires: Dealing with People Who Drain You Dry.* Healer, heal thyself.

Without Mike's stuff, little as it was, the rooms somehow looked even more bare and empty. For perhaps the first time, she was seeing — really seeing clearly — the space in which she lived: blank walls, windows hung with ill-fitting, hand-me-down curtains from her mother, a couple of dead or dying potted plants, an absence of personal touches. The stark bareness had been disguised for her until now, draped in hopes and dreams, and furnished with the fantasy of what she and Mike might have been.

She'd been in a kind of limbo — renting this anonymous place, not committing to as much as a change of wall paint while she waited to see how the relationship would go, whether they would move in or perhaps even buy a place together. She'd been so busy doing the nothing of watching and waiting that she'd never really set down roots and created a nest for herself.

Oedipus lifted his head hopefully when she hoisted the box onto one hip and walked to the front door, but he sighed and let it drop again when she walked past the rack where his lead hung. Megan marched outside and placed the box squarely in the middle of the front path. Perhaps it would rain soon. She went back inside, locked the door behind her and shot the deadbolt for good measure. Then she approached the other, smaller box and allowed herself to dwell on that other emptiness — the void inside.

She'd never truly felt pregnant, never fully attached to more than the *idea* of having a baby, let alone forged a personal bond with the life that she'd thought was growing inside her. So why did she feel so empty, so hollow? The baby felt more real now, in its absence, than it ever had been in its presence. Inside the second box was the sum total of her purchases for the new baby: two books on pregnancy. It was as if she'd been researching some intellectual enterprise. Where were the bibs and booties that every broody mother starts collecting? Where were the Winnie-the-Pooh wallpaper borders, the tiny teddy bears, the soft shawls and receiving blankets? She'd invested as little into the pregnancy as she had into the townhouse.

A superstitious thought intruded. Maybe she'd jinxed the pregnancy with her lack of attention and connection. Perhaps it was precisely because she'd never really bonded with the little soul inside her that it never took hold, that it shrivelled up and withered away. *Blighted* — that was the word Weinberg had used, maybe she'd blighted it with her doubts and ambivalence.

She told herself to stop being stupid. After all, fully one third of first pregnancies ended in miscarriage. She wondered how she knew this fact. Perhaps she'd read it in one of the pregnancy books; certainly, Weinberg had never told her. They didn't tell you the potentially awful news while they were confirming your pregnancy and congratulating you. They only told you once it had already happened — cold comfort, indeed.

She needed to make some changes in her life, and they

would begin here and now. That very weekend, she'd start looking at new properties. She would choose something that pleased purely her, something with lots of light and airy space. She would buy, not rent, and put down roots — literally as well as emotionally. She would plant a garden with sapling trees, and bulbs destined to emerge far in the future. She would commit to herself and her home. She'd buy paintings and hang them on the walls, clothe her bed in fine Egyptian cotton, stack her shelves with something more than books, stock her cupboards with couscous and cake flour and gelatine — and learn how to cook with them. She would heal herself and feather her nest, and start something new.

This place would be easy to leave, she thought, as she wandered restlessly from room to impersonal room, Oedipus trailing in her wake. In fact, she needed to get out of it soon or she'd go nuts. Everyone had advised her to take a few days off after the miscarriage and operation, to rest and recuperate. But one day at home had been enough to convince her that she needed to be back at work, needed the challenges of clients to distract her from her grief and self-absorption.

She picked up the phone and dialled. "Hi, Patience, it's me. How are you?"

"How are *you*? Are you all right? Can I help you?"

"I'm okay, but I need to come back to work."

She waited for Patience to say it was too soon, that she should rest some more, take it easy. But Patience said nothing and Megan felt a moment's intense gratitude and love for the woman who knew her so well.

"Will you call all the clients we had to cancel, and re-instate their appointments? Starting from tomorrow. Just don't call Tony Thomas."

"Not yet or not at all?"

"Not at all. Not ever."

42
DOUBTS

Having been so determined to be back at work, she was irritated to discover the next day that she wished she were back at home instead. It was so difficult to focus, to screen out all the thoughts about the miscarriage, the break-up with Mike and the case against Trotteur, that she didn't think she was being of much help to her clients. All her attention and energy seemed to have been used up in her first appointment — with Alta Cronjé.

Alta had confirmed that she was doing well, though her energy had seemed low. She said she was keen to get going with her idea to learn more about being a counsellor, and reported that her husband, Johan, said he felt like he had the "old Alta" back again. The pregnancy was progressing well; the doctor had told her it was a boy and Johan was thrilled. Her daughter, Marlien, could hardly wait to become a big sister.

Alta's big news was about the hearing at the Health Profession's Council. She'd been notified that it was scheduled for two weeks' time and if Trotteur had not already been notified of the fact and summoned to appear, he soon would be. Megan wondered if he were in the clinic at this moment, or whether he, too, had taken leave following his injury. Wherever he was, she intended to stay well clear of him.

"I thought, you know, that when this happened, when the time came when I could face him eye-to-eye and take him down, that I would feel great and, like, excited," Alta said, sighing deeply.

"And you don't?"

"Not really, hey. It's a bit of an anti-climax. Mostly I feel tired. Sick and tired of the whole thing. I just wish it was all over, that I could rest and relax."

"You want to get on with your life."

"Exactly. It's enough now, you know? It's gone on for long enough. Too long, actually. I can't handle it if it drags on for ever."

After Alta, the rest of the day seemed to comprise a series of no's to a succession of clients.

"No, Yvonne, even though your husband is in the terminal stages of cancer and is draining the life and love out of you and the children with his bitterness and self-pity, you may not put a pillow over his head and smother him."

"No, Stephen, I do not think that going ahead and having an affair with your daughter's tennis coach will re-energise and enrich your marriage."

"No, Zahira, I don't think that because your teenage son has accessed an online porn site that he's a pervert who should be sent to Boys' Town."

"No, Maria, however sorry he may say he is, I don't think

309

that he'll never hit you again. In fact, if you do go back, I can pretty much guarantee you that he will hit you again, with worse to follow."

Megan had been on the receiving end of a no, too — from Pumla Phahlane.

"I've changed my mind, I can't testify against him."

"Pumla, please, we really need you."

"No, I'm sorry, I can't help you."

"Why? Has something happened?"

"I just— I'm afraid. He— I just can't do it anymore. I'm sorry for that, but please don't contact me again," she'd said, her voice tight with fear, and the line had gone dead.

Now Megan sat with Henk Labuschagne, the self-confessed infidel, who was rambling on about his marriage, his back problems, and his craving to visit the masseuse again, and Megan was battling to present even a semblance of attention. What was wrong with people? Why did they persist in making stupid decisions? And what was she doing here when she could be at home, curled up in bed eating ice-cream, and thinking of nothing? Why had she—

Her thoughts were interrupted by loud banging and shouting coming from the reception room. Then her office door crashed open and an enormous man, red-faced and broad-shouldered, stormed in. Quick as a flash, Henk leapt over the back of the couch and hid behind it.

"It's your fault! All your fault!" The huge man pointed a finger at Megan. His face was glazed with tears and his hands, his whole body was trembling. He picked up a stack of books from the table and hurled them at the shelves behind her desk.

"Crap, it's all crap! That's what I think of it, what I think of *you*. You were supposed to help her, get her better and now look what's happened!"

"Sir, please," Megan said. "What's the matter?"

She could see Patience behind him, speaking softly but furiously into a telephone, no doubt calling security.

"She's dead, that's what's the matter! *And* my little son. And what must I do now — tell me that. What am I supposed to tell Marlien?"

"Marlien? Are you Johan Cronjé? What's happened? Are you talking about Alta?"

At the sound of the name, the man's arms fell limply to his sides and his head dropped and swung wretchedly from side to side.

"My Alta, my love. She's dead. She killed herself."

"What! What are you talking about? I saw her this morning, just a few hours ago. And she was fine."

"She couldn't have been fine. She's killed herself — here in the underground parking. She never came home; I came to find her and she was there. She's still there, in the car, dead and all pale and … She must have done it straight after her session with you this morning. What did you say to her? *What*?"

"Nothing! I … Nothing that would —" Megan stammered. Her chest felt icy and empty, hollowed out by cold shock. "Are you sure?"

Johan Cronjé shuddered, gripped by a paroxysm of wracking sobs. Before she could get herself together or think of a thing to say, three men in security uniforms burst through the door and seized him by the arms, dragging him backwards out of the office.

"Stop!" shouted Megan. "That's not necessary. This man's wife has just died. He's upset. Let go of him right now!" When they hesitated, looking uncertain, she said firmly, "I'm fine. He's not dangerous, you don't have to restrain him. Now, let go of him."

They exchanged a look with each other, then released Johan Cronjé and stepped backwards. Megan took hold of Johan's shoulder, shook him gently and said, "Come, Johan, show me. Take me to her, take me to Alta."

Johan Cronjé wiped his sleeve across his face and stumbled out of the office, followed by Megan and the security guards. They walked down the corridor and made the trip down to the second level of the basement parking in silence. Megan's mind was a whirl of confusion. There had to be some mistake, had to be. It couldn't be Alta.

In the basement, they pushed past the small crowd clustered outside the lifts and walked past the rows of parked cars. Megan's mind detached from the bewildering maelstrom of emotions inside. She noticed the oil patches and tyre marks on the floor, smelled the exhaust fumes, and heard the buzzing of a fluorescent strip light flickering overhead.

In the far corner of the garage was a red Toyota Corolla. Parked behind it was a police vehicle, a blue light flashing mutely on its roof. A female police officer was standing beside the open door on the driver's side of the car. A male officer was unwinding yellow tape from a large reel and cordoning off the area with it.

"Uh-uh. You can't come here, lady," he said, stepping forward to block Megan's path.

"I know her. I'm her psychologist. I saw her for an appointment this morning."

"You were supposed to be helping her and now look, just look!" she heard Johan Cronjé shouting from somewhere behind her. "You were supposed to help her!" The words echoed in the basement.

The officer looked at her with keen eyes, then stepped aside to let her pass with a warning not to touch anything.

Megan made her feet take the final steps to the car, forced herself to look inside.

Alta sat in the driver's seat, her head tilted back against the head-rest, her lips and face chalky pale and blank of expression, her eyes mercifully closed. But what drew Megan's horrified gaze was the blood — dark and sticky-looking. Alta's right arm hung limply at her side, but her left arm lay palm-up in the lap of what had been a yellow dress. Across the wrist were two deep, parallel cuts. Trails of blood, now drying into cracked crusts, led into the red pool which stained her lap and the seat, and spilled into the foot well. Megan retreated from the car, from the sight of her client reduced to this.

"I can't believe it," Megan said hoarsely to the police officers, to Johan Cronjé. "I just can't believe she did this. What did she use?"

"We found this." The police woman held up a plastic evidence bag with a scalpel inside. A smear of blood stuck the sides of the plastic bag together.

"A scalpel? Never! She'd never have used that."

"We found it in her hand, lady. She meant to off herself, for sure. She sliced open her leg, too," the male officer said. He gave a low whistle.

"What?"

"Here." He demonstrated a cutting motion against the inside top of his thigh, near the groin.

The detached part of Megan's mind remembered how once, at a medical conference, she'd discussed methods of suicide with a forensic pathologist who'd stated that never, in her twenty-five years of practising, had she seen a successful suicide by cutting the wrists, because the method was fraught with problems. It was difficult and very painful to cut deep enough to sever the artery. Most attempters used their dominant hand to cut their other arm first, then didn't have the strength to cut the wrist of their dominant hand, especially when tendons were severed. It took a long time to bleed out from the wrists, and the cutter usually changed their mind and got help in time. There was a popular belief that cutting along the length of the forearm — "up the street, not across the road" — made death more likely, but this was more urban legend than fact. A deep slice across the radial artery would do the trick, but it would be slow.

Severing the bigger blood vessel in the leg would bring death much more quickly and surely.

"I don't believe it. I *can't* believe it. I saw her this morning and she was fine. A little tired perhaps, but there was nothing to suggest that she might do something like this."

"Nothing? Nothing at all?" asked the policewoman.

That was when the doubts began to creep in.

Megan walked to where Johan sat on a kerb, crouched over

his knees. When he threw off the hand she tried to rest on his shoulder, she went back up to her office and explained what had happened, in broken sentences, to a shocked Patience. Patience pressed a cup of hot sweet tea on her, but wisely refrained from trying to discuss it.

Megan sat at her desk, ignoring the tea and passing the heavy dandelion paperweight from hand to hand as she thought.

She felt shaken to her core. She must have missed something. But Alta had seemed fine, said she was doing well. There had been no sign, no hint of suicidality.

Or had there?

She thought back to the flowers which Alta had recently brought her. People planning suicide often gave tokens of love and appreciation away, as they said their thanks and goodbyes. What had Alta said that day, that day that felt like a thousand years ago but was really only weeks ago? Something about expressing thanks and appreciation. It was no good, thought Megan, she could not remember and the exact words would not be in her session notes.

She cast her mind back to that morning's session, tried to replay exactly what Alta had said. Was there anything that could have hinted at suicidal intention? No.

Maybe.

Alta had said she was tired, sick and tired of the whole issue with Trotteur. She wanted it to be over. Oh God, thought Megan, oh God. She'd thought Alta was talking about the scheduled Board hearing, that she was eager to get on with the rest of her life, but that had been her own interpretation of what her client had said. What Alta had *actually* said was that she wanted "it" all to be over, that she'd had enough and could not face it dragging on. Given what she'd done afterwards, the words now took on a completely different significance.

In the midst of her own grief and distraction, Megan had missed Alta's, had not seen the hopeless exhaustion, had not heard the despair in those words. She was truly an appallingly incompetent therapist. She'd completely missed Trotteur's psychopathy when it had sat before her in the charming form of Tony Thomas, and she'd now failed to see Alta's active suicidality when it, too, must have been staring her in the face.

What's more, Alta had ended her life at the clinic, right after her therapy session. That must be a message to her therapist.

Megan knew she was responsible. She hadn't saved Alta, not from her trauma, or from herself. It was all over now. Alta was dead. Pumla was refusing to testify. There was no case against Trotteur, no evidence and now no witnesses. She hurled the paperweight at the opposite wall. It dented the soft walling and bounced off, hitting the carpet and rolling under the wingback chair.

She had failed.

43
A CALL

He looks down and finds that his feet are carrying him along the corridors, up stairways and along more corridors, past office after office: gastroenterologists, orthopaedic surgeons, dermatologists, urologists. He is tired — he was up all night, his mind turning over and under — and now his thoughts are on the call he has just received, the call which propelled him out of his office, electrified him with an urge to run.

When his receptionist told him that Mrs Mdluli was calling from the HPCSA, elation filled his chest. This was the notification he'd been waiting for. The hearing had been cancelled due to a lack of evidence and witnesses. They were sorry to have troubled him and wished him a good day and would never trouble his precious time with petty grievances again.

But that was not what the Mdluli bitch had said.

What she had in fact said was that the Board had been notified that the complainant was now unfortunately deceased, but that the hearing was nevertheless going ahead as there was still a signed affidavit from the complainant. In addition, a witness, Mrs

Cronjé's psychologist — who had been treating her for psychological complications following the surgery performed on her by Dr Trotteur — had come forward and wished to make a submission to the panel assessing the case. Dr Trotteur was please to present himself at the Board's offices in Pretoria at the originally stipulated time and date. The relevant documents and statements would be forwarded to him by the day's end so that he could take legal advice, if he so desired.

He'd heard a hint of grim satisfaction in her voice. It made an itch rise inside him. At the centre of the anger, in the centre of himself, there was an itch which needed to be scratched.

Like the itch on his arm.

He needs to see it again.

He pushes back the sleeve of his white coat and stares down at the scarred ugliness. It is repulsive: black stitches knotting his flesh together, the raised red welt already beginning to form a ridged, thickening keloid. As he looks at it, it seems, for the briefest of moments, to move slightly, like the minute, sinuous writhing of a blood-red asp. And it itches so! He rubs at it. Scratches at it.

"Excuse me."

He looks up, realises he is standing in the middle of one of the corridors, blocking the way while he worries at the weal. A woman is trying to get past him.

Aren't they always?

She looks at him with an odd expression. Her eyes flick down to the scar, then back to his face, a mixture of pity and revulsion in her gaze.

"Bitch."

"Excuse me?"

He brushes past her and starts walking again, looking down at his feet. Right and left, right and left. His steps tap out a chant: What to do? What to do? It is a conundrum.

He glances to either side and discovers that he is passing the offices of one Megan Wright, Counselling Psychologist.

It is an answer to the question, he knows it. He knows best, after all.

He walks on, right and left, right and left, towards the wards, no longer looking down, but looking up into the faces of the people he passes. There is something suspicious in their expressions, something accusatory in the way they stare at him with their dull sheep eyes, that makes the itch stronger. He passes a group of nurses, chatting outside the entrance to the maternity unit. He recognises them, lifts a hand — not the disfigured one — in greeting as he walks by. They nod, seemingly respectful, but when he snaps his head around to look back, he sees that they are clustered in a tight huddle, whispering and looking slyly at him out of their ugly, misshapen faces.

Again, he feels the slight, snakelike shifting of the wound on his arm. It is warning him. He tries to stroke it gently, to soothe it still, but the fury and the hot itch are unsated. He scrapes at it with his nails, sighs at the temporary relief.

He walks on, back to his floor, back to his office. There are two men coming towards him. They are doctors, by their white coats. It is Weinberg and Matthee. They talk intently to each other. Are their whispers about him?

"Hello there, Gavin," he says, cramming his voice full of friendly nonchalance.

"Oh, hello Dr Trotteur."

Trotter! Again!

"It's Trotteur," he barks. "It's pronounced Tro-teur, not trotter. I'm not a pig!"

Both men stare at him. Their mouths form no words, but in their eyes he reads mistrust, doubt and censure.

"I'm not a pig, and I'm not blind, you know — I can see what you're thinking," *he spits out the words, and hurries on.*

He needs his office. He needs to sit in his safe chair at his desk, to gaze at the instruments on his wall and fondle the paperweight in the drawer until the cool calmness returns. He blows inside the cuff of his left arm.

It has stilled now. He can send it to sleep.

44
NIGGLE

Something tugged at a corner of Megan's mind.

She wished she could swat it away like a fly, but it would not be ignored. Instead, she tried to focus on the oak trees which formed a living arch over the narrow road where she walked. The first leaves were just beginning to turn yellow, responding to the hint of coolness in the late afternoon breeze. Autumn would soon be here, taking all of three weeks in this crazy-fast town, and then winter would arrive with the first cold snap.

Again, she felt the tug; there was something she'd forgotten, or something she'd not consciously recognised.

Realising that the only way to be rid of the niggle was to allow it to surface into awareness, Megan stopped resisting its intrusion. She gave herself over to the walk, allowed herself to be lulled by the rhythm of step after step as Oedipus trotted ahead, for once undistracted by scents on trees and lamp posts. She allowed her mind to go blank.

And there it was: the scalpel.

Alta's wounds had been made with a scalpel, and that simply made no sense. No matter how hard she tried, Megan could not see Alta somehow acquiring the surgical knife and then slicing herself open with it, not when she'd already been so damaged by such a knife. Then again, perhaps using that particular implement had been a message to the world, to Megan: this is what ruined me, now it has killed me. But no, that definitely did not fit. The woman who put up posters to register her disapproval of corrupt cops wasn't the sort of woman to leave cryptic, ambiguous clues. She would have signed out with a clear and decisive suicide note. And — another memory intruded — she would not have killed herself this way, leaving a bloody mess for her husband or a stranger to discover.

Megan had a vague idea that at Alta's first session, when she'd been assessing the client's levels of depression, they had discussed suicide. She was sure that Alta had said she would never kill herself because she believed it was wrong in the eyes of God, and also because of what it would do to her husband and daughter. And hadn't she also said something about pills and champagne being the way to go?

Megan quickened her step, she'd have to check her notes in the client file, but she felt more and more certain that she was right. Alta would not have done it, and she would never have done it this way. She'd been excited about the new plans for her life, delighted by the pregnancy and happy that her relationship with her husband was improving. She hadn't been tired of life, only of the ongoing issue with Trotteur, and she was hardly likely to have killed herself to avoid the very hearing she'd been working to bring about.

Megan felt energised, though not cheered, by her growing conviction that Alta's death had not been suicide. Whether or not Alta had killed herself, it was still Megan's fault. Either way, she should have seen it coming, and prevented it. At least she no longer felt quite so helpless. There were a few calls she needed to make now, and the first of them was to Alta's widower.

"Alta did not commit suicide, Johan, I'm sure of it. There'll be a post-mortem — there always is unless the death is clearly from natural causes. I'll find out the name of the forensic pathologist from the police and call them, tell them I suspect foul play. They'll check her over carefully, screen for substances, and hopefully we'll find out what really happened."

"You think ...?"

"I think she was murdered, Johan." The image of Alta in the bloodied car flashed before Megan's eyes. She saw again the arm lying palm-up in the lap, the two perfectly neat and symmetrical cuts across the wrist. "And if she was murdered, then I know who did it."

45

COMING UNDONE

When he walks into his rooms, he immediately sees two men sitting in the waiting room. They are not doctors. It strikes him that they do not seem to be with any of the waiting brood mares, either. He raises an eyebrow at Beth behind the reception counter.

"Oh, Dr Trotteur — there you are! These gentlemen have been waiting for you, they're from the South African Police Service."

Immediately, the waiting women lift their heads, look from him to the men, who now stand, staring at him with keen interest. Trotteur glowers at Beth Finch. Has she no discretion? No intelligence? She wilts beneath his gaze — he has that power — and continues in a softer, more acceptably respectful voice.

"This is" — she consults a piece of paper on the counter — "Sergeant Pieterse and Warrant Officer Mtibe, and they wish to speak to you."

"As you can see," says Trotteur, gesturing to the patients waiting in the room, "I'm very busy and now is not a good time." Sometimes one does need to state the obvious.

"We'll only take a few minutes, sir," says Mtibe and, before Trotteur can cut him off, he adds, "We want to talk to you about the death of one of your patients. Shall we go into your office or would you prefer to talk here?"

The eyes of the waiting patients are now wary as they stare at him. One cow turns to another and whispers something. He thinks he hears his name. Humiliation burns and churns inside.

The creature on his arm is awake again, it twists painfully, a fiery cord binding his flesh, but he forces himself not to touch it as he leads the way into the office, closing the door hard behind the two men. He sits down behind his desk and studies them over his steepled fingers. Sergeant Pieterse is a tall, bulky man in his thirties with buzz-cut brown hair. His cheeks are pocked with the pale craters that bear testament to a fierce clash with adolescent acne vulgaris. Trotteur stares at the disfigured skin with distaste before transferring his attention to Warrant Officer Mtibe. What the hell is a Warrant Officer anyway? This man is younger — probably not yet thirty — and smaller. He slouches comfortably in his chair and studies Trotteur with lazy eyes.

Trotteur ignores this insolence and addresses himself to Pieterse: "What can I do for you?"

"We need to ask you some questions regarding the suspicious death of one of your patients, a Mrs Alta Cronjé." Pieterse opens a small notebook and tests a yellow ballpoint pen against the paper.

"Suspicious? In what way?"

"You're not surprised, doc," says the one with the lazy eyes. "You knew she was dead, then?"

"I … I heard about it, yes."

"Who told you?"

"I can't remember who precisely. I must have heard it on the grapevine."

"Uh-hm," says Mtibe, with a sideways glance at Pieterse.

Pieterse writes something in his book, while Mtibe rocks back in his chair and gazes around the office. There is something unsettling about the soft, tuneless whistle which comes from his lips. Just who is in charge here?

"Well, sir," says Pieterse, "you may have heard —"

"On the grapevine," Mtibe interjects.

"— that Mrs Cronjé committed suicide, right here in the basement parking at Acacia Clinic. But that is not so."

"She didn't do it here? She did it somewhere else?" Trotteur asks.

Mtibe's chair comes down onto all four legs with a dull thud. "She didn't do it at all," he says.

"I'm afraid I don't understand." Under the desk, Trotteur rubs hard at his arm. The burning itch will no longer be denied.

"As per regulations, a post-mortem was conducted on Mrs Cronjé's remains," Pieterse says.

"How extraordinary. It seemed like a clear-cut case of suicide. From what I heard."

"On the grapevine," Mtibe says again. A slight smile twists his lips, but there is no humour in it, only menace.

Trotteur feels another itch — this time in the palm of the hand which longs to slice the impudence right off the man's face.

"Well, it's standard procedure, because it wasn't a 'natural causes' death. We also initially thought it was suicide, doc," continues Pieterse, "but the post-mortem kicked up some strange findings." From an inside pocket, he extracts a folded wad of paper

and holds it up. "Post-mortem report and affidavit from the forensic pathologist."

"Terrible," says Mtibe, examining a cuticle and nibbling at the edge of a nail, "what was done to that woman. And not just in that garage."

"Do you want to know what they found, doc? Apart from" — Pieterse reads laboriously from the report — "pale mucosae … reduced lividity … ah, here's it: fatal haemorrhage resulting from penetrating wound on inside of left wrist and forearm dissecting the radial artery and penetrating wound on left inside thigh severing femoral artery."

"I can't see how it concerns me."

"Number one" — Pieterse holds up a thick thumb — "according to the toxicology report, Mrs Cronjé had high concentrations of Ketamine in her blood and plasma levels. Now, you would know —"

"Being a doctor," interjects Mtibe, his eyes fixed on Trotteur.

"Yes, being a doctor, you would know that Ketamine is a very fast-acting general anaesthetic. The pathologist said it was originally a horse-anaesthetic. The report also says that it would have 'stimulated the circulatory system, increasing heart-rate and blood pressure', which I think means —"

"She would have bled faster," Mtibe supplies.

"Bottom-line? She was drugged, doc."

"I'm sure many suicides take something to make their passing easier, to dull the pain," Trotteur says.

Mtibe makes a disbelieving sound and shakes his head. "It was injected, not swallowed. And according to the pathologist, it would have worked extremely quickly, within seconds. If she injected herself with it before she cut herself, she would have passed out immediately and would not have been conscious enough to make those cuts."

"I fail to see what this has to do with me."

"Number two," Pieterse says, holding up his thumb and index finger, "there's also the question of where she would have laid hands on a powerful drug like that."

"That's a drug only doctors have access to, doctor," Mtibe adds.

"And thirdly" — Pieterse holds up his middle finger — "there's the matter of where she was injected, which was in the hairline at the back of her neck, under her hair."

"Almost as if it needed to be hidden," Mtibe says.

"Which doesn't make a lot of sense, not so? If she was offing herself, what's the problem with people finding out she took something first? It might even bring her family some comfort to know she didn't suffer. And it's not an easy place for her to have reached by herself," Pieterse points out.

"Uh-uh, not easy." Lazy Eyes nods in agreement and bites with small, sharp teeth at his nail.

"Plus, there's number four: what happened to the syringe? We couldn't find it in the car, it's nowheresville."

"Perhaps she threw it out of the window," Trotteur suggests. He wants these men with their pitted cheeks, lazy eyes and inconvenient questions gone.

"Nah, I don't think so, doc," Pock Face says, almost conversationally. "Inject herself behind the neck, and then before she passes out, open the window, chuck it outside where someone else might step on it, then close the window again? And why would she do that anyway? And then still have time before she passes out *to make those nice neat cuts? No ways, doc, I don't buy that."*

Trotteur checks his watch impatiently. He has had to transfer it to his right wrist and the movement still feels unnatural.

"Look, this is all very interesting, I'm sure. But I'm a busy medical professional and this has nothing to do with me. I can think of no reason why you should be here, questioning me."

"Can't you?" Mtibe's glittering black eyes blink slowly. They are not lazy at all, Trotteur realises now. They are the eyes of a crocodile lazing in the shallows, waiting to snap its jaws on its prey. "You can't think of any reason why your life would be easier if Mrs Cronjé were out of the way?"

He feels a soft slithering tickle on his hot arm, resists the urge to slap it away.

"Doc, we know that she laid a charge against you at the Medical Board. You stood to lose your licence."

"How did you— Who told you that?" The asp is tightening its coils around his arm.

"Where were you on the nineteenth, between the hours of nine o'clock in the morning and three o'clock in the afternoon, Dr Trotteur?" asks Mtibe.

"It's pronounced Tro-ture."

"Where were you?" The reptilian eyes pin him with suspicion.

Trotteur rubs at his arm.

"I was at home. As you can see, I had an accident and so I cancelled my patients for a few days." It pains him to do so, but he rolls back his sleeve and shows them his scarred arm with its pulsing snake of stitches.

"Now that's very interesting, doc," Pieterse says, squinting at the injury.

"Ve-ry in-te-res-ting," repeats Mtibe, sounding out the syllables grimly.

"Because we have the access log from the basement parking. It registers the date and time every time someone with an access card enters and leaves. And it shows that you entered the garage at precisely 7.55 a.m. and left it again at precisely 9.23 a.m. on the date in question," Pieterse says, flipping back through his notebook and reading off the times.

"Oh. Well, yes, I did actually pop in to catch up on some admin and to collect some files to take home to work on them, I remember now."

"Now he remembers," says Mtibe to Pieterse, who nods. Then he looks back at Trotteur and asks, "Anyone see you, er, catching up and collecting?"

Trotteur stands up abruptly. "This discussion is at an end. I've had quite enough of being treated like a suspect. It's outrageous! I'm not going to answer any further questions without my lawyer being present."

Mtibe shakes his head as if at some deep foolishness. "Lawyers."

"That's okay, doc. We'll call later to set up a time to interview you down at the station. We need to get full statements from everyone in this case — the husband, the pathologist, and you."

Trotteur ignores him, stalks to the door and opens it.

"And of course" — Pieterse flips through to an earlier page in his notebook with his stubby fingers — "from Mrs Cronjé's psychologist."

Trotteur spins around to face him. He cannot believe his ears. Her. Again! The wave of rage that surges up inside him almost fells him. He puts out a hand to the doorframe to steady himself.

"Her psychologist?"

"Yes, she's been very helpful in assisting us with our enquiries. It was her who suggested we talk to you," Pieterse says, brushing past Trotteur into the reception room.

"We like it when members of the public assist us. Makes a nice change." Mtibe walks out then turns, offering his hand to shake Trotteur's.

Trotteur glares at him, and slams the door shut in his face.

He leans against the door, rubbing furiously at his arm. How much would she be able to say? Did death end the duty of confidentiality? Would the husband be able to authorise disclosure? His mind races, then blossoms with beautiful pictures. He imagines Megan Wright with a dent in both cheeks, her lips stitched closed with knots of stiff black thread. The image makes him smile, relaxes the tension in his shoulders a little.

There is a knocking from somewhere distant behind him. He ignores it.

Carefully he folds back his sleeve and inspects his arm. The prickling is unbearable. He tugs at the black stitches along the puckered, red welt. One of them is coming undone. It is unravelling, the black ends of the thread stick into the air like the arms of a miniscule drowner, waving for help. As he watches, they wiggle on the crest of a moving red wave. He pulls one of the tiny black arms right out of its socket. Then he wrenches another until it, too, comes loose. He digs his fingernails right into the flesh and scratches deeply. It feels good, but he can't reach the deeper itch. He stares at the gaping sides of the wound, now oozing blood.

Loose ends must be tied up. Otherwise things begin to unravel and come apart.

46
SCRATCHING THE ITCH

It had been a spectacular sunset — the dusty Johannesburg sky somehow catching and holding the flames of crimson, coral and cerise which licked at the horizon — but night had long since fallen. From the window of her office, Megan could see the lights of the city radiating out in the night, but none of the stars which must be somewhere above. The parking lot, bathed in the yellow glow of security lights, was mostly empty now that visiting hours were over. Her office and the corridor beyond were so silent that Megan could hear the ticks of the second hand on the wall clock.

She spun her chair back to face her desk and once again read the text message on the cell phone in her hand.

> *I was Mrs Cronjé's nurse in the post-op ward. I have something to tell you about Dr Troutter but he must not know Im talking to you. If you see me you must not greet me because Im afraid. Can I visit you tonight after my shift ends at 8pm? I know where your office is. I will*

come there. From Sr Mercy Sibisi

Megan was both excited and nervous. Another witness who might be prepared to testify would certainly strengthen the case against Trotteur, but she was worried about keeping the woman safe. She could not allow a repeat of what had happened to Alta.

Megan glanced up at the clock on the wall: 7.45 p.m.

She remembered joking with Patience about a Sister Mercy, but it wouldn't hurt to double-check. She called the cell number from which the text message had been sent. A smooth female voice announced that "the person you wish to contact is not available. Please call again later." A standard service provider voicemail message.

Megan thought for a moment, then picked up the receiver of the landline, looked up the number of the post-operative ward in the clinic's internal directory, and dialled the extension. It rang for a good half minute before a harassed-sounding voice answered.

"Marula Ward."

"Good evening. Please may I speak to Sister Mercy Sibisi?"

"Hang on."

Megan held the line for several minutes, listening to clattering noises and voices in the background. Eventually the same voice came back.

"She's busy changing a dressing. She'll be finished now-now. Do you want to leave a message?"

"No, that's okay, thanks. I'll call again later."

It was coming up for eight o'clock. Megan guessed that

Mercy Sibisi would still have to complete a handover to the staff of the next shift, and to gather her belongings before making her way from the ward to Megan's office. The nurse probably wouldn't arrive before twenty past eight, Megan estimated. She decided to spend the time compiling a list of questions for the potential witness.

It was just gone quarter-past when Megan heard the sound of the outer sliding door opening. She got up and headed for the door, heard the grate and click of the door sliding closed. As she passed the table with the dried-flower arrangement, a sudden impulse made her reach under and switch on the recording device. Over the last few months, she'd developed a healthy respect for the value of hard evidence.

There was a timid knock at her office door.

Megan reached for the handle and was just turning it when the door flew open, knocking into her and sending her stumbling back. She grabbed the wingback chair and managed to stay on her feet, staring into the red-rimmed, glittering eyes of the tall man who faced her. His shoulders heaved, his lips were pulled back in a tight grimace, and his unwashed hair fell lankly on either side of a face which was noticeably thinner than the last time she'd seen it. The silver scar on his chin stood out clearly against the ashen pallor of his skin. He wore a crumpled blue shirt with sweat stains under the armpits, and a dark streak of what Megan thought might be blood smeared the inside of the left sleeve.

"Anthony Trotteur!" She would not use the title he so little deserved. "Or should I call you Tony?"

She spoke the names loudly and clearly, and in the direction of the hidden microphone in the flowers. Perhaps she would be able to get more than one type of evidence tonight. And if he killed her, she thought wildly, at least they would know who to arrest!

"I need a session with you, Megan. Urgently. There are some things on my mind that I need to get off my chest." He spoke through gritted teeth and rubbed fiercely at his arm.

Megan tried to keep her voice calm and steady, tried to speak past the breathiness which filled her throat. "I can no longer be your therapist, Tony, surely you can see that? Given ... given everything that has happened, it would be totally inappropriate."

"Clause 21 of annexure 12 of the Ethical Rules of Conduct for psychologists, in the Health Professions Act 56 of 1974 stipulates that 'a psychologist shall not abandon a client by terminating the professional relationship PREMATURELY OR ABRUPTLY'!" He shouted the last words at her. He was clearly losing control.

Holding eye contact and keeping her voice as steady as she could, Megan said, "The code also says that a psychologist may not see a client where there is a conflict of interest or a dual relationship, Tony."

"Both of which you already did — at my expense! And more." He wagged an admonitory finger at her. "You're a regular rule-breaker."

"Look, we obviously need to talk about these matters, Tony, but right now —"

"Stop using my name in every sentence like some second-hand car salesman! Where did you learn that repeating the person's name would forge a bond — Psych 101?"

"You're very clever to spot that."

"And now you're trying flattery. Just shut up, you cow! You have to see me, have to, have to." He scratched at his arm with the nails of the other hand. He caught her glance, grimaced again, and said, "It's the itch, Megan, it's making me a little crazy." He almost sang the last word. "And it's moving again. It's in the rules. You may not refuse treatment to a client in crisis, shrink. And I" — he held his arms wide open and Megan saw the bright red stain of fresh blood on his shirt sleeve — "am most definitely in crisis."

"Given the circumstances, I'm sure an exception can be made. There's something in the code about not having to see individuals from whom you consider yourself at immediate threat. But —"

"Do you feel threatened by me, Megan? Are you scared?"

There was an eager glint in his eye. He was obviously getting his rocks off at the thought of her fear.

"No," she said firmly. "I'm not scared. But I am in a hurry and I don't have time to see you now. I'm expecting my fiancé, Mike, at any min —"

"No, you're not." His voice was flat and cold. He started walking slowly towards her. "You're expecting Sister Mercy Sibisi."

"How …?" Megan began, but then answered her own question. "It was you who sent the text message."

"I have something to tell you about Dr Troutter," Tony said in a high falsetto voice. "*Troutter* — I thought that was a masterly touch!" He giggled, chafed his arm against his side, and continued in the high voice, "'But he must not know I'm talking to you'. Have you still not learned to check people's identity, Megan? They say that intelligence is the ability to learn from experience. So what does that say about you?"

He took another step forward and Megan automatically retreated. Her mouth was dry and her palms clammy. No one would be coming to save her.

"You're not the only one who can use a pay-as-you-go cell phone. But you do have to learn to pay as you go. There's a price to everything, Megan, you need to learn that. Happily, we have plenty of uninterrupted time ahead of us, and a nice, quiet, deserted section of the clinic in which to have our first lesson. Our first, and last." He rubbed his hands together, as if in anticipation of a treat.

Megan snapped her head to the side, as if she'd seen something at the window. Involuntarily, his glance followed hers. She bolted suddenly for the door, but he was there ahead of her, locking the door and dropping the key into his trouser pocket.

"Uh-uh," he said, his wild eyes at odds with his indulgent smile. "We have some unfinished business to settle, you and I — some scores to even. And you know how I like things to be even." He pointed a finger, blood crusted along the ridges of its nails, at the couch behind her. "Please, do sit down."

"Tony, I —"

"I said, SIT DOWN!" He shoved her back so that she fell onto the couch. "You know, for a psychologist, you have really bad listening skills."

The scar on his chin stretched and curved as his face twisted between a rictus of anger and a contorted travesty of a smile. His eyes were wide now, the floating irises more unnerving than ever.

"Tony," she began again, desperately deploying all the containment skills in her meagre therapeutic arsenal. "I can see that you're upset."

"*Upset* doesn't begin — doesn't *begin* — to capture what I'm feeling! I itch, Megan, I burn. I'm a burning man." He paced back and forth on the carpet in front of her as he spoke, rubbing and scratching at his arm relentlessly.

"Angry, I mean," Megan said quickly. "You're really angry with me! You think I've betrayed you. You're feeling abandoned. Another woman who was supposed to nurture you has abandoned you, just like those mothers all that time ago."

"Stop it! Stop talking, you dirty, stinking girl! Stop your words in your hole and swallow them. Talking can't help you now. We're beyond words — can't you see that?" He turned his face to hers. "I'm very tired, Megan, very, very tired. I haven't been sleeping well. Too many things are troubling me, bubbling me …"

As he breathed in hard through his nose, the nostrils pinched together. His features were etched with a desperate appeal — for what, Megan wondered desperately. For understanding or acceptance? Or for something more malevolent?

"Tony, I'm trying to understand."

He ran his hands over his face, then rubbed his eyes with balled fists. For a moment, he looked like a tired little boy, about to cry.

"We're. Beyond. Words. 'The rest is silence' — don't you

know your Hamlet? But before we have that rest, we need to get to the flesh and bones of the matter."

He reached the hand of his uninjured arm into a pocket, and pulled out a hard-plastic spectacles case. Keeping his eyes on Megan, he opened the case. Inside, on red velour lining, lay a scalpel. He picked it up and held it for her to see. The light winked off its sharp blade as he turned it between his fingers. He sat down in the wingback chair opposite her and placed the scalpel on his right thigh, its tip pointed at her. With head cocked, he stared at the instrument for a moment, then adjusted it minutely so that it lay precisely straight.

"Now, the flesh and bones of this bloody matter are that I received a call today. Two calls, in fact. A call to the ear and a call to the eye. The ear call informed me that the Board is going ahead with its hearing against me, that there is a new witness. That new witness, that interfering busybody of a bitch would be you."

He picked up the scalpel, pointed it at her and then laid it very precisely down again in the same position as before.

"Then there was the other call — a visit from Mr Pock Face and Mr Crocodile Eyes, in the flesh. It wasn't a pleasant experience, Megan. I was Mr Humiliated today. They had all sorts of facts and theories and absences and even a little evidence. And guess who the chief instigator, the tittied trouble-maker and agent provocative is? You."

Again, the ritual with the scalpel.

"And now I am Mr Mega-Pissed-Off! You have wounded me, Megan, inside and out. Outside and in. Just look."

He undid the button on the blood-stained sleeve and

pushed it back up his arm. Megan gasped. The wound was vivid red, swollen and inflamed, puckered in places with black stitches, while in other spots the lips of the wound gaped. Fresh red blood was seeping over the rusty crusts and scabs, and a dark flush radiated out across his long forearm.

"You did this." His voice was almost a whisper. "You cut me, to the core. Does it move you, now, Megan? It moves me. It moves on me. There!" He held his arm out to her. "Did you see that? Just then?"

Megan nodded, having no idea what she was agreeing to, but unwilling to anger him with opposition.

"Well, that couldn't go unavenged, could it? An eye for an eye, and an arm for an arm — isn't that what the old Good Book says?" He cradled his wounded arm against his chest with his other arm and rocked it slightly from side to side. "I had to give that tale-telling bitch what she deserved. I had to shut her pie hole forever. I so wanted to sew her lips shut — yours too — but that would have been bit of a giveaway." He giggled again. "But the cuts had a certain balance, don't you think? A scar for a scar. With interest, of course. And now it's your turn."

47
SCALPEL

"**D**o you mean...?" Megan's voice was a croak. Her throat was tight and dry with fear, and she battled to say the words. "Are you talking about Alta Cronjé?"

"What a disappointment she was. What a stupefying waste of my talent," Trotteur sneered.

"Your talent?"

"She was all lopsided and uneven when she came," he wagged his head from side to side, "and ungrateful when she left. All you bitches are ungrateful. There's no end to your demands — you're never satisfied. Don't know a good thing when you've got it." He frowned down at his arm, then scratched idly at the wound and tugged at the end of one of the stitches. "Freud would say that's because you don't have a good *thing*, only an o-thing. Would you agree, Megan?"

"What did you do to Alta, Tony?" Say it loud and clear for the microphone.

"I did what was necessary, which was what she deserved."

"And what was that?"

"When I got that letter from Miss Efficiency at the board, how I burned, Megan. How dare she? That dirty, stinking ..." He blew out a long breath and his features, which had briefly contorted with rage, once more smoothed themselves out into the bland mask. "But how very kind they were to tell me the name of my accuser. I hadn't known until then, you see. And with you sticking notices up in hospitals and sending my patients prying, spying emails — yes, I know everything, you see! — how was I to know who had been pouring poison into your ears about me? But now I knew. And I knew the sort of person *you* were, too. You wouldn't let sleeping dogs lie. Bitches! All the sleeping, lying she-dogs who wouldn't stop their yapping. I had to do it for them."

His tone was flat, his face blank of expression. It was alarming how his emotional state swung between extremes, how his language was deteriorating into a word-salad. He was clearly experiencing a severe psychotic break.

"Them?"

"Yes, them! Pay attention, Megan." His irate stare burned into hers.

"Who exactly?"

"The first one took money like the whore she was."

"Stacey Cole."

Trotteur shrugged. "Cole-hole," he said, his voice a sing-song. "Then there was that other one who would not shut up."

"Nirvana Reddy?"

"If you say so — it's not like her name matters. But that one I regret, I very much regret." He sighed deeply, then, piping his lips, blew air up and down the length of his wound. "I had to be quick, you see, there was no time for finesse, for my preferred technique. She had to be excised, but there was no time for excisions. *More* excisions, I should say, it's important to be exact, for I had already done some on her sweet, young flesh." He flashed a manic smile at Megan.

"It was you, the hit-and-run!" she gasped.

"As I say, it is a lasting regret — not the fact of it, but the way of it. Too loud and messy and fast. Too fast, really, to see the fear or feel the power. I like it to last a little longer." He licked his lips and leered lasciviously at her. "I'm a goer and a stayer, Megan. I hope to have a chance to show you."

He brought his injured arm up close to his face, and crooned to it. "Shhh-shhh. Be still, little one." Then he calmly picked up the scalpel, deftly inserted it into one of the stitches and with a quick, upwards flick, cut it open. He laid the scalpel back down on his thigh and pulled the thread out of the inflamed flesh. "Aaah," he sighed, his eyes rolling in pleasure. "You have no idea how good that feels. Almost as good as cutting her."

"Her — who?"

"Her — any. Does it make a difference?" he said indifferently. "One mound of stinking, rotten flesh is very much like another."

"How did you kill Alta?"

"Simplicity itself. When I knew who she was, I looked up her address in my patient files. I had to pull hers from the archives because, of course, she was no longer a patient of mine. Went to her house early every day and waited outside.

Watched, followed, planned. Planning is essential. Well begun is half done." He chanted the last words in a sing-song voice. "And the anticipation is not without its own pleasure. On the third day, she arose again and came here. Well, I knew she wasn't coming to visit me, she'd left me, so she must be coming to see *you*." He picked up the scalpel, pointed it at Megan, wiped it on the material of his trousers and then laid it down again in the precise centre of his right thigh.

"I waited behind her car, until she came back down. Waiting for her to come" — he snickered — "that sounds rude! Waiting for her to come, that was the hardest part, Megan. The ground was so dirty and stinky. But then she came, I leapt up, embraced her like a lover — just in case anyone was watching — and pushed that needle in, deep into the back of the neck." He sighed and smiled at the remembered pleasure. "Such soft flesh there, just below where the hair begins, it's like a woman's inner thigh. Then I placed her in the seat behind the wheel, though I was in the driver's seat all the way, you could say."

Megan winced as she pictured the scene in her mind's eye. His smiles and satisfied sighs sickened her, and she didn't trust his unnatural calm. At any moment, he might spin into another rage.

"But then came the moment of uncertainty and revelation, Megan. I wasn't sure, you see, that I would be able to cut her, to slice her up" — his right hand dissected the air in front of him — "as she so deserved. And I wasn't sure what poison you had poured into *my* ears. What if I could never cut again?" His eyebrows rose high and his lips pursed in a parody of bewilderment. "Of course, I had come prepared, I had a gun in my jacket pocket and was prepared to use it, if necessary. But only with reluctance. Guns are so messy and so instant. The cut's the thing that does it for me: a sweet slice of life! So, imagine my delight, Megan, imagine my delirious joy when I discovered that I most certainly could cut her." Again, the horrible smile.

He leaned back in his chair, but Megan could tell that he was still coiled as tight as a spring. His dark eyes glinted with excitement.

"I suspect that you planted some command in my mind that I couldn't cut patients. Perhaps you never imagined I might want to cut outside of the operating theatre? That was a tad limited and short-sighted of you, Megan." He might have been chastening a careless intern. "Because she was no longer my patient: and nothing stopped me when I simply lifted the scalpel and sliced her arm." He mimicked the motion, snatching up the scalpel and slashing at the air twice. "Such beautiful cuts they were: deep, even slices. And then her thigh, so near my original work. And the blood left her and the words never would. So simple and so neat a plan. Though, I see now of course that I was a little too neat: the missing syringe. Like the dog that didn't bark in the night. Ah well." He hummed a few tuneless notes. He seemed less wild now and had stopped scratching his arm. "There was at least that fitting and pleasing symmetry, that my contact with her, my beginning and her end, should be bookended by such beautiful cuts, at this place."

He looked up at her. "Nothing to say? Cat got your tongue? That can be arranged — nothing simpler. Please stand up and go stand there," he said, almost pleasantly, indicating the spot in front of her desk.

She complied quickly, eager to get further away from him.

He stood up, moved a pace closer and glared at her. "Speak, please. You've always had so much to say, don't stop now." The smile was gone. "I am all ears."

Megan could feel the danger rising. She scanned the surface of the desk for a weapon. It was covered in files and piles of useless paper. The container of pens was out of easy reach, but perhaps if she flung herself backwards?

"I ... I ..." What could she say? What words could calm this storm?

"Yes, you, you! *You* are to blame!" His voice rose in pitch, his face twisted into a grimace of bitter anger. "There is no way around it, no way over it, and no way under it" He slid the scalpel into another stitch, cut it, removed it. The wound gaped like a slack mouth drooling fresh blood. "If you hadn't meddled, it wouldn't have been necessary to silence her. And if you hadn't wounded and scarred me, it wouldn't be necessary to silence you!"

In one swift movement, he sprang at her, the scalpel pointed at her face.

48
CLOCKED

Trotteur rammed Megan backwards onto the desk, and threw himself on top of her. Her arms flailed, sending papers, pens and the telephone flying. Trotteur pinned her down with his body, shoving his left hand up against her throat to cut off her scream of terror as he held the scalpel to her face with his right hand. The point pricked her cheek.

His face loomed above hers, the obsidian eyes glittering. "You, too, are not a patient Megan. Your dirty little trick kicked in before I could make you one of mine, so I can slice and dice you any way I like. And you *do* have a couple of holes that need fixing. I promise you we'll get to them all, in time. But I need to begin with this right here." Drops of spit sprayed as he growled the words. "This dent, this blemish, this rogue would-be dimple has always bothered me. It detracts from the ice and the fire. It cannot be allowed to continue."

Megan's shout came out as a strangled gargle. Her left leg was trapped under his, she kicked out her right leg, but it could find no purchase and jerked uselessly in the air. She bucked and twisted under him, trying to throw him off. Her hands beat and clawed against his body, but the reach of his longer arms kept his face just out of her reach. The pressure against her throat increased. She couldn't breathe. Black spots stippled her vision. The edges of her sight frayed into advancing darkness as she gasped for air.

"The only question is whether I should give you another hollow *here*" — he pressed the blade against her other cheek — "so that you're nice and even. Or whether we should rather cut this one out?" He returned the scalpel to her dimpled cheek.

The blackness was sucking Megan into itself. The choking noises in her throat seemed to be coming from far away.

"I think we definitely need to excise this disfigurement. And what I say goes. You know what they say, Megan: doctor knows best."

He dug the scalpel into the dimple and began to cut a deep circle. Megan felt the pressure, then the pain. It blazed ice-cold, then searing hot. She welcomed the burn; it pulled her out of the encroaching darkness, and fired her with rage and returning strength.

Trotteur sucked in a breath and shivered in delight. There was a fractional loosening of the pressure at her neck as he pulled back slightly to admire his work.

"Not quite perfect," he said, tilting his head from side to side like an artist examining a canvas. "It needs a little more just here."

As he brought the scalpel back down and fixed his eyes on the bleeding wound in her cheek, Megan pulled both her arms inside of his with a quick movement. With her left hand, she batted outwards at the arm holding the scalpel. There was a sharp slice of fire on her upper arm, and then she heard the scalpel clatter against the bookshelf behind her. At the same time, her right hand grabbed at the injured arm still pressing against her throat, digging her fingernails into the bloodied mess on his forearm.

Trotteur gave a high-pitched scream of pain.

Megan brought her other arm across and clutched at the wound with that, too. She began to tear the edges apart. The hand on her throat slackened its grip as she felt the remaining stitches give way under her ripping grasp. Trotteur punched her against the side of her head with his free arm, and then began to wrench at her arms, trying to pull them off his wound.

Megan's head swam. Once more the black sea of darkness threatened to suck her down, but she clung to the ragged, bloody arm as though to a life preserver, clawing her hands deep into the gash, grabbing and gouging at the flesh.

She crushed his arm with all the strength left in her right hand, while her left reached into his pocket and grabbed the key. She brought it up, stabbed it into his arm and twisted.

Trotteur howled and lurched back, wrenching his arm free of her hand and the key. He clutched his arm against his chest and Megan seized the moment of distraction to dash for the door, clambering right over the back of the couch and knocking the side table over.

She was within steps of the door when he slammed into her from behind, sending her crashing into the side of the wingback and onto the floor. He forced her onto her back and sat on her hips. This time he put both hands around her throat.

"I. Haven't. Finished!" he screamed at her. "I haven't finished! And now I have no knife so I'll just have to dig it out with my fingers."

He reached out with clawed fingers and twisted her head to the side so that her bloodied cheek was uppermost. She felt the pain vividly, but it was as though it was happening to some distant place in her body, some place no longer fully part of her. Her eyes were riveted on what she saw lying under the chair: light and hope trapped in solid, square weightiness. She reached out a hand and closed it around the heavy glass cube. Then she brought it up and held it threateningly in his field of vision.

"Get off me! Get back!" she hissed.

He looked from her hand to her face and then laughed — a loud merry peal. "You're threatening me with a dandelion? Oh, please," he mocked. "You won't use that. Miss Knows-Right-from-Wrong. You're a fucking psychologist. Help and heal and do no harm and all of that." He kneeled back on his haunches and laughed harshly. "*I'm* your client, a desperate man asking for help. You must help *me*. Fuck the women, fuck the retards and the rejects and the defectives!"

"You're the reject, Tony," she croaked. "You could never see that, but you're the defective one, the permanently damaged and inadequate one. Perfectly imperfect — that's what you are, what you've always been. No wonder nobody wanted you."

With a silent scream of rage that contorted his face, he lunged at her. Megan pulled her arm back and swung the paperweight forward, full-force against the side of his head, smashing a sharp corner into his temple with a jarring blow.

There was a single moment when Trotteur looked down at her, surprise rippling across his face. Then he shook his head, and swiped at the air in front of him as if trying to clear a fog. Megan thudded the weight against his head again, and he merely looked stunned as he toppled sideways off her.

Gasping, trying desperately to take a deep breath, she rolled over onto her side and pushed herself up off the floor, onto her knees. Her fingers were still locked onto the bloodied paperweight. Trotteur lay twitching on the carpet. A trickle of blood from the side of his head split into two rivulets; one ran down his cheek and neck, and dripped onto the carpet, while the other ran into the outer corner of his left eye, staining it red. His dark eyes were open — they seemed to bore into hers — but he made no movement to wipe away the blood.

Megan stared at him for several long moments. Perhaps a minute, perhaps several. Tears welled in her eyes.

"Bastard!" she rasped. "How's it feel when you get hurt, *doctor*?"

There was no reply, though she thought she saw hatred glimmering in his eyes. She was about to crawl away when he moved.

Without thought, without hesitation, her arm swung back and then flew forward as a silent spasm arched his back and convulsed noiselessly through his body, raising one stiff arm into the air. A corner of the heavy glass cube hit his head behind the ear. The force of the blow reverberated up Megan's arm, and she felt, rather than heard, the splintering of bone beneath her hand.

She collapsed back against the chair, her chest heaving.

Suddenly, the pain rushed in. Her throat burned, her head throbbed, her cheek was on fire.

She studied the still form of Trotteur carefully. His eyes were closed and there was no movement in his body except for a faint rise and fall of his chest. She looked down at her hands. The fingers of her right hand still grasped the paperweight, now clotted with blood and matted gore. With a sharp cry, she dropped it, and it rolled to the floor with a soft thud. Her hands began to shake, and the tremor grew and spread until the whole of her was shivering violently.

There was something she had to do now, something she must do. She would be able to remember if she could just stop trembling.

She concentrated hard, forced herself to look away from the blood and the glass, to think past the pain. She focused on her knees, the sharp folds of the clean fabric of her trousers. And it came to her: she must phone the police. But first she must phone an ambulance. Stupid! She was already in a medical facility. She just needed to call downstairs.

She could hear the phone now, in this profound silence; the continuous beeping tone told her the receiver was off the cradle. Turning her head, she could see that it lay to the side of the desk. It seemed an impossibly long way off. But she had to get herself over there and make the call. Time mattered with head injuries. Minutes could mean the difference between life and death.

She glanced back at Anthony Thomas Trotteur.

Raising her head, she watched the clock on the wall. The long, slender hand counted off the seconds. It snapped to each progressive line and seemed to quiver as it hit the marks. The minute hand was shorter and more rigid; it moved with a steady firmness. Perhaps the seconds collected strength as they coalesced into minutes.

Under her constant gaze, the movement of the clock's hands appeared to slow down. Tears slid down her cheeks, burning the cut Trotteur had carved into her face. She pressed her hand to it. And thought.

And waited.

Sitting very still, and as quiet as she would be if unconscious, she watched the hands of the clock inch forwards.

After a long while, she groaned, pulled herself up the side of the wingback and tried to stand. Her legs no longer shook, but her knees seemed to have melted and would not hold her. She sank back down onto her hands and knees, crawled over to the telephone, and made the call that would summon help.

Then she lay down beside the chair, curled in upon herself, rested her head on her bleeding arm, and stared at the unmoving legs of Anthony Thomas Trotteur.

49
LOCKED IN

The October air was still, dusty and rich with the heady, sweet perfume of Syringa blossoms. The small group stood in the cool shade beneath the arch of dark branches and emerald leaves, listening to the silence of the *veld* reverberate in the quiet lull after the man in the grey suit stopped talking. Tiny blossoms drifted down to add to the fragrant carpet already beneath their feet. A blossom landed on one of the russet curls on Megan's shoulders. She picked up the tiny flower and examined the delicate white petals, their undersides striped with the palest lilac, and the distinctive black slash of stamen standing out from the centre.

"I always told her it was an invasive weed, but she said weeds were just plants growing in the wrong place. It was her favourite tree. She said it was the smell of spring." Johan Cronjé gestured at the tree. "So, I thought she would want her ashes scattered in spring, under a Syringa. It's why I waited all these months."

He wiped his eyes with the back of a hand, then lifted the little girl off his waist and gently set her down beside her grandmother, who laid a gnarled hand on the child's brown hair. Marlien Cronjé looked confused. She scrunched at her lacy dress with one hand and clutched at a stuffed rabbit with the other.

Her father stepped forward, opened the small wooden box, and scattered the ashes around the base of the tree. There was no breeze, the ashes fell where they were strewn beneath the fragrant arms of the tree.

Their pastor had said the formal prayers. Now family and friends went up, one by one, laying flowers at the base of the tree, softly murmuring their own prayers, whispering their own goodbyes. Megan walked up to the trunk and hugged it tightly. She could imagine the startled gazes being exchanged behind her, but she thought Alta would understand, and approve. Then she laid down the three, fragrant, dusky-pink roses which she'd cut from the enormous rose bush in the beautiful garden of her new house that morning.

"I'm sorry," she whispered to the tree and the three flowers and the ashes beneath. "I'm so very sorry."

She walked back to where the others stood. While they took their turns, she breathed in the exotic fragrance and took in the beauty of the farm: the sandstone farmhouse glowing golden in the sun, the long grasses bending in the breeze, the distant specks of cattle. A dog barked somewhere in the distance.

When the ceremony was over, Johan walked over to speak to Megan. Marlien was back on his hip. She sucked on one of the rabbit's ears and stared curiously up while Megan and Johan spoke the well-worn words that both lied and comforted.

"Would you like to come back to the house for tea or coffee?

We've got some cake and savoury tart too."

"And *koeksisters!*" Marlien said with a shy smile.

Megan felt something tug at her core. She kissed her forefinger and touched it to the tip of Marlien's nose. Another, bigger smile appeared.

"Thank you, Johan, but no. I must get going. It's a long drive back to Jo'burg and I have an appointment to keep."

They said goodbye with a brief, tight hug, then Megan walked across the dusty grass to her car, the pain of the man and child heavy in her chest.

The road back to the city sliced through dry fields barren of anything at this time of year, but the odd dust devil. The parched earth seemed to be holding its breath for the coming summer thunderstorms, and the ploughing and planting which would follow.

There was plenty of time for Megan to think. She marvelled at the kindness of Johan, who seemed to bear her no grudge. She'd been less forgiving of herself. Alta's death was set at least partly against her account. She reminded herself that future women had been spared: a potential saving set against a definite loss.

She'd survived, emerged the victor, but she'd been marked by the events of the year, and of that day five months ago. She touched her cheekbone, felt the dent — deeper, now — and traced the crescent-shaped scar: the outside marks of what had happened. The other scars were internal, invisible, but probably just as permanently disfiguring. She'd changed, become less like herself — or less like the self she'd once thought she was.

She still believed in free will, in choice — perhaps more so now than ever — but she was no longer so sanguine or confident about her ability to help others change. Sometimes, they didn't want to. Sometimes they were wedded to their pathology — in love with it — and would no more be parted from it than from a lover. That was their choice, and it was beyond her control.

Her beliefs about herself had been profoundly shaken. Once — it seemed a very long time ago, now — she'd been sure that if given a choice about the big things, she would always take what she'd once so naively called "the high road". But now she knew different.

That night in her office with Trotteur, she'd possessed a moment of total power over another, and like Prometheus stealing fire from the gods, she'd grasped it. Yes, she'd used it to save herself, and to protect those unknown future women whom she'd judged as more deserving than the man who'd been her own client, but she wasn't at peace with the choices she'd made that night, and was still distressed at how automatically and instinctively her actions had come. But she knew, too, that given the chance to relive that moment between her and him, she would choose to do the same again.

She'd used her freedom of choice to play God, to reach a verdict, to act as judge and avenger. Now she was on her way to confront the consequences of her decision.

The place she arrived at was very different from the farm she'd left two hours earlier. She parked on hot asphalt, not dust; there were plastic plants in linoleumed corridors, rather than trees in the *veld*, and instead of the fresh blooming of spring, here there was only dead sterility. She stopped to ask directions, found the room she was looking for, and entered.

He lay on his back on the high bed, his body immobile. His arms rested on top of the bedspread, the hands pulled up into curled claws of spasticity. On one forearm, a thick red keloid scar marked a trail down the pale whiteness of the flesh. The other arm was punctured by a needle connected to a tube running to an IV bag hanging on the stand next to the bed. Another tube had been fed into one nostril and taped in place on his top lip with white surgical tape. A third tube snaked into the corner of his mouth. His face was lopsided: the right side sagged and drooped, pulling down the ends of mouth and eye. Two monitors blinked and softly beeped behind the bed.

A nurse bustled into the room and greeted Megan with a nod and a smile.

"Ooh, how nice, you have a visitor today," she said brightly in the direction of the bed. "And how are we today?"

It was clear that she expected no answer from her patient, she didn't even make eye contact with him. If she had, if she'd stood still and looked very carefully, she would've seen that the dark eyes were staring directly at Megan.

"And you've brought flowers," the nurse said, nodding at the small potted plant Megan held. "An African violet, isn't that pretty? It's a kind thought, luvvie, but he won't register it. No lights left on in the top storey, see?" She tapped the side of her head with a finger. "Are you family of his?"

"No."

"Do you know, you're only the second visitor he's had since he's been here? No family or friends or anything. Sad, isn't it?"

"Who was the other visitor?"

"His lawyer," the nurse said, flicking a finger at the bottom of the IV bag where clear fluid dripped slowly into the plastic tubing. "He's the one who organised the transfer here for long-term care. They don't have chronic facilities at most of the clinics any more. The lawyer said there are a mother and father still alive."

"Really?"

"Yes. Lived in Durban, I think he said — or was it Cape Town? Anyway, neither of them's been here to see him." She leaned over her patient and administered drops into his eyes. "Not that he would know the difference, would you, Mr Trotter? Poor thing — I really pity him."

Perhaps it was just her imagination, but Megan thought there'd been a flash in those dark eyes.

"Excuse me, luvvie, I just need to move him so he doesn't get bedsores. Every two hours we rotate him, just like a lamb on a spit."

She laughed loudly at her joke, and used the sheets to manoeuvre her mute and inert patient onto his left side. He now faced a beige metal cabinet. Its scratched surface was completely bare; no doubt the drawers would be empty. Anthony Trotteur didn't need a place to store books, or grapes or get-well cards.

"What's the prognosis?" Megan asked.

Tucking the bedclothes tightly around her patient to hold him in place, the nurse said, "Well, it's never good with these cases, is it? Ninety per cent of these vegetative patients die within the first six months. Usually it's pneumonia that gets them. But he's got this far, he might surprise us and go on for a lot longer. There we are, all right and tight. I'll be back later to do the bed-bath, but I'll leave you alone now so you can have a nice visit." Patting her patient on the shoulder, she left the room.

Megan walked around to the side of the bed, so that she could see his face again. His eyes didn't move. Could they?

"Hello Tony."

Carefully, she placed the African violet on the bedside table, in his line of vision, and squatted down on her haunches beside the bed so she could look directly into his eyes. They'd lost their old sherry sparkle, they seemed duller, the colour of unpolished dark wood. His skin had an unhealthy pallor and he smelled odd — an unpleasant mix of camphor and geriatric sourness.

"The doctors aren't sure about your condition. 'Persistent vegetative' seems to be the general consensus. But one doctor thinks you might have locked-in syndrome, *coma vigilante*. There was a bleed in your brainstem, plus, of course, the damage to the left temporal area, your speech centres, Broca's area.

"I wonder which you would prefer? To be hopelessly brain-dead, or to be fully awake and aware, but trapped in a paralysed body — unable to communicate, unable to do anything. The endless ache of a pain no one else can see, the torment of an unscratched itch, and completely unable to make anyone else understand. I think that would be a living hell, Tony, like being buried alive."

She reached out and gently moved a strand of hair out of his sagging right eye.

"And totally at the mercy of others — women, mostly."

She stared at him intently, trying to see if there was any flicker of a response.

"If you're locked-in, then I'm sorry about that. At least, I think I am. I'm not sorry I'm alive, and I'm not sorry that no other woman will be suffering at your hands. But I do regret that it came to this. And not just for you — for me too. I'm changed, and I don't think I'm the better for it."

The focus of his gaze shifted fractionally. She was sure he was looking at her scar.

"Yes," she said, touching it. "I'll always have that mark to remind me of you. I wonder, can you — you who were always so obsessed with how things looked — can you believe me when I say that *this* is the least of the ways in which I'm damaged?"

Somewhere down the corridor, a telephone chirruped. Megan rummaged in her handbag and brought out an enamelled powder compact.

"Do you want to see how *you've* changed, Tony? Here, Look."

She opened the compact, blew the traces of translucent powder off the mirror and held it up to his gaze. She was sure he could see it. The dark eyes stared, narrowed minutely and then closed.

"No, it's not pretty. And definitely not perfect. But I didn't come here to torture you, Tony." She snapped the compact closed and put it back into her handbag. "I came to tell you that you were right."

His eyes opened again, the one with the drooping eyelid was

slower to move and didn't open all the way.

"Do you remember that debate we had about unconditional acceptance? You said it wasn't possible to separate the doer from the deed, and so unconditional acceptance was impossible. 'Idealistic psychobabble claptrap,' I think you called it. I argued with you. I thought I was right, Tony, truly I did. But I was wrong, I see that now. We are what we do, and that's true for me, too. I have to live with that."

She sighed.

"I was wrong about something else, too. Do you remember what you said about change? That there are two ways to help — either by strengthening the weak, or by weakening the strong? You said it's easier to destroy the bad and the unhealthy, than it is to strengthen the good, remember?"

She leaned forward so that she was very close to him, and stared into the dark, fathomless eyes.

"You were right," she whispered.

Glossary

In South Africa, we have eleven official languages, and words and phrases from these are frequently used and understood by all.

Babelas — (pronounced *bub-buh-luss,* Afrikaans) a hangover

Bunny chow — a hollowed loaf of bread filled with cooked meat, vegetables or beans in a curried gravy

Doc Khumalo — a famous and skilled South African soccer player who played midfield for Kaizer Chiefs

Eina! — (pronounced *ay-nah*, Afrikaans) ouch!

Eish! — (pronounced *aysh*, originally derived from Xhosa) an exclamation expressive of surprise, agreement, disapproval, shock, outrage, horror or excitement

Gevaar — (Afrikaans) danger

Howzit — a greeting, the informal South African way of saying, "Hi, how's it going?"

Ingozi — (isiZulu) danger / caution

Indoda engalungile — (isiZulu) a bad or untrustworthy man

Ja — (pronounced *yah*, Afrikaans) yeah / yes.

Koeksisters — a delicious Afrikaner confectionery made of plaited yeast dough, deep-fried and drenched in syrup

Lifts — elevators

Mlungu — (isiXhosa, isiZulu) a white person

Now-now — in a short while (in the future), or very recently (in the past). Not to be confused with "now" (in the next moment) or "just now" (some few minutes ago, or later — sometime in the future, ranging from in the next few moments, to never, depending on how slowly you say the 'just'!)

Rooibos — (Afrikaans) literally "red bush", a healthy and caffeine-free South African tea made from the Cyclopia genistoides bush

Russian & chips — a large grilled sausage served with thick-cut fries doused in vinegar

Samoosas — (pronounced *suh-moo-suh*) a triangular deep-fried pastry of Indian origin containing a spicy filling of meat or vegetables; in England called a samosa.

Sangoma — a traditional healer who can also divine your future by throwing bones and other small objects, and interpreting their meaning.

Sawubona — *(isiZulu)* Hello / Good Day

Yebo sawubona; unjani? — Yes, I see (acknowledge) you. How are you?

Ngikhona — I'm fine.

Sisi — (isiZulu) literally "sister". A respectful way of greeting a woman.

Tannie — (Afrikaans) literally "auntie", a respectful way of greeting an older woman who may or may not be related to you

Wabenzi — (originally Swahili, from Kenya) a colloquial term used to describe a rich person (usually a government official) who drives a luxury vehicle (usually a Mercedes Benz) purchased with improperly gained funds

Yebo — (isiZulu) yes

Veld — (Afrikaans) wild grasslands / prairie

Zuma — former State president of South Africa, charged with multiple counts of corruption

Dear Reader,

If you enjoyed this book, please consider leaving a review on your favourite online site. Every review is valuable in helping other readers discover the book.

Would you like to be notified of my new releases and special offers? My newsletter goes out once or twice a month and is a great way to get book recommendations, a behind-the-scenes peek at my writing and publishing processes, as well as advance notice of giveaways and free review copies. I won't clutter your inbox or spam you, and I will never share your email address with anyone. You can join my VIP Readers' Group over at my website: www.joannemacgregor.com.

I'd love to hear from you! Come say hi on Facebook (www.facebook.com/JoanneMacg/) or Twitter (@JoanneMacg) or reach out to me via my website, and I'll do my best to get back to you.

– Jo Macgregor

Acknowledgements

My sincere thanks to Dr. Mariette Hurst, specialist in Forensic Pathology, for her invaluable help in the details of death and post-mortems; to my fabulous beta-readers Nicola Long, Sarina Hateley and Heather Gordon-Cotterill, and to my editor Danél Hanekom for her assistance and support through the years. I deeply appreciate each one of you!